TETON SUNRISE

TETON ROMANCE TRILOGY BOOK 1

PEGGY L HENDERSON

This is a work of fiction. Names, characters, places, and incidents are either the product of the author's imagination, or used fictitiously, and any resemblance to actual persons, living or dead, events, or locales, is entirely coincidental.

All rights reserved. No part of this book may be reproduced in any form or by any means without the prior written consent of the author.

Copyright © 2013 by Peggy L Henderson

ISBN: 9781092225472

FOREWORD

Dear Reader

Teton Sunrise is the first book in a trilogy of books about life as it might have been for one family in the harsh wilderness at the base of the Teton Mountains long before the area was settled. Each book is a standalone, but they also build on each other. Events and characters in one book play a role in subsequent books.

Teton Sunrise is a complete love story for the hero and heroine in this book, although we see them again in subsequent books. The life they led was not easy. It was harsh, and often brutal. The events that occur in the epilogue, which involve some of the supporting characters in this book, are necessary for the continuation of this trilogy...

Evelyn Lewis' secret dream of marrying her brother's best friend is shattered when he leaves their home town to seek his fortune elsewhere. For six long years, she's waited and wondered if he would return. After the shocking murder of her parents, her brother is the only family she has left. Refusing to accept a betrothal to a man she

FOREWORD

doesn't love, she decides to take control of her destiny and confront her parents' killer.

Growing up, Alexander Walker has known only violence at the hands of his cruel father. After the death of his mother, he embarks on a journey into the uncharted wilderness to test his resolve as a fur trapper and mountain man. When an impulsive decision leads him back to his childhood home, he finds more than he bargained for.

Amid the rugged Teton wilderness, fate suddenly throws Alex and Evelyn together. The quiet protective boy she remembers is now as strange to her as the world she's been forced into. Wary of the hardened man he has become, Evelyn must put her trust in him in order to survive. Alex's memories of Evelyn are of a pesky little girl, but he can't deny his growing feelings for the beautiful and spirited woman she is now. His biggest obstacle in winning her heart may not be her uncertainty of him, but a fear that has haunted him all his life.

In a primitive and brutal world, can Alex and Evelyn forge a love as solid as the mountains, or will the past come back to haunt them both?

PROLOGUE

St. Charles, Missouri, 1822

Evelyn Lewis rescued the wooden bucket from under Miss Millie's legs just before the cow would have knocked it over. She pushed the milking stool she'd been sitting on out of the way, and straightened her back.

"I'll be back later to let you out into the pasture," she said, patting the bovine on the back. Millie swished her rope-like tail, and resumed munching contently on a bushel of fresh hay. Evelyn doused the lantern that hung on a peg on the stall's wall, and headed for the barn door. Thin ribbons of golden light found their way through the cracks between the wooden boards, creating striped patterns along the hard packed dirt floor. It was well past sunup. Apparently, she'd been in the barn longer than she had thought. Her mother was surely waiting for this morning's milk.

She leaned her shoulder against the heavy barn door with the intent of pushing it open when her brother's loud and excited voice reached her ear. Evelyn stopped to listen.

"Let me see that advertisement, Alex."

Alex! Evelyn's heart sped up. He hadn't stopped by the farm in almost a month. The passing of his mother had to have been quite a shock.

Evelyn remembered folks saying that poor Mrs. Ada Walker was probably in a better place. People in town whispered, speculating whether Silas Walker had finally struck his wife hard enough to kill her. It was common knowledge that he beat his wife on a regular basis. Even Alex had shown up here, sometimes limping, other times clutching at his ribs, or holding a piece of raw meat to a swollen eye.

"I met that fella, William Ashley, after I read the notice in the St. Louis Gazette. He's startin' up a fur company."

Paper rustled, and Henry cleared his throat, then read out loud. "*Seeking enterprising young men to ascend the river Missouri to its source, there to be employed for one, two, or three years.*" He paused. "You're actually going into Indian Territory? They hire men only eighteen years old?"

"Yes. I signed up. Mr. Ashley hired me on."

Evelyn's heart pounded in her ears. She quickly held her hands over her mouth to quiet the gasp that escaped her lips. Alex was leaving? For up to three years? That seemed like a lifetime. She blinked rapidly. She couldn't stop the tears from falling. Alex couldn't leave.

"I wish I could go," Henry said excitedly. Then his voice dropped with a twinge of disappointment. "But Pop depends on my help on the farm. Evie's only thirteen. She can't help out in the fields."

"Maybe in a few years," Alex suggested. "After my ma's passing, I ain't staying here. This is the perfect chance for me to get away."

The barn door suddenly pulled open, and Evelyn jumped back in surprise. The milk sloshed over the sides of the bucket in her hand, soaking her skirt.

"Evie!" Henry sounded equally surprised to find her

standing there. Her eyes darted quickly from her brother to Alex. In the month since she'd last seen him, he'd grown some more. Her brother was still taller, but Alex was not as skinny. His shoulders seemed to have gotten wider, and his arms more muscular. She wiped a hand down her skirt, hoping neither of the boys noticed how her face had flushed.

"Did you hear the news, Evie? Alex is going to be a fur trapper. He's leaving for St. Louis today." Henry's joy grated on her nerves. She ventured another quick look at Alex. He glanced her way, but the expression on his face was unreadable. His dark, almost jet-black hair hung over his forehead, partially covering his blue eyes.

"Guess your plans are going to have to change, Evie," Henry continued, almost in a mocking tone.

"My plans?" she echoed.

Henry snorted. "Come on, Evie. We all know you fancy yourself in love with Alex. I bet you're hoping he asks you to marry him someday, when you're all grown up."

Evelyn's mouth fell open, mortified that Henry would spill her deepest, most guarded secret in front of the very person who shouldn't be hearing it. She sucked in a deep breath of air, then raised her chin. With one hand on her hip, she glared at her brother. There was only one way to save face. With her eyes narrowed, she advanced on him, and said, "I have no such notions, Henry Lewis. Why, I would much rather marry a warthog than someone like Alexander Walker." For emphasis, she glared at Alex, then pushed past her brother through the barn door. She paused and lifted the milk pail, tossing its contents at her brother's face, then stormed toward the house. Her long braided hair whipped behind her back, the tears streaming uncontrollably down her face. The last thing she heard before escaping into the house was her brother and Alex laughing loudly behind her.

CHAPTER ONE

St Charles, Missouri 1828

"You did what?"

Evelyn Lewis spun around on her heels so quickly she nearly lost her balance. The wooden ladle in her hand dropped to the ground with a dull thud, splattering brown gravy and vegetables on her dress and over the floorboards. Ignoring the mess, she stared at the man who stood across the room. Her eyes widened in shocked disbelief.

"Why would you do such a thing, Henry?" Evelyn's voice rose almost to a shrill screech. She stepped away from the hearth, and stormed toward her brother. How dare he bring such news without proper warning, or even discussing it with her first? Henry Lewis raised his hands in front of his chest as if he was about to fend off a formidable adversary, and took a step back.

"Now don't get all riled, Evie. I'm doing this for you," Henry said, squaring his shoulders and standing his ground.

"For me?" Evelyn held her fists to her hips, and glared at her brother, standing only inches from him. She leaned forward. "How is a marriage to Charlie Richardson going to benefit me?" she demanded.

Henry tentatively placed a hand on her shoulder, and his lips rose in, what looked like, an uneasy smile. He inhaled a deep breath.

"Listen to me, Evie," he said calmly. "I've had several requests for your hand in marriage over the last few months. We've known Charlie since we were children. He's always been smitten with you. He seemed like the best choice to me."

"Well I refuse to marry him," Evelyn snorted. She shot her brother a narrow-eyed look. "You know I detest him. Ever since that time he pushed me into the creek when I was eleven years old, do you remember?" She poked a finger in her brother's chest, her other hand balled in a tight fist at her hip. "Why, if it hadn't been for . . ." Her voice trailed off, and she stared wide-eyed at Henry. She'd almost spoken *his* name. Her shoulders slumped, and she lowered her gaze to the ground. Tears threatened behind her eyes, and she blinked to curb the flow. After everything that loathsome man had done, why did every thought of him bring tears to her eyes?

Because he murdered your parents! Alexander Walker murdered your parents, and all you want to remember is the eighteen-year-old boy you fancied yourself in love with as a naïve young girl.

It was the last memory she had of him; the day Alex and Henry laughed at her as she ran from the barn to the house, completely humiliated. He had left that day to venture into the unknown wilderness beyond the Missouri. A year had gone by, and she clung to the hope that he would return. Two years had passed, and no one had neither seen nor heard from him. After the third year, even Henry had suggested that savages might have killed Alex.

Evelyn was well aware of Charlie Richardson's infatuation with her. He'd often tried to talk to her when he saw her in town, and he'd stopped by the farm for one obscure reason or another. To keep him at arm's length, she had pretended to show an interest in several other young men who came calling. None of them held her attention for long. One dark-haired, blue-eyed quiet boy continued to creep into her mind. But that was before . . .

Evelyn had first noticed Alexander Walker as more than just her brother's best friend that day when she returned from carrying a basket of her mother's eggs to a neighbor's house. Charlie Richardson had spotted her on the trail along the creek between the two properties, and followed her. Relentlessly, he'd called her freckle face and made rude comments about the fact that she was thin and lanky, and hadn't started filling out in the chest like some of the other girls her age had done. She'd tried to ignore his taunts, and pretend indifference, but he had continued until she couldn't stand it anymore. Turning around quickly, she'd barely taken notice of his stunned expression before her fist connected with his nose.

Horrified at what she'd done, even as her insides filled with self-satisfaction, Evelyn had spun on her heels and ran toward home. Charlie had caught up with her quickly, and grabbed her by the arm. She was no match for his larger size, and he had dragged her to the creek's edge, then forcefully shoved her into the cold water. Alex Walker had appeared out of nowhere and grabbed Charlie by the shirt collar. With seemingly effortless ease, Alex had hauled Charlie away from the creek bank, and slammed his own fist into Charlie's face. Blood spurted everywhere, and Charlie held his hands over his face while he ran off. To this day, his nose was a different shape than it had been before Alex hit him.

Alex had reached for her hand, and pulled Evelyn from

the water. She remembered staring up into those blue eyes of his, and her youthful heart had fluttered in her chest. He hadn't said a word to her, and turned to disappear into the thicket just as quickly as he had appeared. Evelyn stared quietly after him that day, lost for words for the first time in her life.

"Evie, are you listening?" Henry's voice, and a gentle shake on her arm brought her back to her senses. She sniffed, and blinked again.

"There's more I need to tell you," he said tentatively. He ran a hand across his lower jaw; a sure sign that he was nervous about something. "But I think you'd better sit down first."

Evelyn's eyes narrowed suspiciously. She still wasn't done discussing that she wouldn't marry Charlie, and by the look on his face, Henry wanted to present her with more bad news.

Henry held her elbow and guided her to one of the wooden chairs at the table in front of the hearth. She allowed him to pull the chair out for her, then sat and folded her hands in her lap. Seconds later, she rested them on top of the table. After Henry was seated across from her, she squared her shoulders and sat up straight.

"So, what else have you to tell me? I'll listen, but the matter of my marriage to Charlie is still not settled."

Henry cleared his throat, and shifted his weight in the chair. He stared at his hands resting on the table for a moment, then inhaled a deep breath and met her eyes.

"I sold the farm to him." He paused, then clarified, "To Charlie."

"You what?" Evelyn sprang from her seat so quickly, the chair toppled over behind her. She braced her hands on the table and leaned forward. If steam came from her ears, she wouldn't be surprised. Heat rose up her cheeks as it always did when she was angry.

"This is my home, Henry. This was Ma and Pa's home. It's your home. How could you sell it? We're not destitute." Tears of anger welled up in her eyes, and her brother's face blurred.

"And it will remain your home, Evie."

"I will not marry Charles Richardson," she stated heatedly, and stomped her foot. Her hands fisted in front of her, and she resisted the urge to strike out and hit something.

Henry stood from his chair. "You have no choice, Evie. He will be here in the morning to claim his property, and to take you to the church to wed you." His palm swiped across his forehead.

Evelyn sucked in a deep breath. She stared across the table at her brother as if she was seeing him for the first time. Her heart slammed against her ribs, and a sinking feeling swept over her. This was really happening. Henry's face showed no hint that he was merely joking with her.

"What about you? What are you going to do, Henry?" she finally asked, her voice lifeless. Her gaze dropped to the ground. Henry was her legal guardian. He had every right to choose a husband for her. She never thought her brother would pick the man she would marry, especially not without asking her first. She and Henry had always been close. The fact that he took matters of such importance into his own hands hurt deeply.

Henry stepped around the table, and stood before her. He touched a hand to her shoulder. "I'm sorry, Evie," he said softly. "Perhaps in time you'll come to understand that I have your best interest in mind. Charlie will be a good husband. He will protect you and take care of you."

Evelyn ducked around him to avoid his touch. "I wish you would have consulted me on this matter." She turned on her heel to face him. "Why wouldn't you allow me to pick my own husband?"

"You haven't been interested in anyone, Evie," Henry said, moving to the hearth. He stared into the dying flames of the fire. "Every suitor who has come around, you've repelled. You're nineteen years old. It's time you married."

Evelyn was about to argue that she had no desire to marry, least of all a man who sparked no desire or warm feelings in her. Before she could speak, Henry turned to her and stared through narrowed eyelids.

"You can't still be holding on to your childish fantasies about Alex, can you?" he asked. "After what he did?" His jaw muscles tightened, his eyes cold.

Evelyn straightened her back. "Of course not. How could you think such a thing? I just haven't found the man I wish to marry." She glanced away from his perusing eye.

"Evie." Henry spoke her name slowly. He waited until she made eye contact with him. "Alexander Walker is not the boy you remember. The quiet youth has turned into a savage." He spoke the words almost viciously. "It's no surprise, either. Look at his father, and how violent he was. The man killed his own wife. Alex has always had it in him to become just as ruthless, and I'll wager that the wilderness has made him ten times more so."

"I have no thoughts or feelings other than hatred and loathing for Alexander Walker, you can rest assured of that." Evelyn spat his name as if it was poison on her tongue.

"He was my best friend," Henry said as if to himself. He stared at Evelyn, his eyes unfocused. "He was my best friend, and he murdered . . . Ma and Pa in cold blood." His voice cracked. Evelyn moved quickly across the space that separated her from her brother. She placed a comforting hand on his arm, the tears falling freely down her cheeks.

"I held Pa in my arms while he gasped his last breath,

Evie." The horrible memory was clearly written on Henry's face. "If Charlie hadn't come along when he did, and shot at the damn bastard while he ran like a coward, Alex might have killed me, too."

"I know," Evelyn whispered, and wrapped her arms around her brother's waist. He held her tightly, a shudder passing through his body. Right now, she couldn't be mad at him for what he had done. Right now, her brother needed consoling. The death of their parents a month ago had shaken him badly, as it had her. Evelyn was still not completely clear on the events that had transpired that fateful day.

At her mother's request, Evelyn had stayed the week with an elderly friend of the family whose husband had taken ill. While the woman tended to her husband, Evelyn cooked for her, and took care of basic chores around the house. Charlie had sent a boy with a message for her to come home straight away; that something horrible had happened. She'd found her parents dead, her mother's throat slashed with a knife, and her brother hovering like a little child over their dead father.

Apparently, Henry had already gone to the fields with the team of mules while his father finished some work in the barn. No one had seen nor heard from Alexander Walker in nearly six years.

At about the same time, Charlie had come to pick up a piece of harness that Evelyn's father helped him repair. According to Charlie, Alex came charging out of the house and headed straight for him. Luckily, he carried his hunting rifle with him. Raising the rifle, he had shot Alex in the chest, but the shot must not have killed him, for he ran off into the woods, and once again disappeared. The sound of gunshot had alerted Henry, who came back from the fields in time to hear his father's final gasp for air.

Evelyn eased her hold around her brother's waist. "Without the farm, what are you going to do?" she asked again.

Henry took a step back. He gripped her upper arms. Staring intently into her eyes, his facial muscles hard, he said, "I'm going after the bastard who killed our folks."

A quiet gasp escaped Evelyn's throat. Her eyes grew wide with disbelief. "You can't go after him, Henry. He'll kill you. You know nothing about the wilderness."

"He has to be brought to justice, Evie," Henry said, his fingers biting almost painfully into her skin. "I'm going to make him pay for what he did."

"I can't lose you, too," Evelyn pleaded. "Don't do this, Henry. How will you even find him?"

"I've hired some men to take me up the Missouri into what's known as the Yellowstone country. These men know the wilderness. They'll help me find him."

"When?" Evelyn asked, her voice uncharacteristically shaky.

"I leave at first light."

A sudden feeling of the world spinning and turning upside down came over her. In a matter of a few short minutes, her life was no longer her own, and she had lost everything she still held dear to her heart.

CHAPTER TWO

Evelyn pulled the hat she wore further down onto her head and tucked some loose strands of hair under the cap. She wrapped Henry's old wool coat tighter around herself, a slight shiver passing down her spine. Inhaling a deep breath, she hoped the fierce pounding of her heart would ease up, even as her apprehension grew. Her breath swirled in front of her as the early morning sun rose higher in the eastern horizon. She glanced at the many boats anchored along the banks of the Missouri River. The docks were already teaming with dozens of men loading and unloading cargo.

Her eyes traveled along the line of flatboats, barges, and longer keelboats until she spotted Henry standing with a rough-looking group of men near the plank of a keelboat. He looked out of place in his wool trousers and jacket, while the others were dressed mostly in buckskins and furs, many of them wearing fur hats. Each one of them appeared to be well armed with rifles and an assortment of weaponry hanging off their belts. Where had Henry found such an objectionable bunch of men to take him into the wilderness? Evelyn absently rubbed her fingers against the palms of her suddenly sweaty hands. She glanced over her shoulder at the path she had just come from. There was still time to turn around.

Squaring her shoulders, Evelyn raised her chin. She was not about to turn back. She had already made up her mind last night about what she was going to do. Having lost her appetite after Henry's announcement that he planned to pursue Alex, and that he had given her away in marriage to someone she barely tolerated, she'd retired to her room. Tears of despair had rolled freely down her cheeks, followed quickly by tears of anger. A plan had slowly formed in her mind. She would not be left behind. Even if she remained at the farm that had always been her home, it would no longer be her home.

If Henry was going to apprehend Alex, then she wanted to be there to look him in the eyes and demand answers. Why had he killed her parents after everything her ma and pa had done for him while he was growing up? Her mother had tended to the injuries inflicted by his father as best as she knew how, and treated him like a son. Often, he'd spend several days at the farm before returning to his own family. How could he kill the people who had been so kind to him?

Alex has always had it in him to become just as ruthless as his father, and the wilderness has made him ten times more so. Henry's words echoed in her mind. If that were so, then how did Henry figure to apprehend him? Henry was a farmer. He could shoot an occasional buck or snare a rabbit when called for, but he was not a killer. One glance at the men who stood with her brother gave her the answer she needed. Perhaps her brother had chosen wisely when he hired the men who now surrounded him. Not only would they protect her brother, they would also hunt down Alex and bring him to justice.

Her lips curved in a quick smile. Henry would be spitting mad when he found out that he couldn't get rid of her so quickly. She glanced down at the britches she wore. She had spent the better part of the night altering a pair of Henry's old pants and shirt to fit her slighter form. By wearing men's clothes, combined with the heavy coat she wore, she hoped to keep her gender disguised at least until they were far enough away from St. Louis, and it would be too late to turn around.

Her ploy had worked before when she was younger. Many years ago she'd donned Henry's old clothes when her mother forbade her to watch the men castrate calves. Her mother had been adamant that it was not something for a girl to watch. Her disguise had been successful then, so why not now? This would be her only chance to follow her brother. Once she confronted Henry, he would have no choice but to bring her along. Scanning the hustle and bustle of men and horses along the shoreline, her eyes rested on the keelboat that her brother and his companions had just boarded. Now she only needed to figure out a way to get onto that boat without notice.

Slowly, she made her way to the docks, keeping her head down and her hands in her coat pockets as she walked. Amid the multitude of people going about their business, no one seemed to take notice of her. She moved between boxes of cargo, making her way toward her objective. If she could somehow manage to get on board the boat without being seen, she could hide among the freight goods until the vessel was well on its way up the Missouri. Her fingers wrapped around the bread she had rolled in a piece of cloth and stuffed into her coat pocket. At least she would have something to eat later on.

"Hey, boy!"

Evelyn stopped in her tracks. Her heart leapt up into her

throat. Slowly, she looked up to see who had shouted at her so gruffly. She expelled the breath she'd been holding when a young boy scurried past her to stop in front of a burly man wearing a sweat-stained cotton shirt and dirty britches. He looked as though he could lift an ox.

"Yes, sir," the boy said eagerly.

"Take these here sacks up into that there boat." He pointed to some burlap bags at his feet, then toward the boat Evelyn wanted to board. He tossed a couple of coins into the child's open hand. The sacks looked much too big and heavy for the one boy to carry.

"Here, let me help you." Evelyn quickly stepped up next to the boy, seizing her chance to get on board the boat. She made sure to keep her head down, lest the big burly man noticed her.

"I ain't sharing my coins with you," the boy said in a warning tone, and stuffed the money into the pocket of his britches.

Evelyn smiled. "I don't want your coins. I'm only trying to help." She bent over the sacks, and lifted one end while the boy lifted the other. Despite his surly disposition, he shot her a grateful look.

By the time they were halfway up the gangplank with a heavy sack between them, perspiration beaded Evelyn's forehead even in the chill of the morning air. "What is in these sacks?" she groaned, the muscles in her arms burning from exertion.

The boy shrugged. "Dunno. Gunpowder, most likely."

Evelyn stepped off the plank and into the boat, when a dark figure blocked her way. He was clad in buckskins and a fur coat that seemed much to heavy an article to wear in early May. She shot a hasty glance at the bushy-faced man, whose head was covered by a coonskin cap, then lowered her gaze just as quickly. A foul odor that reminded her of a decaying chicken and rotten eggs emanated from the man's clothing and Evelyn coughed, trying to keep the bile from rising up her throat.

"Allow me," the man said, his words laced with a thick French accent, and without waiting for a reply from either her or the boy holding the other end of the sack, grabbed hold of their burden.

"Run along, boy," the Frenchman said brusquely, nodding to the boy. Wide-eyed, and with a hint of fear in his eyes, the youth turned and darted from the boat. For a spilt second, Evelyn thought to follow him. The man's dark stare seemed to seep right through her, and her throat went dry. She was almost sure that he was one of the men she had seen standing with her brother at the dock earlier. Was he one of Henry's hired men?

The man dropped the sack to the ground. His hand snaked out and he wrapped his fingers around Evelyn's wrist. She pulled back reflexively and dug her heels into the slick wooden planks of the boat's deck.

"You should not be lifting such heavy burdens, *mademoiselle*," the Frenchman said, leaning toward her. Evelyn's heart jumped, and she sucked in a deep breath. Her head shot up, and she stared into the man's black eyes. His mustache twitched, and his lips curved in a leering smile.

"Release me," Evelyn hissed, bracing against the man's hold on her wrist. Although not painful, his grip was nevertheless firm as if she'd been shackled in irons.

"Do not draw attention to yourself," the man warned in a low tone. "Even a blind man can see that you are not a boy. Why would a beautiful woman disguise herself as a man?"

"That, sir, is of no concern to you," Evelyn said between gritted teeth, still pulling against the man's unyielding grip.

"You plan to stow away on this boat. What will you do when you are found out?" The man raised a bushy eyebrow.

He jutted his chin toward the deck behind her. Evelyn didn't need to turn her head to know there were only men aboard this vessel. "You will be a most welcome surprise to twenty eager men."

Evelyn groaned silently. How had this man seen through her disguise so easily? Her heart sank. Her plan had failed. The best she could hope for now was to free herself of this man's clutches and leave. Perhaps she could find another boat that would travel up the Missouri, and catch up with her brother that way. Looking into the Frenchman's hardened features, the meaning of his words suddenly became crystal clear to her.

"I ask you again to release me," Evelyn said with all the confidence she could muster. Her eyes darted around the boat. Perhaps if she spotted Henry, she could call out to him and he would save her from this man's clutches. Instead of doing what she asked, the Frenchman yanked her closer. She squeezed her eyes shut and held her breath.

"Tell me why you are on this boat," he demanded.

"Very well," Evelyn huffed. "My brother is on board," she answered truthfully. "I only wish to join him. He is all the family I have left. He means to leave me behind while he goes off in search of the man who killed our parents. He gave me in marriage to a man I despise." She glared up at the unkempt woodsman. "Does that satisfy your curiosity?"

The Frenchman studied her for a long moment, his eyes roaming her face. Evelyn shifted her weight from one foot to the other under his unrelenting perusal. "You understand, *mademoiselle*, that what you are getting yourself into may be far worse than marrying a man you do not love."

"Then let me go, and I will return to my home," Evelyn pleaded. Did she really regret her impulsive decision to follow Henry into the wilderness? She had to admit that this man was telling the truth. What had she been thinking? She'd only wanted to get away from Charles Richardson, but the consequences of her actions hadn't occurred to her. Until now.

The Frenchman's smile widened. Surprisingly, his teeth looked white and clean, even if he did stink as if he hadn't bathed in years.

"Laurent Berard at your service, *mademoiselle*," he said, and bowed slightly. He still held to her wrist. "I offer you my service as your chaperone, until you choose to reveal your presence to your brother."

Evelyn's eyebrows rose. She stared in stunned disbelief. Was he joking with her?

"Why would you offer me your protection?" she asked slowly. Her mind raced, trying to decide whether to trust this man.

"You are the sister of Henry Lewis, are you not?" the Frenchman asked, and casually led her away from the side of the boat. Evelyn stood her ground for a moment, but when the man tugged firmly on her wrist, she took a step toward him.

"Yes," she said softly. So he was one of Henry's men. Somehow this gave her courage. If Henry trusted this man to lead him into the wilderness, then shouldn't she trust him as well? He hadn't seemed all that threatening. He'd simply warned her, and reminded her that her plan might be less feasible than what she had envisioned. Truth be told, she had no idea what to expect on this journey. Perhaps a chaperone, someone to protect her, was just what she needed.

"You will continue to act as a boy," Laurent said in a low tone, his eyes darting around, seemingly watching everyone around them simultaneously. "You will remain here with the cargo, *comprenez-vous?*" He gave her a hard stare. Evelyn nodded.

"*Tres bon*," the Frenchman said, his lips twitching. "In a

few days' time, I will inform your brother of your presence here on board. By then, he will not be able to turn you away. In the meantime, do not look at anyone, or speak to anyone."

Evelyn nodded again. She couldn't believe her turn of good luck. Despite this man's gruff appearance and obvious lack of personal hygiene, he seemed genuinely kind and helpful. Perhaps he hoped that Henry would pay him extra for taking care of her.

* * *

"Of all the foolhardy things you have ever done, Evie, this one takes the cake," Henry almost yelled, his angry red face inches from hers. His eyes darted from her to Laurent, who stood several feet behind her, and lowered his voice. "What on earth are you thinking?"

"I refuse to marry Charlie, Henry. If you're going after Alex, then I want to go with you." Evelyn stood her ground, her hands clenched firmly at her sides. For the last three days, Laurent Berard had kept her secret. He watched over her, brought her food and water, and made sure no one came too close to her to realize she was not a boy. He had apparently decided that it was time to relinquish his responsibility as chaperone to her brother.

Henry's reaction was no less than Evelyn had expected. He was livid. She had never seen him so angry, even after the grief of their parents' death had eased, and when he cursed Alex Walker to hell and back. The six other men he had hired stood off to the side, their heads together, whispering amongst themselves. One man glared at Evelyn, an almost evil grin on his face, and an unmistakable hungry look in his eyes. She averted her gaze, feeling trapped like a mouse in a barn full of cats.

Henry's jaw clenched, and his eyes darkened even more.

His upper body tensed, and for a moment Evelyn wondered if he was about to strike her. Instead, he abruptly turned, and rubbed at his jaw with his right palm. He spun back around to face her, and shot a murderous look at Laurent.

"I don't know what I'm going to do with you, Evie," he finally said. His voice had calmed considerably. "I was trying to look out for you when Charlie asked for your hand in marriage. Coming into the wilderness is dangerous to say the least. A woman here is unthinkable."

"I want to be with you, Henry," Evelyn said and stepped up to her brother. She placed her hand on his arm. "You're the only family I have left. I don't care about the dangers."

Henry sucked in a deep breath. "All right," he finally said, and offered a tentative smile. "Let me . . . let me talk to these men." He gestured with his chin over his shoulder in the direction of his hired help. "I'll no doubt have to pay them extra to bring you along, but I don't see an alternative at the moment."

Evelyn flung herself at her brother and wrapped her arms around his neck. "Thank you, Henry," she whispered. "I won't be a burden to you. I'll stay out of trouble."

Henry peeled her away from him, and shot her a look that told her in no uncertain terms that he didn't believe a word of what she said. Several of the men behind him sniggered. The one who'd been leering at her licked his lips. Evelyn stepped away from her brother and looked in another direction.

"Go back to where you've been hiding out, Evie. It's already getting dark. We'll talk more in the morning." He shot a meaningful look toward Laurent, who nodded. Taking her arm, the Frenchman led her away from her brother.

"That went very well, don't you think?" Laurent asked cheerfully as he led her back to the cargo area.

Evelyn sank to the ground between several burlap sacks,

satisfied that Henry agreed to take her with him. She relaxed against a bag. She had barely closed her eyes, when gunshots and loud shouting startled her out of her contentment.

"Laurent?" She sprung to her feet. The Frenchman was no longer at her side. Stumbling over a crate in the dimming evening light, she looked ahead to the front of the boat. Men ran in all directions, shouting and firing their weapons.

"Henry?" Evelyn screamed. Someone bumped into her, knocking her to the ground. A heavy body fell over her legs.

"Get off me," Evelyn demanded and pushed at the man. Startled, she realized that he didn't budge. When she looked closer, lifeless eyes stared up at her. Evelyn scooted backwards on her rear, gasping for breath and swallowing the bile that rose up her throat. She pushed and shoved against the dead man until she succeeded in yanking her legs out from under his heavy body.

She stood on shaky legs, her eyes frantically searching for her brother. Finally she spotted him at the helm of the boat. He met her eyes, a look of panic in his gaze. One of his hired mountain men suddenly darted in front of him, a knife in his hand. With a forceful thrust, he buried the knife in Henry's belly, and pushed him overboard.

"No!" Evelyn screamed, and she raced to the front of the boat. Her hat flew from her head, and her long hair spilled around her face and down her back. A forceful grip on her arm broke her momentum and she was hauled up against a solid form.

"Do not make the same mistake your brother made, *mademoiselle*," a voice she'd come to trust breathed in her ear. There was no hint of warmth or kindness in Laurent's tone.

"What do you mean?" Evelyn squirmed against the Frenchman's hold on her. He wrapped one steely hard arm around her waist, and dragged her away from the middle of the boat.

"Let me go," Evelyn demanded, gritting her teeth. "You have to help Henry."

"Your brother is dead, *mademoiselle*. Did you not see him fall overboard?"

"How do you know he's dead? We have to try and find him. You were hired by him to take him safely into the wilderness."

Laurent began to laugh. It started as a low rumble in his chest, then grew louder as he threw his head back.

"Your brother was a fool. And you, *ma petite*, are an even bigger fool."

"You vile, evil creature," Evelyn shouted, and pounded her fists against the Frenchman's chest, which only seemed to amuse him more. All around her, the gunfire slowly ceased, and the shouts of the men quieted.

"I believe we killed everyone," someone said gleefully behind her. Evelyn turned her head as far as it would go. The man who had leered at her earlier stood in front of Laurent. The hungry, savage look in his eyes startled her.

"Let's bring this boat to shore," the man yelled to no one in particular, then fixed his evil eyes back on her. Evelyn shuddered. "Who knew that the greenhorn would offer more than just a fat wallet?" His hand reached out and he weaved his fingers through Evelyn's hair. "What a delectable morsel we have here."

"She will fetch a good price at rendezvous," Laurent said.

"I'm thinking we need to sample the goods before then," the man sneered. Laurent stepped back, keeping a firm hold around Evelyn's waist.

"If I had not offered her my help, she would not be here now," Laurent said firmly. "When we get to rendezvous, you can bid for her just like everyone else. Until then, she will not be touched."

The other man opened his mouth to speak, and Evelyn heard a pistol being cocked right next to her.

"She will not be touched, or you will meet the same fate as her brother," Laurent said in a menacing tone. "She is worth more as pure as she is."

Evelyn listened as the men argued, but her mind and body were too numb to respond. Henry was dead. The last of her family was gone. She lowered her head, unwilling to look into the eyes of the evil men who had done this to her and her brother. Tears rolled silently down her face.

Henry. Why did you have to do this? Why couldn't we just go on as before? As much as she wanted to see her parents' killer brought to justice, it had cost more than it was worth. Evelyn wished a stray bullet had hit her during the gunfire. Death was certainly preferable than what she knew was in store for her.

CHAPTER THREE

Alexander Walker rolled from his stomach to his back, and stared up at the cloudless sky. Stars twinkled brightly overhead; the only light illuminating an otherwise moonless night. Gripping his Hawken Rifle in his left hand, he laid it across his chest, fingering the familiar smooth trigger. He cradled the back of his head in his right hand, and closed his eyes.

The rhythmic chirping sounds of crickets surrounded him, almost drowning out the faint rustle of leaves in the underbrush. Probably a rabbit or vole scurrying around. The screech of an owl in a nearby tree silenced the crickets momentarily, and Alex seized on the opportunity to listen for anything unusual. Thankfully his companions had followed his suggestion and camped about a mile away. If his plan was going to be successful, he wanted to do it on his own, not with a bunch of crazy, trigger-happy trappers to ruin everything and possibly get them all killed.

Alex shifted his weight and stared into the blackness of the night. Visions of an auburn-haired girl crept into his mind. He gritted his teeth. Of all the times to be thinking about her, why now? *Focus, dammit!* He grimaced, and rubbed at the sore spot on his chest where the bullet from a hunting rifle was still lodged in the flesh below his collarbone. If the shooter's aim had been a little better, it would have been a fatal shot.

This spring he had gone to St. Louis for the first time in six years to restock his supplies, which he ordinarily would have purchased through the Rocky Mountain Fur Company – his former employer. Now that he was a free trapper, he had to find his provisions elsewhere. While in the city, he'd made an impulsive decision to visit St. Charles. A young woman walking along the docks by the Missouri River had caught his eye. There was something oddly familiar about her. It had taken him a few minutes to try and recollect where he'd seen her before, when he suddenly realized who she was.

Henry Lewis' sister, Evelyn, had blossomed from a spindle-legged girl into a beautiful curvaceous young woman. Her auburn hair was coiled properly atop her head and shimmered golden like the changing autumn aspen leaves in Jackson's Hole. She paid no notice to the many men who stopped their work to watch her walk by. She had glanced his way momentarily, but there was no recognition in her eyes. She'd quickly averted her gaze and stuck her pert nose in the air. *Can't blame her, now can you, Walker? You must look a sight.*

Alex absently ran his fingers through the thick bushy hair that covered much of his face. No one else had recognized him, either. What the hell had he been thinking? Six years away from civilization, and they would welcome him back with open arms, with him looking like a wild savage? He'd barely escaped with his life after his unknown attacker shot him. Curiosity about Evelyn Lewis after seeing her at the riverfront led him to her folks' farm. He wasn't sure what he'd find there, but a strange desire to see her again had overruled any common sense at the time.

No matter how often over the last several months he told himself to get her out of his mind, he couldn't shake the memory of Evie's beautiful face. After seeing nothing but Injuns and trappers who looked as wild and unkempt as he, Henry's little sister had been a feast to his starving eyes. She had to be married already, he told himself forcefully. Regardless, she was not for the likes of him, and he was never going back to St. Charles.

A sudden grunt and loud scraping noise to his left made him groan silently. Gritting his teeth, Alex raised his head slightly and focused his eyes into the darkness. A human form inched awkwardly on the ground in his direction.

Dammit! He could think of only one person who didn't have the brains to do what he was told. The movements were too loud and clumsy to be made by an Injun. Why the hell hadn't that fool Yancey listened and stayed behind with the others? The stupid greenhorn had been following him around like a stray dog ever since his return from St. Louis a month ago.

Alex listened for any other possible sounds that weren't made by the nighttime creatures of the wilderness. Nothing. All seemed quiet at the moment. Slowly, quietly, he laid his rifle on the ground. In one lightning fast move, he leapt to his feet and pulled his hunting knife from his belt. Before the man crawling toward him had a chance to react, Alex bent over him, and pinned him to the ground with one foot on his spine. He gripped his opponent's hair and forcefully yanked back. Hoping to prevent a scream from his victim, Alex held the sharp blade of his knife to the man's throat.

"You'd be dead if I was a Blackfoot," Alex growled quietly into the man's ear. "I should do us both a favor and kill you right now." For emphasis, he pulled the man's head back further. Alex held him in what was, no doubt, a painful position for another minute. "When I let go, keep your mouth shut," he warned. Loud, quick gasps for air were his answer.

Slowly, Alex eased his hold on Yancey's scalp, and pulled his knife away from the greenhorn's throat. Disgusted, he pushed the man's head into the dirt.

"You don't start listening, you're gonna be dead, and get the rest of us killed, too," Alex said coldly, and walked away to retrieve his rifle.

"The others dared me to sneak up on you," Yancey gasped, a quiver in his voice.

"Keep your goddamn voice down," Alex hissed. "I ain't in the mood to die tonight because of your stupidity." He glared into the darkness. For all he knew, the fool had already alerted the band of Blackfeet who were camped not a hundred yards away. Their campfires had burned down long ago, and Alex was ready to execute his plan. For two days, he'd tracked this group of Injuns who had stolen not only his saddle and packhorses, but those of several of his companions as well. Luckily, no one had lost their hair in the skirmish with the Blackfeet that day, but he wasn't about to let them get away with his horses.

Last fall, after nearly six years of working for the Rocky Mountain Fur Company, he'd finally decided to strike out on his own, and his pack animals carried all his worldly possessions, not to mention a year's worth of back breaking work in the form of beaver pelts that he planned to sell at rendezvous in a few days. He'd be damned if he was going to lose it all to a bunch of cutthroat Injuns. His friend and mentor, Daniel Osborne, had convinced him that he'd be better off as a free trapper rather than busting his back to stuff the pockets of William Ashley and his partner. Even after the company was sold to Jed Smith and the Sublettes, who were all experienced mountain men, he still had to turn in every beaver pelt he brought in while in their employ.

"Keep low and stay behind me," Alex cautioned the inexperienced Yancey, and led the way back to his hiding place behind several downed lodgepoles. He dropped to the ground and leaned his back against a log, motioning to the greenhorn to do the same.

"When do we attack?" Yancey whispered almost eagerly.

"We don't." Alex emphasized the word *we* in his quiet reply. "You're gonna keep your sorry hide right here."

"I've heard that the Indians call you Shadow Walker because you're known to attack when they least expect it, but you can't go against all those savages on your own," Yancey protested.

Alex inhaled a deep breath and clenched his jaw. If he had any sense at all, he'd have followed through with his threat and slit the greenhorn's throat a few minutes ago and been done with him. Memories of his first year in the mountains pushed to the forefront of his mind. Over the years, he had gained a reputation as a fierce fighter when his life or the life of one of his companions was threatened. Thanks to the man he considered to be his mentor, he was also an excellent tracker and marksman. But hadn't he been the same stupid youth six years ago? Eager to prove that he had what it took to be a mountain man, he hadn't listened to the more experienced trappers any more than Yancey was listening to him now.

A twig snapped in the darkness just beyond Alex's hiding place, and he tensed instantly.

"Wha—"

Alex clamped a hand over Yancey's mouth before the fool could finish his word, and cursed silently. Slowly, he reached for his rifle. Another twig snapped softly, this time only a few feet from his hiding place. Alex inhaled a deep breath, waited another five seconds that felt like an eternity, then sprang to his feet and swung the butt end of his rifle like a club through the air. With a dull crack, it connected with the solid form of a man's head. Dropping like a felled log, Alex's adversary hit the ground.

"Sweet Jesus," Yancey gasped. "What was that?"

"Unless you plan to go under tonight, you'll do what you're told and stay put," Alex growled, then leapt lightly over the log he'd been crouched behind for the last several hours. It was time to steal his horses back before the sentry was missed.

* * *

Evelyn swayed precariously on the back of the horse she'd sat on since before dawn. Her head pounded fiercely, and she thought for sure her skull would split in half at any moment. Her limbs felt about as heavy as lead anchors, and trying to focus her vision on anything became impossible. This morning was no different than all the others she had endured since that fateful night on the boat. The six mountain men had killed not only her brother, but all the rivermen on board, then brought the vessel to a halt at the riverbank.

Two more men had shown up at dawn with horses and mules. This raid had obviously been well planned out. After unloading much of the cargo from the boat onto the animals' backs, they had set off away from the river, heading west. The forest around them was dense and often so heavily overgrown with underbrush, that traveling became nearly impossible in places. After only an hour, Evelyn had become hopelessly disoriented.

The idea of escaping her captors occurred to her every day, but she was never allowed a moment's privacy. Laurent watched over her like a hawk, telling the other men in no uncertain terms that she was his prize, and that he would kill anyone who tried to come near her. At night, he tied her wrists to his own, and she was forced to sleep pressed up against him. On the first night, she had lain awake with fear, wondering when he would take liberties with her, but not once had he touched her in ways that were inappropriate.

While a small part of her had been glad that Laurent kept those other wretched men away from her, he had made it quite clear what would happen to her when they arrived at a place they called the rendezvous, whatever that was. It sounded like a gathering of some sort. The packhorses and mules were laden with the goods they'd stolen from the boat and would use in trade, and she was apparently the most profitable commodity.

One day had blurred into another as they trekked through the mountains. She couldn't recall the last time she'd washed her face, much less the rest of her body, and her hair hung in limp strands down her back and past her shoulders. Laurent and the others no longer smelled bad, probably because she herself stank as much as they did.

The horse underneath her suddenly stopped, and Evelyn slowly lifted her head. She forced her heavy eyelids open, and tried to focus on her surroundings. Snow-capped mountain peaks rose in the far-off distance. The shouts and laughter of men, the barking of dogs, and horses' whinnies all mingled into one distant echo. Spread out before her as far as she could see were countless tents of all shapes and sizes, along with makeshift structures made from logs and tree branches and covered with hides. Campfires crackled everywhere, enveloping the small valley in a cloudy haze. Several deer carcasses in various stages of butchering hung upside down from wooden racks, and the distinct smell of whiskey blended with the countless other unpleasant odors wafting through the air. White men dressed in buckskins and furs mingled with Indians who wore not much more than loincloths. Evelyn lowered her head again. No doubt they had arrived at their destination, and her horrible fate awaited her shortly.

"*Mademoiselle*, the journey is over," Laurent said gallantly, moving his horse up alongside the one she'd been given to ride. Evelyn didn't respond.

"Why so sad?" he asked, and lifted her chin with his dirty fingers. "Today, you will meet with your future husband. It is not often that these men have the pleasure of bartering for a white bride. In fact, I believe it is almost unheard of. You will be the talk of this year's rendezvous."

Evelyn gave a listless laugh. Hadn't she left St. Charles in order to escape marriage to a man she didn't care for? Charles Richardson was looking pretty good to her right about now.

"Future husband?" she asked, her voice raspy and foreign-sounding to her own ears. "Don't you mean you're selling me to be a whore to these . . . these beasts?" She jutted her chin in the direction of the large camp, and almost lost her balance. If she fell from the horse, perhaps she would break her neck, and her troubles would be over. As if he had read her thoughts, Laurent snaked his hand around one of her wrists, steadying her seat.

"*Mademoiselle* Lewis, are you ill?" Laurent asked. He leaned forward in his saddle and studied her face. Was that concern in his eyes? Evelyn blinked and looked away. The man, if he could even be called a man, didn't have a shred of compassion in him. Why would he be concerned for her health all of a sudden?

"Don't worry, Mr. Berard," she spat, not hiding the contempt in her voice. "I'm well enough that you can sell me like a pig at market. No one will know, or care, whether I feel ill or not. I only hope that whatever ails me kills me quickly."

Laurent's face hardened, and he abruptly yanked on her horse's reins and kicked his own mount forward. Following the rest of his men into the loud and boisterous camp, cheering men quickly surrounded the new arrivals. Evelyn tucked her chin toward her chest and closed her eyes. She couldn't understand a word of what was said around her, and she didn't want to know. Instinctively she kicked out her leg when a sudden hand groped at her upper thigh. The roar of laughter all around her became deafening.

"I have waited weeks for this moment, Laurent," a menacing voice next to her startled her. She opened her eyes to see Oliver Sabin leering at her. He had made it no secret that he wanted her since the night he killed Henry. "You want to barter her, let's get on with it. I have a packhorse laden with trade goods, and I'm ready to barter for her now."

Several other men who apparently stood close enough to hear the exchange cheered. It seemed to only encourage Sabin, and he grabbed for Evelyn's arm.

In a move faster than Evelyn could comprehend, Laurent pointed a pistol at Sabin's head.

"Those trade goods you speak of belong to me as much as they do to you, *mon ami*. Remember that I was part of that raid, and the cargo belongs to us all equally."

"Yet you keep the woman for yourself," Sabin shouted angrily.

"I am the one who found her aboard the boat, so therefore, yes; she is mine to do with as I please. She was not part of the raid." Laurent didn't waver. His hard stare dared any of the men to contradict him.

"But very well," he continued after several tense moments, and shrugged. He lowered his weapon, and reached for Evelyn's arm, pulling her from the horse. A wave of dizziness swept over her when her feet touched the ground, and for a moment she thought she might black out. Laurent tightened his grip on her arm to steady her.

"Spread the word that Laurent Berard has brought this beautiful white woman who goes by the name of Evelyn Lewis to rendezvous, and I will entertain all offers for her." Like a theater actor, he swept his hand out in front of him in a dramatic gesture, pronouncing Evelyn's name in his peculiar French accent. He scanned the large crowd of men that had formed around them.

"Bidding will begin in one hour." His words were barely audible above the eager shouts of dozens of rough and eager-looking mountain men. Evelyn couldn't bear to look. Her heart pounded in her chest, and her head felt as if it was made of lead. All she wanted to do was sink to the ground and allow sleep to overtake her. Perhaps then this nightmare would end.

Laurent led her further into camp, stopping next to a group of willow bushes.

"Rest here, *mademoiselle*. You will need all your strength." He pushed her to the ground.

Evelyn raised her head and glared at him through unfocused eyes. "If you have even one shred of decency in you, you foul, disgusting excuse for a human being, you'll take that pistol you're so fond of and put a bullet through my temple."

Laurent stared down at her, then burst out laughing. "I cannot do that, *mademoiselle*. You are much too valuable for that."

Evelyn shot him a look of pure contempt, then turned her head and closed her eyes. Tears of despair squeezed through between her closed eyelids, and rolled down her cheeks. Glad for the fever that ravaged her body, making her mind nearly numb with delirium, she leaned back against the branches of the willow. She'd barely closed her eyes when a sharp tap on her shoulder startled her awake.

"It is time, mademoiselle," Laurent whispered in her ear.

"What?" Evelyn croaked. She forced her eyes open. Men stood all around her, eager and hungry looks in their eyes. She'd just closed her eyes. Was the hour up already?

Laurent helped her to her feet, and she stood facing dozens of rough and unkempt-looking mountain men. A shiver ran down her spine. Sabin stood at the front of the group. Evelyn tried to lift her chin and square her shoulders, but it was too much of an effort. She tuned out Laurent's voice as he asked for someone to make him an offer. The voices became louder and more boisterous, and Evelyn shut out the noise as best as she could.

A sudden loud uproar from the men made her lift her head to see what the renewed commotion was all about. Men stepped aside, and Evelyn's gaze locked on a man pushing his way to the front. Broad-shouldered but of average height, he carried himself with a certain confidence that seemed to be lacking in most of these other men. He was just as unkempt as the rest of them, his long thick black hair falling nearly to his shoulders, and most of his face obscured by a bushy beard.

"What did you say?" Laurent exclaimed next to her.

"I'll give you half a year's beaver pelts for her," the man said in a deep and resonating voice. The roar of the men around him increased. He didn't look at her, but instead glared at Laurent as if he intended to kill the man with his stare alone.

"You can't barter pelts for her. They belong to the Rocky Mountain Fur Company." Sabin sneered and tried to block the other man's way. "B'sides, since when have you ever wanted to trade for a woman?"

"Since I decided I want this one," the dark man answered gruffly. "And my pelts are mine to do with as I choose."

He stepped forward and grabbed Evelyn's arm, pulling her away from the half-circle of men. He stopped and turned toward Laurent.

"I'll settle up with you in a little while." His tone implied more than paying for what he had just bought.

Evelyn darted a frantic glance at Laurent, whose mustache twitched as he smiled triumphantly. She tried to pull away from the menacing man's grip, but he held firm. She had no strength left in her. Her head pounded, and her world began to spin. Her legs felt like bread pudding, but she forced one foot in front of the other as he dragged her away from the crowd

Evelyn didn't care anymore what happened to her. Her mind was too tired, and her body weak from the fever that had plagued her for two days. She simply wished she could curl up and die. Her legs suddenly gave out, and she stumbled. Before she hit the ground, the gruff mountain man who now owned her scooped her in his arms. For a moment, Evelyn stared up into the trapper's deep blue eyes, which were partly obstructed by thick strands of black hair. His dense black beard covered most of his facial features.

Evelyn blinked, trying to keep him in focus, but his face suddenly became a blur.

"Alex," she whispered, just before her world went dark.

CHAPTER FOUR

"What the hell were you thinking, bringing her here?" Alex roared and charged at the man who stood next to his horse, unwrapping the leather girth straps from around the animal's belly. Laurent Berard spun around on his heels. Before he could react, Alex grabbed the Frenchman by the front of his shirt, his momentum sending both of them against the horse. The animal sidestepped nervously, and Laurent nearly lost his balance. Alex grimaced, his face inches from his wide-eyed opponent. His fists dug into the slightly shorter man's collarbones. Laurent stared back at Alex.

"I had no choice, Walker," he said between gritted teeth, and grabbed hold of Alex's wrists in an attempt to loosen the grip.

Locked in a duel of strength, Alex refused to back away. He leaned toward Laurent in an attempt to unbalance him, but the Frenchman had squared his legs in a way that made it impossible to budge him. The slow smirk on Laurent's face only served to infuriate Alex more.

He was tired as hell, and had been looking forward to a

nice long nap. Two nights ago, he had successfully stolen back all the horses that the Blackfeet had stolen from him and his six traveling companions. He'd ended up with a few extra animals that he planned to trade at rendezvous. The party of Blackfeet was too small to dare an attack on this large gathering, so he wasn't worried about being followed. Hundreds of trappers from all over the Rockies were already congregated here, along with countless Indians from various tribes. Alex hadn't much cared to find out who had already arrived. He would look for acquaintances later. He especially wanted to seek out Aimee Osborne, and ask her to remove the buckshot from his chest.

After an all-night ride to reach the site of this summer's rendezvous, a small valley some hundred miles from the mountain range the Shoshoni called the Teewinots, Alex had been looking forward to a day of sleep. He and his fellow trappers had arrived in camp before dawn, and after tending their stock, had simply spread their bedrolls on the ground. There would be time to set up a more permanent camp later.

He'd just fallen asleep when that meddlesome Yancey called to him, his voice full of excitement and going on about the talk in camp over a white woman who apparently had the misfortune of being caught on the river by a group of thugs. Alex had rolled over under his blanket and threatened to put a bullet in Yancey's head if he didn't leave him in peace.

"The Frenchman, Laurent Berard, is making a big show of bartering her to the highest bidder," Yancey continued. "He wanted it announced throughout camp that he had a white woman by the name of Evelyn Lewis. I think this sort of thing is downright barbaric, and..."

Whatever else Yancey had said was lost to Alex. A jolt of adrenaline had surged through him at hearing the name. It was impossible that Yancey had misspoken. What were the odds that there was another Evelyn Lewis? If it was the same girl who haunted him in his dreams, how could she possibly end up here, of all places?

Alex didn't waste time to contemplate the question. He made sure his pistol was loaded and stuffed in the belt around his waist, and fingered the elk antler handle of his knife. Dashing through camp, he weaved between tents and lean-tos, and soon saw where all the commotion was coming from. Dozens of men gathered in a semi-circle, whooping and hollering. Laurent's distinct voice, trying to calm the crowd, reverberated over the others.

She barely looked like the girl he remembered seeing in St. Charles a few months ago. Her hair that had shone like spun gold that day at the docks now hung listless and dull from her head. She appeared pasty and frail. Her slight body, dressed in men's breeches and shirt, swayed like a young sapling in the wind, an occasional shiver coursing noticeably through her. Every now and then, her head jerked up, revealing her terror-filled eyes.

Rage such as he'd never felt before coursed through Alex. His blood pounded through the veins in his temples, and the muscles tensed throughout his body. He wanted to kill each and every one of these men who leered at the helpless girl, their intentions only too obvious. There was only one way he could get Evelyn safely away from these men, and Alex pushed his way through the crowd. He didn't stop to give another man a chance at her, and offered a price that he felt confident no one would meet. If need be, he was prepared to double his offer. One look at Evelyn Lewis, and he knew he'd give his life for her at that moment. The naked fear in her eyes reminded him of his mother each time she faced his drunken father. Alex hadn't been able to keep her safe. He was not going to fail this time.

"What has gotten into you, *mon ami?*" Laurent shouted, startling Alex to loosen his grip on the man's shirt. With a forceful shove, he pushed the Frenchman away from him, releasing his hold. Laurent hastily straightened his shirt, and glared at Alex, then his mustache twitched and he smiled broadly.

"How the hell is it that she is here, Laurent?" Alex demanded. He inhaled a deep breath to calm his nerves, and turned his head slightly to the side.

"It is not something I planned, I assure you," Laurent said, and pulled his coonskin cap from his head, slapping it against his thigh.

"Jed Smith asked you to go to St. Louis to try and find out what those thieves from the American Fur Company were up to, not to abduct white women to barter here at rendezvous."

Laurent scoffed. "You know as well as I that I would never wish such a fate on any woman, much less one as lovely as Mademoiselle Lewis. She gave me no alternative but to bring her along."

"Explain yourself, Laurent." Alex glared at the Frenchman.

Laurent nodded. He turned and pulled the saddle from his horse's back, and tossed it against a nearby tree trunk. "Walk with me, my friend," he said quietly, and his eyes darted around as if looking for someone. "I do not wish to be overheard." He headed in the direction of the woods, leaving Alex no choice but to follow if he wanted some answers.

"I trust the young lady is safe?" Laurent asked after several minutes of silence.

"I left her with Aimee Osborne," Alex grumbled. His chest suddenly tightened at the memory of Evie in his arms. Just before she lost consciousness, she'd looked him in the eyes and recognized him. Alex was startled to see renewed fear in those green eyes of hers. He'd never been close enough to Henry's sister to notice the color of her eyes, not that he'd ever been interested in that sort of thing before.

"She will be well cared for." Laurent nodded in approval. "I could do nothing for her while we traveled over the mountains," he added quickly, and shot a hasty look at Alex. "I could not reveal my cover. Surely you understand."

Alex's eyebrows pulled together. "Start at the beginning, Laurent."

Laurent nodded. "I met up with Oliver Sabin's crew shortly after I arrived in St. Louis," he began. "A quick demonstration of my knife and pistol skills, and they were more than willing to hire me on."

"Sabin and his men have been sabotaging Jeb Smith's supply boats for years," Alex remarked. "How did Evie . . . Evelyn Lewis end up on one of those boats?"

Laurent's twitching lips and twinkling eyes didn't escape Alex's notice. He clenched his jaw.

Laurent cleared his throat. "Her brother sought the services of Sabin and his men."

"Henry Lewis?" Alex raised his eyebrows. He remembered his childhood friend's eagerness to join him on his adventure in the wilderness, but duty to his family prevented him from going along. Had he finally decided to give up his life as a farmer? That still didn't explain how Evie ended up with Laurent.

"Shortly before the boat departed, I noticed a young woman disguised as a boy get on board. I intercepted her. You can appreciate my surprise when she revealed her name, and that she was trying to follow her brother."

Laurent stopped walking. He turned fully toward Alex. A wide smile spread across his face. "I have done you a great service, *mon ami*." His teeth gleamed white in the sunlight.

"What the hell are you talking about?" Alex avoided Laurent's much-too perceptive stare.

"Mademoiselle Lewis. She is the lady you have talked about, no? You refuse to return to St. Louis. I have brought her to you."

Alex cursed under his breath. He should have never discussed his time in St. Charles. The meddlesome Frenchman had insisted on knowing why Alex had returned to Jackson's Hole with a bullet in his chest. His body had been combating a fever, and in his delirium he must have talked about seeing Evelyn. Laurent had relentlessly pestered him for information afterwards. Laurent, a free trapper, had been his friend for years, and Alex had spent several winters at the Frenchman's cabin that he'd built at the base of *Les Trois Tetons*.

"I don't want her here." Alex forced the words from his mouth. "She should be at home, safe on her folks' farm."

"And marry the man her brother chose for her? A man she does not love?"

Alex's head shot up. His eyes narrowed. "Why would Henry choose a husband for her. Where is he, anyhow?"

Laurent studied him before he spoke. "Henry Lewis is dead. Sabin killed him. There was nothing I could do to prevent it. I have done my best to keep the little *mademoiselle* safe from Sabin and his men. I knew you would be here when we arrived, and I made sure her name spread through camp. I was certain that you would come and claim her as your own when you heard."

Alex ran a hand up the nape of his neck. The last thing he wanted was Evie here in the wilderness, near all these trappers and mountain men, and least of all, near him.

"Why couldn't you simply scare her off that boat?" Alex's mind churned. What was he going to do with her? There was no denying that she stirred feelings in him that were as foreign as an encounter with a friendly Blackfoot. He'd felt similar stirrings the day he saw her in St. Charles, and although her appearance was vastly different today than the woman he had seen then, holding her in his arms had ignited a longing deep inside him unlike anything he'd ever felt.

Laurent let out a bark-like laugh. "Walker, do you really believe that she would have simply returned home if I had chased her off that boat? She would have found another vessel; mark my words. That little *mademoiselle* has a spark in her that is not so easily squelched."

Alex gnashed his teeth in frustration. He remembered Henry's little sister as a plucky girl, annoying and meddlesome. She'd often tag along when he and Henry went off into the woods. He'd simply chosen to ignore her back then.

"Why would she follow Henry into the wilderness?" he wondered out loud.

Laurent's eyes widened briefly. He tilted his head to the side and then leaned toward Alex. "Why, to kill you, my friend."

* * *

Evelyn slowly forced her eyelids open. Her lips parted slightly, and she raked her teeth against her dried lips. Her tongue stuck to the roof of her parched mouth, and she couldn't swallow. She moaned softly, and forced her legs to move. A sharp pain seared up her spine, and when she tried to bring her hand to her face, her arm felt as if lead anchors were attached to the limb.

Blinking, she stared up at what appeared to be the covering of a cone-shaped tent. She turned her head and glanced at the animal skins that served as walls in the dimly lit space. Evelyn groaned and braced against her elbows to raise herself up off the ground. A thick furry hide covered her, which fell from her shoulders. She shuddered at the sudden blast of cold air against her skin.

Evelyn sucked in a startled breath, and hastily pulled the cover back over herself. She was nude! Her heart pounded fiercely against her chest, and she gasped for air. *Dear God! What happened?*

Holding the fur tightly against her body, she rolled to her side and sat up. The blood rushed from her head, and she braced one hand against the ground to stave off the dizziness. She tried to blink away the black swirls in front of her eyes. Frantically, she scanned the interior of the tent, hoping to spot her clothing. More furs were piled in heaps across from her at the other side of the tent, and several large leather pouches leaned against each other. An assortment of wooden bowls littered the ground.

The beating of her heart increased. Memories of the weeks of traveling through the mountains with those vile mountain men flooded her mind. Henry was dead. The Frenchman, Laurent, had sold her like a steer at auction to the highest bidder. That barbarian who bid for her had carried her off, much of his face covered in thick black hair. Those blue eyes of his had stared down at her as if he could see right through her. They were familiar eyes; the eyes of the boy she had lost her youthful heart to all those years ago. He looked exactly like the savage Henry predicted he had become.

No! Please, no! She had stared directly at her parents' murderer. Evelyn pulled the fur covers further up her neck and squeezed her eyes shut. How long had she lain here, and what had Alex done to her while she was unconscious?

CHAPTER FIVE

Evelyn gingerly pulled her legs up underneath her and sat up fully. She made sure the blanket was wrapped tightly around her. Loud voices and boisterous laughter drifted from outside the tent, dogs barked, and a horse whinnied in the distance. Several times, gunshots went off somewhere nearby, and she cringed. Getting caught in the crossfire on the boat was still fresh in her mind. These men . . . these trappers were nothing but uncivilized savages.

She continued to scan the dim interior of the tent, searching for her clothing. A small part of her wished the illness had killed her. Her body no longer felt feverish, but her face flushed hot with shame at the thought of what that wretched beast had probably already done to her. She tried to block out the images that came to her mind, and was glad that she had no recollection of it. She could no longer be seen in civilized society after what fate had dealt her.

Wiping away the tears that rolled down her cheeks, Evelyn inhaled a deep breath. She refused to dwell on what had happened, and didn't want to think about what lie ahead. Was there any hope to get out of her predicament? Alex

Walker now owned her and could do with her as he pleased. There would be no one here to help her.

"What did he do with my clothes?" she mumbled through gritted teeth, her frustration growing when she couldn't spot anything that even remotely resembled something she could wear. She didn't dare move from her spot on the soft pile of furs and animal skins. After weeks of sitting and sleeping on nothing but hard ground, the furs beneath her were almost as comfortable as her bed back home.

The tent flap suddenly moved, and bright light streamed into the interior. Evelyn shrank back, and held her breath. She clutched the cover tighter to her body. To her surprise, the head of a young girl with long dark hair appeared through the opening. She stared at Evelyn, and her lips widened in a smile. She turned her head and yelled over her shoulder, "Mama, she's awake."

The girl stooped over and stepped into the tent, letting the flap fall closed behind her.

"We were wondering when you were going to wake up," she said, and sat on the ground next to Evelyn. Her bright smile hadn't faded. She reached a hand up and held her palm to Evelyn's forehead. "Your fever's gone, too. Mama was hoping the willow bark tea would do some good. She didn't know why you had a fever, but she'll be glad to see you're better now."

Evelyn stared at the girl. She looked well groomed, her dark hair braided in one long rope down her back. She wore clean buckskin britches and a blue cotton shirt, and almost reminded Evelyn of an Indian maiden. Her startling blue eyes, however, were a sure indication that she was white. A soft hint of lavender drifted to Evelyn's nose. What she wouldn't give for a bath with some soap.

"I'm Sarah," the girl continued. "What's your name?"

Evelyn cleared her throat. "Evelyn Lewis," she said, her

voice raspy. Her throat felt as dry as a parched cornfield in summer. She clutched the fur covering tightly to her chest.

"Oh, here are your clothes," Sarah said as if she just remembered something, and reached into the large pouch that hung from her shoulder. "I washed them for you, and mended a few of the holes."

Relief swept over Evelyn as the girl held out her britches and shirt.

"Where am I?" Evelyn asked, and licked at her dried lips. Who was this young white girl?

"You're in my mother's medical tent," Sarah answered. "She's a healer who takes care of all the injured and sick trappers that come to rendezvous each summer. Some of those dumb men just don't know how to stay out of trouble. They always have to prove how tough they are, and most of the time they end up getting shot or worse. It's a good thing Alex brought you here. You had a very high fever."

Evelyn's heart jumped at the sound of *his* name. Alex had brought her to someone for care?

"How long have I been here?"

"Since this morning. You slept almost the entire day. Mama had to remove your clothes and bathe you in cool water to try and bring your temperature down. She made you drink willow bark tea."

Evelyn's eyebrows furrowed, and she shook her head slightly. The thought that another woman had undressed her gave her a small sense of comfort. Perhaps she hadn't been violated after all.

"You don't remember any of it?" Sarah asked.

"All I remember is that . . . that brute carrying me off, after . . ." She left the rest unspoken, and hung her head. An overwhelming feeling of fear and loneliness swept over her. She'd never been away from her family's farm in all her nineteen years, and now she found herself thrust into a brutal world she didn't understand, amidst people she didn't know. Worst of all, she was now the property of the very man who had slaughtered her family.

Sarah laughed, bringing Evelyn's head up. What did the girl find so amusing?

"Brute?" she echoed. "Alex can be a little gruff, I guess." Sarah paused to think. "You're lucky, though," she continued, and stared at Evelyn with a serious look in her eyes. "I don't know why Walker would up and trade a half-year's worth of pelts for you. I've never heard of anyone paying such a high bride price. He's always been a loner, and unless you count Whispering Waters, he hasn't made it known that he had any interest in a wife. He'll treat you far better than most of those other men, I'd imagine."

Evelyn shifted her weight on the furs. This girl spoke of Alex as if he were a fond friend. "Lucky?" she spat. "You think I'm lucky because some uncivilized barbarian bartered for me? Lucky that I watched my brother be murdered, and was then brought here against my will?"

Sarah's eyes widened. "No." She shook her head. "I didn't mean it like that." She touched a tentative hand to Evelyn's arm. Evelyn jerked away.

"Please . . . please grant me some privacy so I can get dressed," she whispered. A painful lump formed in her throat, but she couldn't swallow.

"All right," Sarah said softly. "I'll go see what's keeping my mother. She'll want to check on you to make sure you're better." She scrambled to her feet and turned to leave the tent. Just before she reached the opening, she glanced back at Evelyn.

"You don't have to stay with him, you know. It's not as if he owns you, but it might be safer for you, having a man to protect you." With those words, she scrambled through the tent's opening and disappeared from view.

Evelyn stared after the girl. What did she mean by Alex didn't own her? He had bartered for her. Was she simply free to go? Her spirits lifted with that thought, then quickly plummeted again.

Where are you going to go, Evie? You're in the middle of nowhere. You could never hope to find your way home on your own.

***

Evelyn dressed quickly, inhaling the fresh scent on her clothes. She ran her fingers through her hair, holding a handful of amber strands in front of her to inspect. To her utmost surprise, her hair was clean and soft, no longer greasy and matted. Other than wearing her brother's britches and shirt, she felt almost normal again.

"Why on earth did you wait so long?" A woman's stern scolding from just outside the tent reached Evelyn's ears. "You could have told me about this when you brought that poor girl to me. But I guess those few hours don't matter anymore, either. I swear, Alex, you are about as smart as a bear with its paw in a beehive."

A jolt of adrenaline washed over Evelyn at hearing his name. He must be right outside. Would he seek her out? She still didn't quite believe Sarah when she said she was free to go.

"I didn't feel inclined to head up to the Yellowstone for a little buckshot under my skin, Aimee." Alex's deep, rich voice sent a shiver up Evelyn's spine. It was not the same voice she remembered from years ago, but then she'd never heard Alex talk a lot except when he and Henry thought they were alone.

"Well, it would have been much easier to get this slug out of you when this was still fresh. Now I have to make an incision and open that wound all over again. Sarah, go tell Matt or Zach to fetch me a bottle of whiskey."

"I can get it, Mama." Evelyn recognized Sarah's voice.

"You'll do no such thing, young lady." The woman's voice replied heatedly.

"You know I ain't gonna drink that stuff, Aimee, so there's no need for whiskey. Just cut me open already and get rid of the damn buckshot." Alex's voice hardened noticeably.

"You stupid fool. I wasn't going to make you drink the whiskey. I need the alcohol to disinfect your wound. And since you're being so rude, I won't feel sorry for you when it stings." Although the woman's voice held no hint of warmth, Evelyn had the distinct impression that the banter between her and Alex was lighthearted and friendly.

"You still use them funny words that no one understands," Alex replied, and the woman named Aimee laughed.

Overcome by curiosity, Evelyn sank to her knees by the tent opening. Slowly, she lifted the flap to the side, just enough to peek out. Several yards away, a fire blazed and crackled, and Evelyn noticed the handle of a knife sticking out from the flames. To the right, a woman sat bent over a man lying on the ground. Evelyn's eyes rested on the woman's long golden hair. Dressed in similar clothes as Sarah, this woman's appearance was even more out of place here than her young daughter.

"Does Daniel know you've been shot in the chest?" Aimee asked.

"Ain't seen him yet," came the gruff reply.

"What happened? Did you annoy some Blackfoot warriors too much, or did you get under the skin of another trapper?" Aimee taunted.

"I don't know who shot me," Alex scoffed. "It happened while I was in St. Louis some months back."

Evelyn inhaled a deep breath. Charlie had shot Alex when

he ran from her home after killing her parents. He'd fled into the woods. Any doubt she ever had that Alex had killed her folks vanished instantly. What she was hearing confirmed Charlie's story. He might not be the man she wanted for a husband, but surely he wouldn't simply shoot a man for no reason.

She moved the tent flap back a few more inches to see better. Alex lay on a blanket on the ground. The woman kneeling over him obstructed most of Evelyn's view, but muscular arms reached up and under his head. His flat, well defined abdomen moved up and down in quick rhythmic succession like someone who was out of breath from exertion.

"Hold still, Alex, or I'll stake you to the ground," Aimee said. She reached for the glowing knife in the fire. "Where's Sarah with that alcohol?" She looked up just as Sarah and two youths who looked identical emerged from around another tent.

"Here's your whiskey, Mama." One of the boys handed her the bottle. "Which one of us needs to chaperone Sarah now? There's a horse race about to start, and we want to go watch."

"You can both go, Matt," Aimee said, taking the bottle from him. "Sarah can stay here with me and help."

"I want to go to see the race, too," Sarah protested, and held her hands to her hips.

The boy named Matt boxed his brother in the arm and nodded, and both of them took off running.

"Come back here," Sarah called. Then she glared down at her mother. "That's not fair. Why do they get to have all the fun?"

"Sarah, right now I need you to quit your complaining and help me. Clean that area right here on Alex's chest with the alcohol so I can make an incision."

The young girl huffed in protest, but obeyed her mother. Despite everything, Evelyn couldn't help but smile. Sarah reminded her of herself when she was younger. She'd often defied her mother and gone off to see what the men were doing. It always seemed that the women were left to do the tedious chores while the men went off to have fun.

Silently, Evelyn observed what was going on a few yards from the tent. The woman's back was turned to her, so she couldn't see exactly what Aimee was doing, but when Sarah stuck a branch near Alex's head and told him, "Here, bite down on this so you don't scream like a baby," Evelyn had no doubt that the healer woman was cutting into Alex's flesh. An involuntary shiver ran down her spine. Silently she prayed that the knife would inflict all the pain it possibly could. This man did not deserve her sympathy.

"There. That wasn't too deep," Aimee said after a few minutes. "Let me sew this up, and you'll be good as new. Like a seamstress, Aimee's arm moved up and down, a needle and thread in her hand. With a quick snip of a pair of scissors, she cut through the ends of the string. Had she actually sewn Alex's skin back together?

Sudden anger coursed through Evelyn. Why was she hiding out, watching this woman care for the man who had shattered her world to pieces? Her eyes fell to the knife lying on the ground next to Aimee. Without contemplating her actions, Evelyn pushed through the tent opening and lunged for the weapon. With trembling hands, she held it in a tight grip and took a step back. Aimee jumped to her feet, and so did Alex. Blood covered his chest.

"Why do you help him? You should have driven this knife through his black heart," Evelyn shouted, her wide eyes darting from Aimee to Sarah.

Aimee held one hand out in front of her, the other motioned for Sarah to stay back. She shot a quick look at

Alex, whose eyes briefly widened in surprise before his brows furrowed. He took a step toward her, and Evelyn thrust the knife out in front of her. Quicker than she could blink, Alex's arm snaked out and his hand wrapped around Evelyn's wrist. With a soft cry of surprise, she dropped her weapon.

"Hello, Evie," Alex said slowly. "I figured this would be the sort of greeting I would receive. You certainly didn't disappoint."

She pulled away from him, but his hand of steel held tightly to her wrist. His grip intensified, and his cold stare sent a wave of dread down her spine.

"You vile, evil monster," she spat. "You killed my parents. After all they did for you, why did you kill them?" She swung back with her free hand, then brought it forward in an attempt to strike his face, but Alex's reflexes were faster. He grabbed her other wrist, then pinned both her arms to her sides, stepping closer to her. His bushy face was mere inches from hers. Evelyn stared up into his deep blue eyes, her heart pounding fiercely in her chest.

"Let's get one thing straight, Evie," he said in a low, menacing voice. "I don't know who gave you or Henry the idea that I killed your folks, but whoever is accusing me of that is a liar."

"Release me, you savage." Evelyn gritted her teeth. The more she squirmed, the tighter he squeezed her wrists until his hold was almost painful.

"Alex, let her go," Aimee said softly. She stepped to his side and placed her hand on his arm. "You're hurting her."

As if Aimee had slapped him, Alex's head whipped around to look at the blond woman, breaking his intense eye contact with Evelyn. Then he glared at his hands gripping her wrists. He released her as if she'd burned him and took several steps back. His eyes wide with surprise, he cursed under his breath, and turned toward the fire. His hands balled into tight fists at his side.

Aimee reached out and placed her arm around Evelyn's shoulders. Too stunned to move, she stood there for a moment and stared at Alex's back. Every muscle along his spine tensed.

"Come on, Miss Lewis," Aimee said in a soothing voice. "I see there are some misunderstandings here, but I know we can work them out. Let's get you back to the tent. You've been through quite an ordeal and need to rest."

Her mind reeled with what Alex had said, but Evelyn allowed the woman to guide her back toward the tent. She rubbed at her sore wrists, and cast one final look in Alex's direction. He stared back at her, his eyes filled with anguish and remorse so intense it reached out and gripped her around the heart.

CHAPTER SIX

Alex sat along the banks of a slow-moving creek that meandered through the valley some distance from the main camp. Savoring the solitude, he absently tossed rocks into the water, the deep plopping sound amplified in the stillness of the morning. Fog hovered over the tall meadow grass, giving the entire area an almost ghost-like appearance. In the distance, the jagged snow-capped mountain peaks of the Teewinots stretched toward the sky. The rising sun cast a golden coppery glow across the tops of the three tallest peaks, the lights and shadows changing from one minute to the next. *Gold and copper, just like Evie's hair when the sun touched it just right.*

Alex hurled a large stone far out and over the water, the projectile landing somewhere in the grass on the opposite bank. Clenching his jaw, he pushed himself up off the ground. The wound on his chest throbbed dully. He welcomed the pain.

Let her go, Alex. You're hurting her. Aimee's words from the previous day repeated over and over in his mind. How much pain would he have inflicted on Evie if Aimee hadn't stepped in to stop him?

You're no better than that bastard who fathered you.

Alex cursed under his breath. He'd left his family, or what little there had ever been of one, behind six years ago, and for good reason. His old man was a drunkard who violently beat his mother. Even though he could never prove it, Alex knew without a doubt that his father had killed his mother in a drunken rage. Many times, Alex had walked away with bruised ribs and black eyes while trying to defend his mother. Back then, he'd been too young and scared to do anything other than absorb the blows that were meant for her.

He tried to push the painful memories of his childhood aside. He should have just killed the bastard when he had the chance. Instead, he'd left St. Charles to make a new life for himself in the wilderness. His mother had always begged him not to become like his father whenever Alex spoke of seeking revenge. After her death, he'd respected her wishes and simply walked away. He'd found his escape by joining the Rocky Mountain Fur Company.

Alex clenched his jaw and kicked at some dried clumps of dirt in the grass. He'd acted no differently with Evie than how his father had always treated his mother. He could have easily broken her arms. A shudder passed through him. Determined not to become like his bastard father, Alex had never touched a drop of alcohol, even though it was available in abundance among his comrades. Last evening had been proof that he was just like the old man after all when his temper got the better of him. Violence had been the old man's answer to everything.

Alex scoffed. The life he led now was more violent than anything he could possibly encounter in St. Louis or St. Charles. In order to survive in the wilderness, he had learned how to kill, and he had learned it quite well. *Be quicker and more brutal than your opponent.* That was the law of survival in these untamed mountains. But to lose control so quickly with a defenseless woman? A woman he wanted to protect, and who stirred foreign feelings deep within him; one who planted thoughts of a home and family in his head. All the things he'd never considered before.

A loud plop followed by a splash in the water several feet from where he stood startled him from his thoughts. Alex wheeled around, his knife drawn. He relaxed instantly and sheathed his weapon. Sarah Osborne strode toward him with a determined look on her girlish face. She tossed another rock in his direction into the water. Was there something going on with Evie? She wouldn't try and attack Aimee, would she?

"Walker," Sarah called.

She'd grown since he'd last seen her more than a year ago. She had to be about the same age now as Evie had been when he left St. Charles to start his new life. Long-legged like a young deer, Sarah walked with the proud confidence of her father.

"Good thing you're here, Walker." Sarah stopped right in front of him. She glanced past him toward the creek.

"Is Evelyn causing problems?" Alex's eyebrows furrowed.

Sarah stared at him for a moment, her own forehead wrinkling. "No, but Mama asked me to come find you."

There was only one other reason Aimee would want to seek him out that he could think of. "The stitches are fine," he said.

"It's not about the stitches." Sarah turned her head to the side and studied his face. "Do you know what this is, Walker?" She held out her hand, displaying a rectangular cake of soap.

Alex glanced at it, then back at the girl's face. She behaved more like her mother all the time. She had the same determined look about her when she set out to do something. The fact that Sarah was up to something was quite apparent.

"'Course I know what it is." He frowned.

Sarah thrust the soap at him. "Then use it," she said firmly. She nodded with her chin toward the creek. "I suggest you take off your shirt and britches first, though."

Alex raised his eyebrows.

"Well, you can't bathe properly with your clothes on, now can you." She expelled an exasperated breath of air. "I won't look."

"What the hell do I want to bathe for?" Alex argued.

Sarah held her hands to her hips. "For starters, you smell worse than a grizzly that's been wallowing in bison dung," she said. "I'm sure Miss Evelyn won't tolerate your smell for long."

"What concern is it to her what I smell like? It keeps the bears away. Your father taught me that."

"Walker, you've been in the wilderness with those comrades of yours much too long. Papa wouldn't dream of coming home smelling like you do. Mama would toss him out like yesterday's dishwater. You can cover yourself in bear grease and beaver musk all you want when you're out running your traps, but when you come home, you'd better look and smell presentable. Which," she glared at him through narrowed eyes, "brings me to my next task." She produced a straight edge and a pair of scissors from the pouch hanging from her shoulder.

"After you're done bathing, you're getting a haircut and a shave."

"You ain't comin' near me with those scissors and that blade," Alex said and took a step back. He warily eyed the sharp objects in the girl's hand. He had no doubt that she knew how to use them as effective weapons if need be.

Sarah laughed. "What's the matter, Walker? Scared of a mere girl? Don't worry. Papa lets me shave him all the time. I haven't cut him . . . much."

Alex rubbed at the coarse hair on his face. "What the hell are you trying to do to me?"

"You've got a wife now, don't you? Shouldn't you make yourself more presentable to her? I bet in her eyes, you're no better than the rest of these trappers who forgot what it's like to live among civilized folk. Miss Evelyn is more than likely going to just toss you aside. I swear, Walker, don't you know anything about how to show a woman some respect?"

Alex glared at the young girl. He'd never considered that by bartering for Evie, he'd bought himself a wife. Keeping her was out of the question. Hell, she was scared to death of him as it was.

And for good reason, Walker.

If yesterday had been any indication of how quickly he could lose control, she was no safer around him than his mother had been around his father.

"Mama told me to give you these." Sarah pulled clean britches and a cotton shirt from her pouch. She pushed the clothing at his chest, then turned to leave. She stopped abruptly to face him again. "Mama also told me to tell you that, after what happened yesterday, you and Miss Evelyn need to have a talk and clear up some misunderstandings. I'll be waiting over by that stand of willows." Sarah held up the scissors, and marched off.

Alex stared after her. Had he truly lost all touch with civilized society? Yesterday, Evelyn had called him a vile monster. She hadn't recognized him in St. Charles several months ago.

As a young girl, Evelyn Lewis had been infatuated with him, and he'd taken no notice. Alex shook his head and gave a short laugh. She'd been the last person on his mind over the years. He'd regarded her as his best friend's pesky little sister, nothing else. He ignored that she often watched him when she thought he wasn't paying attention. Just some silly little girl's fanciful notions. *She's not so little anymore, Walker.*

Alex stared at the clear water in the creek, his reflection a blur as the water meandered by. No, Evie was certainly not a little girl anymore. Perhaps for both their sakes, it would be wise to make himself more presentable, at least until he figured out what to do about her. Against his better judgment, he slowly unbuckled the belt from around his waist. Pulling his shirt up and over his head, he gritted his teeth against the sharp pain the action caused to the incision on his chest.

* * *

"I'll return within a few hours. If you need me for anything send one of the boys. I have already told them to stay near camp to watch over Sarah." Daniel Osborne bent over to give his wife a lingering kiss on the lips, then favored her with a soft smile before he turned and strode from camp.

Evelyn sat near the morning fire, silently observing the couple. The love and devotion between these two people was evident in everything they did; a soft touch, a warm glance, a quick smile. Evelyn marveled at the difference in appearance and behavior between this mountain man and the rest of the trappers she had encountered so far. Daniel Osborne was a rare man, she concluded. And his wife Aimee was an even rarer woman. That they had successfully made this wilderness their home and raised a family was astounding.

"If you see Amos Harris, tell him if he wants his boil lanced, he'll have to come see me today," Aimee called after her husband. "I'll start packing so we can be on our way bright and early."

Evelyn's head snapped in Aimee's direction. Her heart jumped in her chest suddenly.

"You're leaving?" she asked, setting aside the wooden bowl in her hand. Her appetite vanished.

Aimee nodded. "Tomorrow morning. We have to return home. Daniel's done trading his furs." She cast a worried look in Evelyn's direction.

"I see." Evelyn lowered her gaze to the ground. She raked her teeth across her lips. What would become of her? For the first time in weeks, she'd felt completely safe, even around Aimee's husband, Daniel. He was well groomed and less intimidating than the rest of these trappers that milled around camp.

Alex had disappeared the previous evening after she nearly attacked him with the knife, and she hadn't seen him since, which had suited her just fine. He was nothing more than an overbearing brute, as wild and uncivilized as the Indians she'd seen. Evelyn rubbed absently at her wrists, which bore the marks of his firm grip.

"Will you take me with you?" Evelyn stood abruptly and stared at Aimee. Her bold request was rude and imposing, but she didn't know what else to do. She had no one, and nowhere else to go.

Aimee studied her, then her eyes focused on something behind Evelyn, and her face brightened in a wide smile. "Alex, you're just in time for breakfast. Would you like some coffee?"

Evelyn wheeled around at the sound of his name, her heart lodged in her throat. A man who was a stranger, yet looked oddly familiar strode into camp. She stared at him, open-mouthed. An older version of the Alex she remembered, the quiet, mild-mannered youth from her childhood dreams now walked toward her. His face was clean-shaven, and his dark hair trimmed to below the nape of his neck. The grease-stained buckskins he'd worn the day before were gone, replaced by a clean cotton shirt and what looked like newly sewn buckskin britches.

"Mornin', Evie," he said, his voice barely audible. His blue eyes held her gaze.

Evelyn tried to speak, but she couldn't bring forth a single word. Her mouth had gone completely dry.

"He was rather disagreeable, Mama, but as you can see, the task is accomplished." Sarah rushed into camp from the same direction Alex had come from, a triumphant grin on her face.

"Come along, Sarah," Aimee said, and grabbed her daughter's arm. "You and I have work to do." She faced Alex. "If you'll excuse us."

When Sarah opened her mouth, Aimee shot her a warning glare, and pushed her daughter away from camp toward their tent.

Evelyn curled her toes inside her shoes as if it would root her to the ground. An overwhelming urge to run after Aimee and Sarah swept over her. Instead, she glanced up at Alex, who hadn't moved, nor had he stopped looking at her. Heat rose up her neck and into her cheeks from his intense perusal. How many countless times had she thought about him over the years? He looked just as she envisioned him. No. He was even more handsome than what she'd imagined. How could the face staring back at her be the same face as the hardened mountain man she'd seen yesterday? The face of a murderer?

Alex cleared his throat. "I . . . ah, brought you this." He held out a bundle of tan-colored cotton material. "Traded for it this morning. Thought you might like something else to wear other than your brother's old britches. I hope it's enough to make a dress."

Trying to steady her hands, Evelyn reached for the muslin

material that he offered. Her fingers grazed his, and she jerked back. In one quick move, Alex's hand reached out, and his fingers wrapped around her hand to keep her from pulling away. He stepped closer and lifted her arm, slowly rotating her wrist. Evelyn held her breath. Memories from the evening before flooded her mind, when Alex had squeezed her wrists to the point of cutting off her circulation. Aimee wasn't here this time to stop him.

A dark frown formed on his face, and the muscles along his jaw visibly tightened. Alex stared from her face to her hand from beneath his lashes, his blue eyes darkening. His other hand reached out, and he slid the sleeve of Evelyn's shirt up her arm, fully exposing her wrist. His work-roughened fingers gingerly touched her skin where red marks encircled her. His light touch felt like a caress, sending shivers racing up her arm.

"Evie, I . . ."

Evelyn yanked her hand from his grasp and took a step back.

"You what, Alex?" she said heatedly. Shielding the turmoil that raged inside her with anger, she fisted her hand at her hip and leaned forward. "You're going to tell me again that you didn't kill my parents?" She pointed at his chest. Her eyes narrowed, and she continued, her voice growing louder with each word. "That bullet hole proves that you were there. If Charlie's aim had been better, you'd be dead, Henry would be alive, and I wouldn't be in this awful place."

Evelyn spun around, and buried her face in the muslin she still held in her hands. If Charlie had aimed better, her entire life would be different. Alex would be dead.

"Charlie Richardson? That corncracker is the one who shot me?" Alex's voice boomed behind her. Evelyn wheeled to face him. Anger blazed in his eyes, where moments ago she'd seen a spark of tenderness.

"You deserved it, and more," Evelyn shouted, advancing on him.

"Like hell I did." Alex stepped toward her until they stood mere inches from each other. He towered over her, his eyes smoldering anger as he stared down at her. His grimace was more than intimidating.

Evelyn's eyes widened. It was the same look he wore yesterday just before he grabbed her. No sooner had the thought entered her mind when his hands clamped around her upper arms. She tensed. For a moment, she was sure he would shake her, but his grip eased instantly, and his features softened.

"Evie, I didn't kill your folks." His voice had gone normal again. There was an almost pleading tone to his words.

"What were you doing at the farm, then?" She wanted to back away, but his eyes compelled her to remain rooted to the spot. The warmth from his hands radiated into her arms, and he stood so close, the scent of leather and clean male skin assaulted her senses.

Alex's eyes raked over her face. He didn't respond for the longest time. When he did, his lips curved in a soft smile, completely transforming his features right before her eyes into those of the boy she had lost her heart to all those years ago.

"I wanted to visit old friends," he finally answered.

Evelyn blinked. Her eyebrows scrunched together, and she shook her head slightly. She wanted to believe the Alex who stood before her. It had been so much easier to be distrustful of him when he looked like an uncivilized savage.

Don't fool yourself, Evie.

Just because his clean appearance reminded her of the boy she remembered from her childhood didn't mean he was innocent. He had become a hardened mountain man. An innocent man wouldn't have run away, would he? He still held her arms, sending inexplicable waves of heat crashing through her. She tightened her grip on the muslin in her hand.

Alex finally released her, but he didn't move away. Instantly, the skin where he'd touched her turned cold. Evelyn shivered, wishing he hadn't let go, yearning for him to hold her. How could he elicit such feelings? Alex's features blurred in front of her, and tears rolled down her cheeks.

"Then who killed my parents, Alex?" she whispered. "Who would want them dead?"

Alex cursed under his breath. "What would Charlie have to gain by killing your ma and pa?" he asked suddenly.

Evelyn wiped the tears from her face. Charles? The thought had never entered her mind. "I . . . I don't . . ." Evelyn's eyes widened. Had the truth been in front of her all along? "He bought the farm, and Henry betrothed me to him."

Alex's eyes blazed anew. "He may own your farm," he said between clenched teeth. "But for now, you belong to me."

CHAPTER SEVEN

Laurent Berard whistled loudly through his teeth. His eyes widened, the disbelief clearly written on his face. He jumped so fast from his seat on the ground, Alex thought a spark from the nearby campfire had burned a hole in the Frenchman's backside. His mouth expanded in a broad smile and his eyes twinkled with mischief. Alex groaned silently as he strode closer into camp. Yancey wisely hadn't left his spot in the dirt, but his jaw dropped and his eyes popped as if he'd seen a two-headed beaver. The three other men in camp gaped openly. Two sniggered, and the other coughed dramatically.

"A woman in your life is agreeing with you, *mon ami*," Laurent said loudly. He clasped Alex's arms and squeezed heartily. He angled his head first one way and then the other, and sniffed the air. "You look and smell as pretty as a young *mangeur de lard* fresh from the east." The three men at the fire burst out laughing.

Alex yanked his knife from his belt and held it to the Frenchman's throat, glaring at his friend. Laurent released his arms and tilted his chin to the side to avoid the sharp tip, but the threat of a knife in his jugular apparently didn't diminish the man's amusement. Alex had known that his comrades would mock the change in his appearance. If any man other than Laurent had referred to him as a pork eater, he would have considered it a great insult, but even coming from his friend, that didn't mean he had to take the friendly barb lying down.

"Is she a nice robe warmer, Walker? Must be better than an Injun squaw," one man called loudly. The others didn't hide the eager expressions on their faces, waiting for Alex to satisfy their curiosity about the woman everyone assumed he had taken as his wife.

"She'll do," Alex answered gruffly. He glared at Laurent, his jaw clenched. The others nodded approval and slapped each other on their backs. Ignoring his comrades, Alex lowered his knife and motioned for the Frenchman to follow him away from camp. He didn't need to watch and listen to any more goading. They didn't need to know the reason for his absence from camp the night before. If they wanted to assume he had spent it in the arms of his new bride, then so be it.

The thought of spending a night in the arms of a woman like Evie sent his heart racing in his chest. Earlier, he told her that she belonged to him. If only it were true. The idea of Charlie Richardson laying a hand on her caused his muscles to tense, just as hot rage had flooded him when he watched other eager men barter for her. That he had yet to pay for his acquisition was best kept between him and Laurent.

After his claim of ownership, Evie had told him in no uncertain terms that she would never belong to him, and had stormed into Aimee's medical tent. For fear of his own temper getting the better of him, Alex had thought it wise to try reasoning with her again another time. If Evelyn found out that he had no real hold on her, she was just the type of woman to try something foolish and leave. For her own safety, it was better that everyone believed she was his newly acquired wife, at least until they both could figure out what to do. Now all he had to do was keep his own distance.

"Why are you not with your lovely young bride?" Laurent asked when they were out of earshot from the rest of the men.

Alex stopped in his tracks and faced the Frenchman. He and Laurent had been friends for four years, ever since Alex had helped him escape from a war party of Blackfeet. From then on, they had traveled the wilderness together, trapping and hunting the streams and tributaries of the Snake River Country below the Teewinots, sometimes venturing further north into the Yellowstone. While Alex was committed to the Rocky Mountain Fur Company, Laurent had always been a free trapper. Now that Alex had cut his ties with the company, he was eager to reach the small, secluded valley at the base of the great Teton Mountains. Laurent made his home in that valley, and last winter they had planned for Alex to build his own cabin.

Glancing over his shoulder, Alex leaned toward Laurent and said in a hushed voice, "You know damn well she's not my wife. I didn't pay you anything for her."

Laurent shrugged and grinned. "You have not paid me the amount you boldly proclaimed you would pay for her. All I ask is one beaver pelt." He held up a hand as if warding off an attack. "I will accept nothing more. Then she is yours."

Alex scoffed. Absently, he kicked at the rocks on the ground, stirring up dust. "Do you think I want Evelyn bound to me in that way? She already thinks I murdered her folks. Besides, I ain't no good for her." He stared at the ground.

"*Mon ami*, when will you stop running from your past?" Laurent placed a heavy hand on Alex's shoulder. "You are not your father."

Alex raised his head and stared at the Frenchman. The bruises on Evie's wrists proved otherwise. "What the hell am I supposed to do with her?" He worked the muscles in his jaw. "This arrangement is no better than the slave trade in the east."

"You are mistaken, my friend," Laurent said, an easy smile on his face. "The young *mademoiselle* has been under my protection since she boarded that boat in St. Louis. She consented to allow me to be her guardian. I have not abandoned that duty."

Alex stared at him blankly. "I don't understand."

"As her guardian, it is within my right to choose a husband for her, no? I choose you." He poked a finger in Alex's chest, making him wince when it jabbed his incision. "The bride price is one beaver plew."

Alex blinked and shook his head. His eyebrows scrunched together. Laurent laughed and slapped him on the back. "It is simple, no? If you were to go to the father of an Absaroka or a Shoshoni, and ask for his daughter in marriage, he would name his price. This is no different. Mademoiselle Lewis has no father or male relative to give her away in marriage. As her guardian, that duty falls to me." He paused, staring intently at Alex, but the corners of his mouth twitched.

Alex scoffed, shaking his head at the Frenchman's logic. "Those are the ways here in the mountains. Evie is hardly an Injun. She's the type of woman who would want a church wedding and be married up all proper like."

"Who says you cannot offer that to her? In time? Until the time comes when you go to St. Louis, she is married to you according to the customs of the land. *A la facon du pay.*" Laurent stopped smiling. His jaw muscles tightened, and his lips were drawn in a tight line. "It is the only way to protect her from men like Oliver Sabin. You know this is true, Walker."

Begrudgingly, Alex agreed with Laurent's reasoning. Hadn't that been his intent already when he bartered for Evie? To protect her from the likes of Sabin?

"Why didn't you simply bring her to me? You said you knew I'd be at rendezvous already. Why did you have to put her through the humiliation of a barter?" Alex's voice rose in sudden anger. He hadn't thought to ask these questions the previous day.

"Sabin forced my hand," Laurent shot back. "He wanted the little *mademoiselle* ever since it was revealed that she was on board that boat. I did what I could to protect her. Once we got to rendezvous, all I could do was buy an hour's time. If he had not been so insistent, I would have sought you out myself, and simply given her to you." He stared intently at Alex, then smirked. "Besides, you will be doing me a great favor, too. Now that you have a wife, Whispering Waters will see that I am the man for her, and not you."

Alex groaned silently. Whispering Waters, the Bannock Indian woman he'd met while trading with her father's tribe over the course of several seasons had made it no secret that she would like nothing better than have him offer a bride price to her father. It was also common knowledge that Laurent was in love with her. Alex never encouraged the young woman's interest in him, not only out of respect for his friend, but also because he simply felt no attraction to her.

You sure as hell are attracted to Evie Lewis, Walker. And for that very reason you need to stay away from her.

"What the hell am I going to do about her, Laurent? She thinks I killed her folks. I don't have time to take her back to St. Louis."

Laurent laughed, and slapped Alex on the back. "Bring her with you to the valley. It is the only solution. I will have to meet with Sabin and his men in a few months, but I will accompany you and help build your cabin, just like we agreed last year, my friend. Perhaps one long winter with you, and the *mademoiselle* will see you in a different light, no?" His eyebrows rose suggestively. "You will have many long nights to convince her that you did not kill her parents. There is always time next spring to go to St. Louis and find out who the real murderer is."

Alex stared off into the distance. The snow-covered jagged peaks of the Tetons rose like a wolverine's sharp teeth into the distant sky. These mountains had beckoned to him since he first laid eyes on them six years ago, calling him back year after year. The thought that he would ever want to leave the mountains to return to his old life in St. Charles never crossed his mind.

Alex inhaled a deep breath. He knew what he had to do, what he wanted to do, and both stemmed from the same selfish reasons. If Evie didn't hate him already, she would surely hate him the next time he spoke with her.

* * *

"I wonder what's keeping Alex. He said he'd be here at dawn." Aimee heaved a large leather pouch onto one of her packhorses' backs. "Hand me that rope there on the ground, please, Evelyn."

Evelyn reached for the coiled twine, and stepped up beside Aimee. The comment only served as a reminder that Aimee and her family were leaving shortly, and she would be left to deal with Alex on her own. The shorter blond woman glanced up at her with a smile, which faded instantly. She placed a hand on Evelyn's shoulder, her face etched with concern.

"He's a good man, Evelyn. Alex may have bartered for you, but I know he did so with the best intentions. He's trying to look out for you, no matter what you may think he's done."

"Would you trust a man who might have murdered your family?" Evelyn blinked back the tears that threatened to spill from her eyes. She had thought a lot about what Alex said yesterday, and she had to admit that Charlie did seem to have a lot to gain by killing her parents. The more she had thought about it throughout the day and into the night, it started making more sense to her. Was it possible that he had lied to Henry?

Evelyn hadn't seen Alex since the previous morning. Her anger seethed anew at the memory of his heated statement that she belonged to him. It had taken all of her restraint not to strike out at him. Instead, she'd sought sanctuary in the tent she'd occupied since he brought her to Aimee. Her mind was overrun with a jumble of mixed emotions where he was concerned. One minute he acted quiet and reserved, almost friendly, and the next his eyes would blaze in anger and he became a stranger to her again.

His clean appearance had both shocked and surprised her. It also brought back all the old feelings and emotions about him that she thought had died years ago when he didn't return from his venture into the wilderness. Worse, these feelings seemed to have intensified. Her childhood infatuation had erupted into a grown woman's desire for a man. His touch had evoked the most electrifying sensations in her when his fingers grazed hers as he handed her the muslin, leaving her both confused and exhilarated. Anger had quickly evaporated those warm feelings when Alex proclaimed he owned her.

"Evelyn, I know there are some misunderstandings between you and Alex, but I can't believe he would kill someone in cold blood."

Evelyn stared at Aimee. The entire Osborne family

thought fondly of Alex. Daniel Osborne seemed like a decent man, so unlike most of the other trappers she'd encountered. If he thought highly of Alex, shouldn't she be a bit more trusting?

"How did you come to know him?" Evelyn asked. Perhaps if she knew more about the man he had become, she could think more clearly about her reaction to him.

Aimee grinned. "It was six years ago, when he first came to the mountains. He thought he had to prove to everyone how tough he was. The trouble is, this wilderness quickly humbles even the strongest man."

"What happened?" Evelyn asked eagerly. Henry had certainly never divulged information to her about Alex when she tried to ask discreet questions.

"Apparently he thought he could bring down a fully grown grizzly by himself with a single shot flintlock. His first dumb mistake that day was to go out on his own to set his beaver traps. Then he provoked a bear by shooting at it. You'll have to ask him about the details, but it was a good thing that Daniel came along when he did, or Alex wouldn't have survived his first winter here. He was such a greenhorn back then." Aimee grinned, obviously thinking of a fond memory. Quickly, her face turned serious again. "But he's learned a lot. I would trust Alex with my life, Evelyn. I think you should put a little more trust in him, too. It takes a special kind of man to carve out a living here, and Alex has proven himself as just such a man."

Evelyn gazed at the ground. "It must also take a special woman to endure life here," she mumbled.

"Something tells me you might be just the type of woman who can handle it. With the right man at your side . . ." Aimee left her thought unfinished. She turned her attention back to her horse, and finished securing the pouch to the animal's back before facing Evelyn again.

"Do you want to return to St. Louis?" she asked tentatively.

"Do I have a choice to return?" Evelyn's eyes widened, surprised at Aimee's question. What would she do if she was allowed to return to St. Louis? Marry Charles? She shook her head at the thought, and a cold shudder passed down her spine.

Before she had a chance to contemplate Aimee's question further, a man's voice spoke from behind them. Evelyn pirouetted on her heels, her heart slamming against her ribcage.

"I'll be heading out today, too." Alex clasped hands with Daniel, but his gaze was clearly locked on her. "Heading up the Snake to a small valley between a couple of lakes closer to the mountains. Gonna build my own cabin before winter sets in."

"Sounds like you are ready to settle down." Daniel grinned broadly.

"Looks like it," Alex answered.

Evelyn swallowed back the lump in her throat. Her palms began to sweat. This was the moment she was both dreading and almost anticipating. She stood by silently while Alex said his goodbyes to the Osbornes. Aimee wrapped her arms around Evelyn's shoulders.

"It'll be okay. You'll see. And if you want to return to St. Louis, I know he'll take you back," she whispered.

"Thank you for everything," Evelyn said, forcing a smile. She embraced Sarah, then stood silently by, watching the family ride from camp.

"Ready?" Alex asked, reaching for the leather pouch at Evelyn's feet. "Are these your personal effects?"

"It's what Aimee gave to me, and the cloth from you," she said, drawing in a deep breath when he straightened to his full height. A dark shadow of stubble had grown on his face since yesterday, and Evelyn wondered if he planned to grow his beard again. Far from off-putting, his look at the moment made him appear even more handsome than with a cleanly shaven face.

"Are you taking me back to St. Louis?" The question was out before she could stop herself. Did she want to go back home? There was nothing for her to go back to.

Alex raised his eyebrows. "Going to St. Louis was not part of my plans this season, Evie. I just came from there, remember?" His look challenged her to say more.

She swallowed nervously. "Then what are your plans for me, Alex?" Her eyes narrowed. She didn't want to be reminded that he considered her his property, like he did his pack animals.

"I reckon you're coming with me," he said matter-of-factly. He looked up, glancing beyond her shoulder at something behind her. His eyes narrowed for a split second, and he stepped closer to her. Evelyn drew in a sharp breath, her senses filled with his masculine scent. Her heart suddenly raced in her chest. If only things were different between them. If only he didn't consider her his property.

"What if I refuse? What if I simply say I don't want to go with you? What if I say –"

Before she had a chance to react, Alex snaked his arm around her waist and pulled her up against his hard body. In the next instant, his mouth covered hers, drowning out anything else she wanted to say.

Too shocked to move or react to his unexpected assault, Evelyn stood stiffly in his embrace. She braced her hands against his chest, which only caused him to tighten his hold around her. His hard mouth on hers suddenly softened, and the kiss changed from one of aggression to a much softer exploration of her lips. His free hand cupped the back of her head while his fingers wrapped around her hair, holding her to him.

Heat suddenly exploded within her, and her legs refused to support her weight. Instead of pushing against Alex, her body instinctively leaned into him, and her arms reached up to grip his shoulders. His mouth slid slowly against hers, coaxing her to respond. Evelyn moaned softly, and her lips parted slightly. Hadn't she dreamed about this years ago? The world evaporated around her while Alex held her in his embrace. There was nothing threatening about him. This was Alex as she had envisioned him a thousand times over; Alex returning the love she had felt for him all these years.

Slowly, much too soon, Alex loosened his arm around her waist. His calloused hand slid from behind her neck, his fingers lingering against her cheek. His lips broke contact with hers, and Evelyn stared wide-eyed up at his face. Bewilderment was written in his blue eyes, along with something she hadn't seen before, nor could she put a name to it. He held her gaze, his eyes scanning the contours of her face. Evelyn slid her hands from his shoulders, and took a shaky step backward. Her heart pounded loudly in her ears, and her lips tingled in the aftermath of his kiss.

"Why?" she squeaked. Speaking seemed impossible. She wished she could hold on to this moment forever. A nagging voice somewhere in the recesses of her mind warned her to remain cautious, while her heart told her this was where she belonged.

Alex cleared his throat. He finally broke eye contact, his gaze seeking something behind her again.

"I had to silence you somehow," he said, his voice raspy. His cheek muscles clenched. "Oliver Sabin has taken quite an interest in this camp. I couldn't allow him to hear that you were about to break your ties to me."

Evelyn's jaw dropped. Her world had ended and begun in

that kiss, but to him it had been nothing more than a means to silence her? Heat crept up her neck, and her cheeks burned. She took a shaky step backward. Alex reached for her arm, preventing her from turning.

"You can hate me for bartering for you, Evelyn," he said, his voice tense. "You can hate me for refusing to take you back to St. Louis. According to the ways of the people who inhabit these mountains, you and I are wed just as if we had stood before a preacher in church back in St. Charles." He paused, his gaze never wavering from hers. "But you also have the right to break the tie," he continued slowly, his eyes staring deeply into hers as if trying to read her mind. "I can't stop you from leaving, Evie. If you want to take your chances with men like Sabin, go ahead and cast me aside. But if you want to live, you'll accept my terms."

With those final words, he released her arm and stepped around her, leaving her standing by the cold ashes of Aimee's abandoned campfire, more confused than before.

CHAPTER EIGHT

The majestic snow-covered peaks of the mountain range that Evelyn had seen when Laurent and the other trappers brought her to the rendezvous loomed in the distance. Like sentinels standing watch over the vast valley stretching before them, they rose high into the sky. Aspen trees and conifers were the only obstructions to the magnificent view.

Alex reined in his horse in front of her, and the animal's neck dropped immediately to drink from the narrow creek that gurgled and meandered snake-like through the tall grass. The two packhorses Alex led followed suit, and Evelyn's mount moved eagerly up alongside the others without any encouragement from her. Alex swung his right leg up and over his horse's neck, and disappeared momentarily from view. He moved around behind the animals, his rifle cradled in the crook of his arm. His head turned slightly from side to side, and his eyes seemed to be in constant motion as he scanned the tree line behind them.

Evelyn forced her gaze away from him. He hadn't spoken a word to her since leaving the large encampment of trappers and Indians behind at the site of the rendezvous early in the day. Her stomach grumbled loudly, and she rubbed at her sore back. She'd become accustomed to riding horseback over the long weeks of traveling with Laurent and the other river pirates, but the endless hours in the saddle still didn't agree with her backside. She leaned forward, and inched her left leg backward, intent on pulling it over the horse's back to dismount. Luckily, she still wore Henry's britches. A skirt would be much too cumbersome.

Her boot heel caught in the blanket tied to the back of the saddle, and Evelyn ground her teeth, determined to get off the horse's back. Her leg muscles tightened, refusing to cooperate while she tried to free her foot from the blanket. Suddenly, strong hands clamped around her waist and hauled her from the saddle. Her backside collided against Alex's solid thighs just before he set her feet on the ground. Evelyn whirled around on her heels, grabbing hold of his arms for support while she fought to regain her balance.

"I could have managed on my own," she said, sucking in a sharp breath of air.

"Didn't look like it from where I was standing," he retorted, a smirk on his face. Strands of his dark hair fell over his forehead, partially obstructing his eyes, but his gaze rested intently on her face. She fought the impulse to swipe the hair away from his forehead. Abruptly, as if he just remembered that he still held her at the waist, he released his hold and pulled his arms away, then took a step backward. He reached for his rifle on the ground, and turned away from her.

Alex's shirt couldn't hide how his back muscles tensed while he stood facing toward the creek. Evelyn inhaled a deep breath. Why did he seem so angry and withdrawn again? She had told him before leaving the trapper rendezvous that she accepted the terms he laid out for her.

They had come to an agreement . . . of sorts. He had offered her his protection with the promise to return her to St. Louis the following summer. In exchange, she would travel with him to the place where he planned to build a cabin, and assume all domestic duties customary of a wife.

"I won't share your sleeping blankets," Evelyn had injected quickly. "I'll perform whatever womanly duties you set out for me, but I won't . . . not those duties." Evelyn recalled her embarrassment when her cheeks heated at the thought of sharing a bed with Alex. Would she have agreed to his terms if he had included those demands as well?

His kiss had left her longing for all those things no one talked about, the things that happened between a man and a woman in the marriage bed behind closed doors. Nothing had ever made her feel more like a woman than when Alex pulled her into his embrace and kissed her like a true lover. Charlie Richardson had stolen a kiss once, which had earned him a resounding slap on the cheek. To compare the two would be like comparing a donkey with a blue-blooded thoroughbred.

"What's the matter, Evie?" Alex's lips had widened in a grin that made her want to wrap her arms around his neck and demand that he kiss her again. At that moment she might have consented to anything he asked for. Instead, his next words ignited her temper to flare to the surface again. "You'd still rather marry a warthog than consider being wed to me?" One of his eyebrows rose expectantly.

His question had confused her momentarily, but then she'd remembered proclaiming that exact thing when Henry embarrassed her the day Alex left St. Charles six years ago.

"Why, Alex," Evelyn forced a smile. "Up until yesterday, your appearance led me to believe that you had turned into a warthog." She had exercised all the self-control she possessed to simply force the words from between clenched teeth rather than shout at the top of her lungs. Her hands had balled into fists at her sides, and her body shook as she tried to conceal her embarrassment. He had some nerve to bring up such a humiliating incident.

"Don't worry, Evie. I'll do my best to keep your virtue safe." Alex had chuckled, and walked away, shaking his head. Later he'd helped her mount the horse he'd saddled for her to ride, even offering a tentative smile. Evelyn interpreted it as his way of making peace again, and her heart had gone galloping out of control. If he continued to favor her with such boyish smiles, she might get the wrong impression and think that Alex might even like her just a little.

His stance and demeanor now, standing in the middle of a wilderness meadow by the creek, dispelled any notion that Alex had somehow found her attractive or likable. The simple fact that he agreed to the idea of a marriage arrangement without intimacy should make it crystal clear that he found her lacking. Evelyn couldn't think of a single man she'd ever met who would be willing to comply with such an arrangement.

Somehow Alex still saw her only as Henry's little sister. Would he ever look at her and see a grown woman before him? To his way of thinking, he was probably taking care of her because of his friendship with Henry.

And because you believe he killed your parents. Was this his way of trying to prove his innocence to her? All the pieces seemed to fall into place. Alex had agreed to protect her, and even return her safely to St. Louis in a year. His kindness made it impossible to think of him as her parents' murderer.

"We'll rest the horses here for a while," Alex said after moments of silence. He turned to face her, and Evelyn's heart fluttered in her chest. A soft smile once again replaced the taut lines of his face. He moved around her to one of the pack horses, and untied a pouch from the animal's back. His steel traps rattled and clanked while he adjusted pouches and blankets. Reaching inside the bag, he produced several dried strips of meat, and handed them to her.

"Best I can do for now," he grumbled. He didn't wait for a response, and stood off to the side, breaking off a piece of tough meat with his teeth, and chewed. He held his flintlock close to his chest, cradled in his arm like a child, while his eyes remained in constant motion.

"Are you expecting someone?" Evelyn asked, trying to break the silence between them.

He shot her a look that seemed to question her sanity. "There's always danger here, Evie. This isn't St. Charles. If a bear isn't trying to kill you, a Blackfoot Indian will."

"Then why do you choose to stay here? Why put your life in danger day after day?" Evelyn stepped up to him, trying to hold his attention. His eyes darted repeatedly from her to the forest all around them.

"I'd rather die here than rot in St. Charles," he said, his jaw clenched. This time he held her gaze. "I'm not cut out to be a farmer. Out here," he gestured with his chin toward the mountains, "I can do as I see fit. I answer to no one, and hold no one responsible for me."

Evelyn's brows raised. She hadn't expected him to divulge as much as he had. A certain longing seemed to linger in his voice.

"I'm sorry to tell you that your father died two years ago," she said softly. She placed her hand on his arm, and he tensed instantly. His jaw muscles tightened along his cheeks. "He lost a fight at the tavern with another man. I didn't know if you already knew. His farm is vacant now. The land rightfully belongs to you."

Alex scoffed. Anger blazed in his eyes. "I'll thank the man who killed him next time I'm in St. Charles," he said, his tone icy. "I want no part of anything that belonged to him."

Evelyn dropped her hand. She hadn't realized how deep Alex's hatred for his father seemed to run. Was it all because of the abuse his father inflicted on his mother? She dared not ask.

All four horses suddenly raised their heads from cropping at the grasses along the creek bank, their heads turned and ears pricked in the direction of the forest to the north. Alex stiffened and cocked his rifle. Evelyn suppressed a gasp when two riders and several packhorses emerged from between the trees. She grabbed hold of Alex's arm and stepped behind him. Visions of Oliver Sabin caused her heart to race with fear. Alex lowed his weapon, and his body relaxed as quickly as it had tensed. Evelyn tentatively peered out from behind his broad back.

As the riders approached, one of the men looked oddly familiar, his coonskin cap partially obscuring his face. He raised his hand in a gesture of greeting, the wide smile on his bearded face showing his gleaming white teeth. Alex raised his own hand in greeting, and stepped forward, and Evelyn had no choice but to release her hold on his arm.

"Hello the camp," the rider shouted. Sudden anger replaced Evelyn's fear. She shot a disbelieving look at Alex, who seemed to have forgotten that she was even there.

"You finally made it," Alex said, stepping out to meet the riders.

"Young Yancey here delayed me," the other man said, his smile widening, gesturing with his head at the other rider.

Evelyn inhaled a deep breath. What was going on here? Had Alex deceived her after all? Laurent Berard, the man who had forced her into the wilderness, the one whose comrades killed Henry, and who bartered her to the highest bidder, rode calmly into camp, and Alex greeted him like an old friend.

***

Alex waited for Laurent to dismount, then stepped up to him and clasped his arm in greeting. Groaning silently, he shot a quick look in Yancey's direction. How had the greenhorn weaseled Laurent into letting him tag along?

"It's such an honor that you agreed to allow me to help build your cabin, Walker," Yancey called. He fumbled with his horse's reins, and appeared to have more trouble than Evie did at dismounting his animal. Just as he set his right foot on the ground, one of the pack mules he led brayed loudly and jerked its head back. Yancey lost his grip on the lead rope. His arms flayed wildly through the air as he tried to regain his balance. With a loud thud, he landed rump first in the grass.

Alex jumped to his side and grabbed hold of the spooked mule's lead rope to prevent the animal from running off.

"What the hell is he doing here?" Alex glared at Laurent. "He should be back home in Philadelphia or wherever he's from, sitting in some fancy parlor discussing the latest women's fashion."

"Monsieur Yancey here needs a taste of the wilderness, don't you think, Walker?" Laurent asked. "He is eager to learn about the fur trade. It will be good for him. I have taken him under my wing, so you need not concern yourself for his safety. I believe you have much more important things that will hold your attention." His eyes darted to where Evelyn stood. Wide-eyed, and with her mouth drawn in a tight line, the look of shock and anger on her pretty face was almost comical. Alex imagined daggers shooting from her eyes at any moment.

Yancey groaned and pushed himself up off the ground, then slapped at the dirt on his britches. Laurent handed him the reins to his horse and stepped around Alex, his wide smile back on his face. He held his arms wide open as if he meant to embrace Evelyn like a long-lost friend.

"Mademoiselle Lewis," Laurent called, pure joy in his tone. Ignoring her obvious look of disdain, he grasped her hand and brought it up to his lips. For a second, she didn't respond. Then she yanked her hand away. She squared her shoulders and stared straight at Laurent, her narrowed eyes blazing with anger. Alex suppressed a grin. She was spitting mad like a cornered bobcat with its paw stuck in a trap. She would start hissing at any moment. His chest swelled with pride and admiration for her.

Laurent appeared ignorant to the impending verbal attack, and glanced over his shoulder at Alex, a question in his eyes. "*Excusez-moi*. Perhaps it is more proper to address you as Madame Walker now?"

"I am not your *mademoiselle*, and I'm most definitely no one's *madame*." Evelyn spoke heatedly, her voice deeper than usual. Her cheeks had turned an almost deep shade of crimson. She advanced on Laurent, her hands on her hips. Her eyes narrowed dangerously.

"You are a lying, evil, despicable excuse for a man. You rob and murder innocent people." Abruptly, she tore her eyes from Laurent and turned her anger toward Alex. "And you," she nearly shouted, stepping quickly around Laurent and advancing on him. "You are in league with him. I started to trust you." She poked a finger at his chest. "But you're no better than he is. He killed my brother, and you knew about it all along. Who are you meeting next? Is Oliver Sabin going to arrive soon, so you can hand me over to him?"

Evelyn stood only inches from him, leaning forward and glaring up at him. Her eyes shimmered with the tears she fought to hold back. Something tightened in Alex's chest at that moment. A warm sensation flowed through him. Here she was, all alone and surrounded by three men whom she thought meant to do her harm, yet she stood her ground. Her renewed fear of him tore at his heart.

Quicker than he would have given her credit for, her arm reached out and up, her intent to strike at him all too clear. Alex intercepted her blow by grabbing hold of her wrist. His first instinct was to incapacitate his opponent, twist her arm behind her back until she begged for mercy, but this was Evie, not some enemy warrior. Instead, he loosened his grip and wrapped his other arm around her waist, pulling her into his arms. A powerful urge to shield her from all the hurt that had been done to her hit him with the force of an arrow to the chest.

Evelyn struggled in his embrace. "Release me, you brute," she hissed, squirming to free herself. His hold tightened, and he struggled to pin her arms to her sides to keep her from trying to strike him again.

"Laurent is not the enemy, Evie. And neither am I," he whispered against her ear. "If you'll calm down enough to listen, I'll explain." The desire to simply kiss her like he'd done this morning overwhelmed him. She'd been so soft and pliant in his arms, her response so unexpected, his restraint had nearly faltered. Would she react the same way now if he tried to repeat his actions? He couldn't put himself through the torment of another kiss, wanting to do so much more, and knowing that Evie mistrusted and most likely hated him.

Although she stopped her struggles, Evelyn refused to relax against his hold. Her muscles remained as tense as a flighty deer, but at least she stopped fighting him. When he was sure she wouldn't try and hit him or bolt, he took a step back. His hold on her eased, and with great reluctance, he released her completely. The sudden emptiness in his arms surprised him. She fit so perfectly against him, it was as if she was meant for him alone.

She can't be yours. You promised to protect her, not hold her prisoner. Evie wanted to return to St. Louis, and it was for the best. He knew how quickly he could lose control of his temper, just as his father had always done. He couldn't risk hurting Evie.

"All right. Explain." Evelyn took a step back, and folded her arms under her heaving breasts. Alex's eyes lingered on her shirt before he forced his gaze to her face. Her emerald eyes still glistened with unshed tears. He quickly glanced over his shoulder. Laurent and Yancey stood checking their gear tied to the pack animals, their backs turned in an obvious attempt to give him some privacy with Evie.

He quickly explained Laurent's involvement with the Rocky Mountain Fur Company, and how he acted as spy against Sabin and his men.

"There was nothing he could do to help Henry, Evie. He had no idea they were about to kill him."

Evelyn wheeled around, leaving him to stare at her back. The sun hit her hair in such a way that it shone like copper against the blue sky. His hand reached out, compelled to run his fingers through the soft strands. He caught himself before he touched her, and dropped his arm against his side, his hand clenched in a tight fist. How he would endure the months ahead without touching her was a mystery to him. Perhaps he should return her to St. Louis now, then she'd be safe from the dangers of the wilderness, and also safe from him.

"If we ride now, we can still cover several miles before nightfall," Laurent called from behind him. Alex cursed under his breath.

Evelyn spun around, and shot him an icy look. She rushed past him to her horse.

"Mr. Yancey, would you care to help me onto my horse?" she called loudly. Yancey shot a surprised look at her before his eyes darted nervously to Alex. Alex cursed again. Before

Yancey had a chance to react, Alex strode to Evie's side, and lifted her unceremoniously into the saddle.

"You're my wife," he said through clenched teeth, staring up at her. Sudden jealousy fueled his anger. "You'll ask me for assistance." He handed her the reins and didn't wait for a reply. Mounting his own horse, he guided his animal through the creek, and wrapped the lead ropes of his pack animals around the horn of his saddle to free his hand to hold his rifle. He set a brisk pace across the meadow heading toward the Teton Mountains. Laurent pulled his horse up alongside his, and Alex ignored the sideways glances the Frenchman shot him on occasion. Thankfully, his friend remained quiet, which allowed him to focus on the sounds behind him.

Yancey rode alongside Evie, commenting on the vastness and the beauty of the wilderness. She remained silent, no doubt pondering what she'd found out today, wondering whom to believe and trust.

"You know the Indians call him Shadow Walker, don't you," Yancey said in a hushed voice.

"What does that mean?" Evie asked, the tone of her voice indicating mild interest.

"Your husband; he's somewhat of a legend among the Indians."

Evie scoffed. "Alex Walker may be a legend among the Indians, but to me he's nothing but a warthog."

Alex's mouth formed a smile despite all his reservations.

CHAPTER NINE

"Would you care for some boudin, Madame Evie?" Laurent sliced a large round sliver off of what looked like a pale, oversized sausage and held it out to her.

"I've asked you before to stop calling me madame." Evelyn shot an annoyed look at the Frenchman. She huddled under a thick buffalo robe, sitting as close to the campfire as she dared. She sniffled, her nose and cheeks numb from the sudden frigid shift in temperature as twilight descended on the camp. A cold gust of wind whipped strands of her hair around her face, and Evelyn swiped it back with an impatient stroke of her hand. She glanced at the clouds moving swiftly across the sky, wondering if rain wasn't far away. The days and nights had been pleasant so far, but today had been unbearably chilly.

The last three days had been spent traveling over high alpine plateaus and meadows covered in sedge and willow. Today, Alex had called an early halt to their travels so that he could go hunting before nightfall to replenish their supply of meat. At Laurent's urging, he had reluctantly agreed to take

Yancey along with him. Laurent had been left behind to set up camp and watch over Evelyn.

Her stomach grumbled, and she warily eyed what the Frenchman offered. Her appetite vanished instantly. During her weeks of traveling with Laurent and his murderous cohorts, she'd seen them eat a variety of unappealing food items. Even during the last three days of moving through this endless wilderness with her present company, the men had offered her foods that made her stomach roil.

"Don't you men ever eat anything that is actually fit for consumption?" Evelyn averted her eyes from the food. It reminded her of the slop she used to feed her mother's hogs.

Laurent held a dramatic hand to his chest, as if deeply offended at her for declining his offer. "Meat is meat. And this is a delicacy, *mon amie*." He glanced around camp and over his shoulder, as if expecting someone to swoop in and steal the *delicacy* from him. He leaned toward her, and whispered, "I have been saving this for when I do not have to share it with the others."

"What is it made of . . . that thing you call a delicacy?" Evelyn asked, more to keep the conversation going than out of curiosity. Laurent was the only person who spoke to her regularly, and as much as she wanted to remain angry with him, his friendly demeanor made him almost likable. Byron Yancey was too scared of Alex to speak to her directly, unless she addressed him first. Alex had apparently decided to ignore her for the most part since they met up with his companions three days ago.

Thinking of Alex as her parents' killer became more difficult with each passing day. Even though he'd barely spoken to her in the last three days, and seemed to avoid her whenever possible, the way he observed her from a distance was almost as intense as if he touched her. Each day that passed made it more impossible for her to ignore his heated glances.

When she caught him staring, her heart always leapt to her throat, and a tingling sensation suffused her insides. Why was he so difficult to figure out? Why did he not engage in conversation with her? Yancey's distance she could understand. The man worshipped the ground Alex walked on, and didn't do anything unless told to do so. Silently, Evelyn agreed with Alex that Yancey belonged in a fancy parlor rather than in this untamed wilderness. The only man truly at ease with her was Laurent.

Sitting next to her, the Frenchman chuckled heartily, and she remembered she'd asked him about the thing he considered a delicacy. "Why, madame, this boudin is stuffed with the meat of bison shoulder, some kidney suet, flour, and pepper. I have cooked it to perfection in bison oil."

Evelyn wrinkled her nose. "You enjoy it then," she said quickly, fanning her hand through the air as if trying to dispel an offensive odor. "I'd rather not eat it."

"You must eat to maintain your strength. What will your husband do to me if he learns that I have allowed his woman to starve?"

Evelyn adjusted her position on the ground, taking care to keep the warm robe wrapped tightly around her. Freezing to death seemed a more immediate concern to her than starvation. Laurent reached toward the woodpile next to him, and added several more logs to the fire.

"If you have some cornmeal or flour available, I can make some biscuits," Evelyn offered. She longed for some bread and greens; anything other than meat. The only time she'd eaten more than meat of various questionable varieties had been during the few days she'd spent with the Osbornes.

"You would make some biscuits or johnny cakes?" Laurent asked, his eyes widening.

Evelyn smiled slowly. His boudin must not be as tasty as he had proclaimed.

"Are there any edible tubers or vegetables to be found here?" she asked, and gestured with her chin into the nearby forest. "I'd be glad to prepare a stew. Alex and Mr. Yancey should be back soon, don't you think?"

Laurent jumped to his feet. "We do not need to wait for their return. Tell me what you need, Madame Evie, to prepare a stew, and I shall provide it for you." His eyes shimmered with hope and eagerness, and Evelyn couldn't refuse him.

"I need a pot over the fire with water, and any greens you can find, and whatever meat you have for flavor. I could use a skillet for the biscuits, flour, some fat, and salt."

"You shall have these things, Madame. Remain by the fire. Laurent Berard will provide you with what you need."

Evelyn watched him rummage through several of Alex's packs, producing all the items she needed. He disappeared into the surrounding forest for a while, and returned with some roots and tubers, and even a pouch filled with berries. With a wide smile on his face, he showed her his finds, then hung the iron kettle over the fire.

"Anything else you need, *Madame*? We will all enjoy your feast tonight." He smacked his lips together, grinning broadly.

Evelyn reluctantly left her warm spot by the fire, and set to work cleaning and cutting the roots, and adding them to some leftover venison that sizzled at the bottom of the pot. A pleasant aroma soon filled the air, and she momentarily forgot about the cold.

Alex and Yancey rode into camp at just about the time when Evelyn deemed her stew to be ready to eat. A small deer lay across Alex's thighs. He dropped the carcass to the ground, then dismounted his horse. Evelyn caught his unreadable stare before he turned his attention to his horse.

"Your wife has graciously offered to cook a fine meal tonight, Walker," Laurent proclaimed loudly.

Alex didn't respond. He finished unsaddling his mount, then hobbled the animal's front legs together and turned it loose with the rest of the horses. He rummaged through one of his packs, and produced a heavy-looking white wool blanket with yellow and red stripes at the ends. Wordlessly, he strode up to her and wrapped it around her shoulders.

Before he had a chance to walk away, Evelyn grabbed his hand. She wasn't about to simply let him walk away this time. "Thank you," she said softly, a hesitant smile on her lips. He stared down at her, the hard lines of his mouth softening just slightly. Her pulse increased.

"Supper smells good," he said. His warm hand unexpectedly covered hers, sending a flood of heat up her arm. She bit her lower lip to prevent a gasp.

"I hope it's better than what Laurent would have us eat," she commented lightly. Her gaze remained locked with his. A quiet yearning shone in the depths of his eyes, and she sensed he wanted to say something. Instead, he pulled his hand away, and the hint of a smile vanished. Evelyn swallowed to hide her disappointment. Why couldn't he simply talk to her?

"Let me know when it's ready. There's something I need to do before it gets dark." With those words he turned and walked away. Evelyn expelled a loud exasperated breath of air through her half-open mouth. Even with his sullen demeanor, she couldn't stop the warm feelings and sensations that flooded her.

Laurent walked up beside her, and his gaze followed Evelyn's as she observed Alex rummaging through one of his packs. Moments later, he strode off in the direction of the woods.

The Frenchman's hand touched her shoulder, and Evelyn turned her head to look up at him.

"He needs time, Madame Evie," Laurent said, offering an encouraging smile. His eyes shone with a warmth she hadn't noticed before.

"Time for what?" Evelyn's cheeks heated. Was she that transparent that Laurent could read her thoughts so easily?

"You have known Alex for a long time, no?" the Frenchman asked.

"He was my brother's best friend. He spent a lot of time with our family," Evelyn answered quietly.

"You cannot truly believe he murdered your *maman* and *papa*."

Evelyn sucked in a deep breath. She shook her head, then peered to where Alex had disappeared into the woods. "No," she whispered, finally voicing the thoughts in her mind over the last week out loud. "I don't believe he killed my parents. Is that why he is so angry? Because he thinks I still hold him responsible?"

Laurent chuckled, and shook his own head. His hand wrapped around her upper arm, and he turned her to face him squarely. "Alex Walker is not angry with you, *petite amie*." He offered an indulgent smile.

"Then why won't he talk to me?" Evelyn leaned toward Laurent, hoping to understand.

"Do you know that he has faced the mighty grizzly bear with a bravery that is rare to see, and he has no fear when in battle against the Blackfeet. But," Laurent hesitated and raised his index finger in front of him. "There is one thing that terrifies him above all else."

Evelyn waited, and when Laurent remained silent, she asked the question that begged an answer. "And what is that?"

"You, *mon cher*." His eyes widened expectantly, holding her gaze.

Evelyn's forehead wrinkled. She took a step back and tilted her head, wondering if she'd understood correctly. She expelled a nervous laugh. "That's ridiculous. Why would Alexander Walker be afraid of me?"

"He would rather face a hundred Blackfeet and ten grizzly bears put together than lay a finger on you."

"Lay a finger on me? Mr. Berard, what are you talking about?"

"You are aware of his father, are you not?" Laurent clasped his hands behind his back. He glanced toward the fire, and leaned over the pot. He raised the lid and inhaled a long drawn-out breath, sighing contently.

"I know his father was a drunkard, and rumor has it he killed his wife. The whole town knew he beat her a lot. Even Alex had bruises on his face on many occasions." Evelyn still didn't understand where this conversation was leading.

Laurent reached for her hand, and held it between his two large, calloused ones. His chest heaved before he spoke. "Madame Evelyn, your husband is afraid that he will become his father."

Evelyn blinked. She hadn't seen Alex indulge in drink. She searched her memory, trying to recall Silas Walker in her mind. She'd seen him on very few occasions, and what she remembered of him was a loud and boisterous man who enjoyed provoking a fight. Alex was the exact opposite. Always quiet. Always reserved.

"Madame Evelyn," Laurent said, squeezing her hand. Evelyn's gaze dropped to where he still clasped her hand between his larger ones. He waited for her to look up at him again. "You can show your husband he is not the man he thinks he is. He has been my friend for four years, and has saved my life on many occasions. I wish for him to find the happiness that has eluded him. He can find that with you, *mon cher.*"

He patted her hand once more, then released her. Smiling broadly again, as if the subject was now closed, he stared at the kettle over the fire, and slapped his stomach. "It is time to eat. Now where is that good-for-nothing *jeunot* and that stubborn man you have the misfortune to call your husband?" He stepped around her, heading toward the woods.

Evelyn stared after him. Her mind swirled dizzily with the information Laurent had given her. She recalled Alex's angry reaction the day she tried to attack him with the knife. Absently, she rubbed at her wrists. The marks he had left were long gone. She remembered his tense stance after Aimee had put a stop to his ever-tightening grip, and the pained look in his eyes afterward. She recalled his fierce embrace, which had quickly turned gentle yet remained strong when he kissed her, and again when he held her during her angry outburst the day they met up with Laurent. Alex may think he would hurt her, but in her heart it became as clear as the water flowing in the nearby creek that he could never do to her what his father had done to him and his mother.

With a new understanding of the quiet, brooding man who had become her husband by a strange twist of fate, Evelyn stirred the contents of her stew pot. Her young girl's dreams of becoming Alex Walker's wife had come true, and she would follow Laurent's advice and make him see that he was not the man he envisioned in his misguided mind.

She spotted Yancey by the horses, and waved him to the fire. He politely accepted her offer, and sat to eat. Alex finally emerged from the woods, carrying several large poles and pine branches. Laurent followed close on his heels. Evelyn ladled stew onto tin plates that Laurent brought her, and added a couple of biscuits from the skillet.

The Frenchman joined Yancey at the fire, but Alex stayed behind, setting to work building, what Evelyn quickly realized, was a lean-to. Tying a large pole horizontally to two young trees that were spaced about ten feet apart, he added smaller poles to create a v-shaped shelter on one side, which he covered with pine branches. Only when he was finished did he come to the fire. He sat and silently accepted the plate of food she offered. She handed him several biscuits, which he eyed appreciatively.

"I'll build a fire near the shelter. It's going to be cold tonight," he said, spooning food into his mouth without looking at anyone in particular. When no one replied, he glanced up, and his gaze met Evelyn's.

"You can move some buffalo robes under there," he grumbled, staring directly at her.

"You built that for me?" she asked, surprised even as her heart soared. She flashed him a wide smile, and Alex's eyebrows scrunched together. Clearing his throat, he said, "Like I said, it's gonna be cold tonight, and probably windy. It'll be warmer for you there."

Evelyn's eyes darted to Laurent, who coughed into his coffee cup, then hastily stuffed a biscuit into his mouth. She shot another look at Alex, but his attention had returned to his food. With a determined intake of breath, Evelyn silently vowed that, starting in the morning, she would win Alexander Walker over just as he had again stolen her heart with his small gestures of kindness.

***

Evelyn shivered under her blankets, and tucked her legs up closer to her torso. A sudden blast of cold air hit her from behind, and in her half-awakened state, she groped for the covers. Just as quickly, a pleasant warmth replaced the frigid cold, and she inched closer to its source until she leaned against a solid wall. Vaguely, she wondered at the oddity, but her groggy mind didn't question it further.

When a steely arm slipped around her middle, pulling her closer, she tensed instinctively, and her eyes opened to the blackness of night. She pushed against her assailant, and kicked her leg back. The strong arm tightened around her waist. Her sleepy mind conjured images of Oliver Sabin. Had the man found their camp? He'd come to claim her after all.

She struggled to awaken fully. "Let go of me," she said through gritted teeth. She thrashed her legs, kicking at him wherever she could, until a heavy thigh fell over her abdomen, holding her to the ground. The man straddled her, and pinned her beneath him. She pushed against his chest, momentary panic flooding her, but she was no match for his strength. His hands clamped around her arms, and he immobilized her further.

"I won't hurt you, Evie," someone whispered softly in her ear. "I'm only here to keep you warm. Don't be afraid of me."

Alex? Evelyn's mind raced at his words. He'd come to share her blankets? Earlier she'd been ready to . . . do what? She wanted to prove to Alex that she was a woman. As her husband, he had every right to be in her bed, but she wasn't ready for this. It was too unexpected.

"Evie, I'm not here to hurt you," he said again, his voice louder this time.

"I told you I wouldn't share your blankets." She forced the lie from her lungs, trying to inhale a deep breath. "Or have you forgotten our agreement already?"

"Dammit, woman. I'm only trying to see to your comfort. Cease your struggles and I'll leave. But I won't release you until you calm down." Alex's breath caressed her cheek, and a delicious shudder passed through her. Unable to see him in the dark, she turned her head to avoid a repeat of the sensation for fear it might give away her body's growing awareness of him. She raised her head slightly, intending to move it to the side. Instead, her mouth grazed against his lips.

"Evie." Alex's whisper was barely audible, just before his own mouth fully covered hers. Evelyn's heart drummed wildly in her chest. Heat raced through her extremities to settle in the pit of her stomach. His kiss remained light and soft, and Evelyn craned her neck to intensify the connection.

Alex released her arm, and his hand ran up her shoulder, caressed her neck, and cupped the side of her face. A low moan escaped his throat, just before he abruptly broke the contact. He inhaled a deep breath, and rolled to the side, completely freeing Evelyn from underneath him. Cold air immediately seeped through her clothing, and she shivered.

"Hold me, Alex," Evelyn whispered, and turned toward him, craving his warmth. A scalding need that had nothing to do with Alex's body heat flowed through her veins.

Alex inhaled deeply. "Evie, I'm not here for the reasons you think," he said, his voice strained. "I . . . come here, you're shivering." He pulled the blanket and buffalo robe that had fallen away during their struggle over her, and she pressed against his chest.

Evelyn lay quietly in his arms. She waited for something to happen, wondering what to say or do. Never before had a man shared her blankets, yet for some reason, lying in Alex's embrace seemed as natural as breathing.

"Turn around and go to sleep, Evie," Alex said firmly. He loosened his hold so she could comply. Evelyn didn't move. Should she dare try and kiss him? She had told him a moment ago that she didn't want to share his blankets. Nothing could be further from the truth all of a sudden. His kiss ignited a need that refused to be ignored.

Gritting her teeth, she finally complied with his request. What if he rejected her kiss if she tried? Turning to her other side, she pressed her back against his chest. Had she imagined a shudder pass through him when she relaxed against him? He slid one arm beneath her head, his warm breath against her neck sending a renewed shiver down her spine. His other arm tightened around her waist as if he meant to draw her inside himself. Nothing had ever made her feel safer or more protected than lying in Alex's arms. For a moment she could imagine that he truly loved her, and wasn't merely here to keep her warm.

"Sleep, Evie, We'll travel early in the morning." His lips brushed against her neck. Evelyn sighed softly and she forced her eyes shut. Lying quietly in Alex's embrace, she smiled to herself. Her mind recalled the gentle way he'd kissed her a minute ago. He was wrong. If he thought he could be cruel like his father, Alex was dead wrong. Here in his arms, nothing would ever hurt her. Content in his embrace, she drifted off to sleep.

***

Horses whinnied, and birds chirped loudly. The sound of men's voices reached her ears. Evelyn blinked and raised her head. Darkness had given way to a sunny morning. She quickly raised herself to a sitting position, and turned her head to peer behind her. Alex was gone. Had he even been here? Had he truly come to her bed in the middle of the night with the intent to shield her from the cold? She touched tentative fingers to her lips, wondering if she'd imagined it all in a dream.

CHAPTER TEN

Alex squatted by the fire, poking at the outlying ashes with a stick. The gray swirls of his breath in the crisp early morning air mingled with the wisps of smoke rising skyward. Laurent silently handed him a tin cup filled with steaming coffee.

"Did you stay warm last night?" Laurent asked, lowering himself to the ground next to Alex with a loud grunt. He sipped from his own cup, and peered at Alex from beneath his lashes.

Alex held the hot cup between his hands, staring at the dark brew. He didn't want to think about last night. He'd been more than warm. Last night had been heaven and hell rolled into one. The early morning cold was a welcome reprieve to the heat coursing through his body like a fever consuming him. He glanced past the fire to where Yancey stirred under his covers, then held the cup to his lips.

"It is good that you have finally come to your senses and decided to share your woman's sleeping blanket. I truly didn't think you would wait much longer. I am surprised, though, that you have left the comfort of her bed so early, *mon ami.*"

Alex didn't respond. Laurent would find out soon enough that he hadn't sought out Evelyn's bed with the intent to truly claim her as his wife. What he had done instead was make a big mistake, something he seemed to be doing a lot lately where Evie was concerned. Communicating with her proved to be more difficult than trying to barter with a tribe of Indians whose language he hadn't mastered. At least with the Indians, hand gestures and signs were sufficient means of getting a point across. Every time he spoke to Evelyn he seemed to make matters worse.

She was already skittish as a flighty deer whenever he came near her, and last night she had thought he'd come to her with the intent to force himself on her. Alex tossed the stick into the fire, sending up glowing orange embers. His coffee spilled onto his britches, and he jumped to his feet.

"Damn it all," he growled, and tossed the remaining contents of his cup over the flames. The fire hissed, and a thick gray smoke plume rose in the air.

"She did not please you, Walker?" Laurent stared up at him, fanning his hand in front of his face. "Perhaps in time, she will learn how –"

"She pleases me just fine." Alex glared at Laurent, and gritted his teeth. "It's me who can't do anything right for her. I've told you before, I ain't no good for her." He tossed his cup to the ground, and crossed his hands over his chest. Staring into the nearby woods, he cursed under his breath.

Laurent grunted and pushed himself up off the ground. He shook his head, and patted Alex on the shoulder. "I hope for your sake you will regain your sight soon, my friend."

"What the hell is that supposed to mean?"

"She is your wife. A woman, a wife, requires her husband's attention."

"Evelyn is my wife in appearance only. She and I both agreed to that. I promised to protect her until I can take her back to St. Louis, and that's exactly what I'm doing." Alex glared at his friend. Laurent cast him a perplexed look. He shook his head and turned, reached for his rifle lying on the ground by his bedroll, and headed into the woods.

"How the hell am I supposed to talk to her?" Alex called after the Frenchman, throwing his arms up in the air. "Every time I try, she gets her feathers ruffled." Laurent kept walking. He raised his arm and waved in a gesture of dismissal. Alex scoffed and turned back to the dying campfire.

Women! How the hell was a man supposed to communicate with them? He threw some more wood on the fire, and glared at Yancey's bedroll.

The greenhorn was still sound asleep. Alex envied the man. Sleep didn't come easy for him lately. He hadn't had a good night's rest since arriving at rendezvous, since Evelyn became his responsibility. Thoughts of her consumed him day and night. Evie Lewis, his childhood friend's baby sister, the woman who stood out among all others the day he arrived in St. Charles, and who had become his wife against her will. The woman he couldn't touch. He had never been so aware of another person as he was of her. By the law of the land, she was his, yet he couldn't have her.

Watching her laugh and smile with Laurent during supper the night before, he'd nearly lost his mind. If he had any sense at all, he would set a course for St. Louis rather than head further into the wilds. Better yet, he should ask Laurent to take her back, then he could push forward with his plans to build his cabin in the remote valley at the base of the Teewinots. That had been his intent for almost a year. He craved the solitude. A woman had never been part of his plans.

"Alex?" A soft voice called from behind him.

He spun around on his heels. How had Evie approached him without his notice? If he didn't start thinking straight, and paid more attention to his surroundings, someone was likely to get killed. These woods were teeming with hostile Blackfeet, eager to add the scalps of white trappers to their belts.

"Good morning," she said tentatively, smiling softly at him. She stood close enough to touch, close enough for him to catch the scent of the soap she used to wash with every day. The flowery fragrance had filled his senses throughout his sleepless night. His heart rate quickened in his chest, and he braced himself for her sharp words that were sure to come, reprimanding him for invading her privacy. Telling him what a varmint he was.

"Mornin'." He cleared his throat and stooped over to pick up the tin cup he had tossed to the ground earlier. "There's coffee." Alex gritted his teeth. What a stupid thing to say! Evie hadn't touched a drop of the bitter brew. He knew she didn't drink the stuff.

"Would you like me to fix some food?" she asked, and stepped closer. Alex straightened to his full height. Her head reached just past his shoulders. Threads of her braided hair fluttered loosely around her face, and he gripped the cup tightly to keep from reaching out and swiping the strands away from her cheek. Her eyes shimmered up at him with expectation. What was different about her today?

"Alex?" Evelyn's gaze turned quizzical, and her forehead furrowed.

He blinked and shook his head, trying desperately to clear his mind.

"I'd like to start upholding my end of our bargain and make myself useful. If you show me where you keep your supplies, with your permission I would like to start cooking the meals."

Alex ran a hand over his face, the rough stubble along his jaw reminding him that he needed to shave.

"Yeah. Sure," he answered lamely.

Yancey chose that moment to awaken. The greenhorn yawned, and awkwardly climbed out from under his blanket. He stretched and scratched at the back of his head. He glanced around, and froze when he noticed Alex staring at him. His eyes darted to Evelyn, and his mouth widened in a smile. Stepping away from his blanket, he stumbled toward her.

"Good morning, Miss Evelyn," he greeting formally, and bowed his head. "Morning, Walker." His attention remained on Evie, and Alex clenched his jaw. "Forgive me for not commenting last evening, Miss Evelyn, but I sure do thank you for the meal you prepared. It was the best thing I've eaten in months."

Evelyn's lips widened in a smile, and she laughed softly. Alex's chest tightened, just as a sudden wave of jealousy hit him in the gut. Rage coursed through him, and he fought the impulse to send his fist against Yancey's jaw.

"You're quite welcome, Mr. Yancey," Evie said. "If Alex will allow it, I plan to do more of the cooking from now on. I'm afraid I've grown quite tired of meat in all its varieties."

Yancey laughed, and nodded in apparent agreement. "That would be most welcome, Miss Evelyn."

"Go and start packing the horses, Yancey," Alex growled, taking a step toward the man, who stumbled backward. "From now on, if you decide to sleep all morning, you're gonna get left behind. We ain't got time for fancy cooking." He advanced on Yancey, fully aware that his demeanor intimidated the easterner. His unwavering stare alone would send the greenhorn running for the woods. Hell, he'd probably wet his pants already.

"I'll get right to it." Yancey stumbled over his words as

well as his feet, and tripped in an effort to get away as quickly as possible.

"See that you do," Alex called loudly. Behind him, Evie expelled a loud breath of air. Alex turned to face her. He was acting like a mule's ass, but at the moment he couldn't stop himself. How could that bumbling fool talk to Evie so easily?

"Did you have to be so rude to him?" Evie glared. Gone was the warm glow in her eyes from a moment ago. He would gladly trade a year's supply of beaver plews to see her favor him with such a look more often. That's what had been different about her, he suddenly realized. Before he could ponder at what it meant, she held her hands to her hips, her eyes narrowing even more. "I just woke up, too. Were you about to give me a scolding as well?"

Alex clenched his jaw. "It's late. We need to head out." He wasn't about to get into a spat with her again. He waved his hand toward the fire. "Do whatever it is you need to do to get ready. I'll be back shortly."

He stepped around her, grabbed for his rifle propped against a boulder near the fire, and strode off in the direction Laurent had taken earlier.

"You are an impossible man, Alex Walker," Evelyn called out behind him, and Alex lengthened his strides.

* * *

Alex picked his way through the forest, stepping over and around downed trees. He didn't bother keeping to a deer trail. It didn't matter. He was only here to clear his head. He gripped the rifle in his hand, and looked ahead out of habit, scanning for any unusual movement. His breath swirled a ghostly gray in front of him in the frigid morning air. The cold was a welcome reprieve to the heat coursing through his body.

What the hell was he thinking, bringing Evie with him to his remote valley? The dangers of the wilderness were real enough, but what would happen if he lost control, and his temper got the better of him like it had done with Yancey? What if he struck her, or worse? He glanced at his hands. He knew his own strength, and what he was capable of. He'd killed enough men with those hands.

Alex clenched his jaw. He swung his rifle like a club at a vine that blocked his way. Rage and fear raced through his body. Laurent made it sound so easy, telling him to let go of his past. Images of his father tormented him. His mother sat cowering in a corner of their small farmhouse, begging for mercy. Silas Walker cursed and screamed at her, telling her she was worthless, and it was her own fault that he had to teach her a lesson.

He squeezed his eyes shut to force the memory from his mind. His arms ached as fresh memories overshadowed the ones of his childhood. He'd spent a sleepless night, holding Evie close to him. As the darkness of night slowly gave way to a gray dawn, he'd watched her sleep. No emotion had ever been as powerful in his life as what flooded his entire being during those few hours. Elation, hope, fear. He had no examples to go by, but understanding what was happening to him rooted itself firmly in his mind, and in his heart. He'd fallen in love with Evie. He was as sure of it just as he knew that the morning sun would rise in the east. He couldn't say exactly when it had happened, but he'd been enamored with her the day he saw her at the docks in St. Charles, the day he got shot. And now she was here, in his mountains. She was his wife, and with every word he uttered, with everything he did, he pushed her further away.

It's for the best, Walker. You're proving over and over again that you don't deserve her in your life. You're just like the old bastard.

Hell. He couldn't even communicate with her. Why hadn't he thought to tell her she had cooked a fine meal the night before? It obviously pleased her to hear it from Yancey.

Alex stopped walking. He stood in a small grassy clearing, the sun filtering through the canopy of the tall lodgepole pines that surrounded him. A soft rush of wind swept through the tallest trees. How far had he gone from camp? And where the hell was Laurent? Birds chirped loudly, adding to the tranquility of the scene. A sudden inexplicable chill ran down his spine; a sense that something wasn't right. He listened for any unusual sounds, and turned slowly in all directions. Cold sweat beaded his forehead. A distant scream pierced the air, and Alex took off running back in the direction from where he'd come. Adrenaline surged through his system. Why the hell had he left camp?

He leapt over a downed log, and dodged tree branches and vines, cursing under his breath. The sound of a gunshot echoed through the forest, and Alex increased his pace. Evie! What the hell was happening?

Hindered by the dense undergrowth of the forest, Alex beat a path through the vines with the butt end of his flintlock. Deeply absorbed in his thoughts, he hadn't paid much attention to how far he'd wandered from camp. He had to be getting close.

A high-pitched yell followed closely after the gunshot. Was the camp being attacked by a war party of Blackfeet? Alex redoubled his efforts, his lungs burning and his heart pumping with renewed fear for what he might find. Looking ahead, the forest opened to the clearing where they'd set up camp the day before. The lean-to he'd built for Evie's comfort stood off to the right.

A loud, predatory roar resonated through the trees. Alex darted into the clearing. His heart sank to the pit of his stomach. A huge grizzly stood on its hind legs about a hundred yards away, its jaw wide open. The beast let out another angry roar. Several feet away, Yancey attempted to scramble to his feet.

"Evelyn," Alex yelled. She stooped down beside Yancey, tugging on his arms to help him on his feet. In her hand was a rifle, and she held it up defensively to ward off the bear's impending charge.

Alex didn't hesitate. While running across the clearing, he aimed his rifle at the beast. Past experience told him that one shot would not kill the bear. He fired, and the shot hit the bruin in the chest, slowing the animal from charging at the people on the ground. In one fluid motion, Alex yanked his pistol from his belt and fired again. This time his shot hit the bear in the eye, splatting blood into the air. The animal swiped wildly at its face, roaring in pain and rage.

Evelyn yelled, standing over Yancey, who hadn't gotten to his feet. She waved the rifle frantically through the air as if her action would create a shield between herself and the mighty predator.

"Dammit, get back," Alex yelled. He dashed around to the animal's blinded side, tossing his pistol to the ground. He pulled his hunting knife from its sheath on his belt, and without hesitation collided with flesh and fur as he leapt onto the creatures back. He drove his knife deep between the bear's shoulder blades, quickly ducking to the right when the bear swiped a mighty paw behind him. The stench of a predator's breath emanated from the beasts mouth, and blood gushed from the stab wound. Alex repeated his action, driving his knife into the bear's back and neck again and again.

Consumed by rage and pain, the bruin danced and darted, swiping fiercely with its mighty paws at the opponent on its back. The animal's massive body began to wobble, and his breathing turned raspy. Alex leapt to the side when the grizzly collapsed to the ground. One final stab to the neck, and he was confident that he had delivered the fatal blow.

Alex's chest heaved, and he leaned forward with his hands on his knees. He breathed deeply, drawing air into his burning lungs, then glanced up. His head turned to where Evie and Yancey hovered on the ground. Behind him, Laurent came running from between the trees.

"*Mon dieu, mon dieu,*" he called, running faster than Alex had ever seen him move.

On the ground, Yancey moaned quietly. Blood covered his face, and clothing. A fresh jolt hit Alex in the chest when he saw blood on Evie's shirt. He reached her in two quick strides, pulling her to her feet.

"Where are you hurt?" he called, his eyes roaming up and down her body. Evelyn's eyes widened, the fear and panic in their depths driving a hot blade right through his chest. She frantically shook her head.

"Dammit, where are you hurt?" he growled. With a shaky hand, he reached to unbutton her shirt. Evelyn clamped a hand around his wrist to halt his action.

"Not me," she said, her voice cracking. "Yancey's hurt. Please, you have to help him."

Relief swept over him like a breeze on a hot summer's day.

"I will take care of the young *jeunot*," Laurent said, already kneeling beside Yancey. "Take the mademoiselle away. This is not a sight for her to see."

"No. Wait!" Evelyn pulled against Alex's hold when he tugged on her arm with a bloodied hand. The flesh across his upper arm burned as if hot needles had been driven into him. He ignored the pain, knowing that the bear's claws had hit their target at some point. He could tend to his own wounds later.

"Laurent will take care of him," Alex said firmly, and held her arm. She shot a frantic look over her shoulder, but didn't fight him when he pulled her away from the gruesome scene. Only when they stood next to the lean-to did Alex stop. Sudden anger replaced his fear.

"What the hell were you thinking?"

Evelyn stood, staring up at him in stunned silence. Her mouth fell open. "I . . . I had to help him," she said, her lips quivering.

"You can't face down a grizzly with an unloaded gun, woman," Alex roared. He held her arms, and shook her for emphasis. "You get yourself to safety. That bear was intent on Yancey. You only made it angrier by waving that stick in its face."

"What would you have me do, Alex?" Evelyn's shaky voice from a moment ago matched his in her angry retort. Her eyes narrowed. "I couldn't just leave him there to be mauled to shreds."

"You're too important to me to let yourself get hurt. Don't you understand? What the hell foolish notion got into your damn female head to—"

Evelyn abruptly stepped closer to him, clasped his face between her hands, and stood on her toes. She leaned up and pressed her lips to his mouth. Alex stood stiffly for a moment, then his hands spanned her waist, pulling her up against him. She pried her mouth from his, her eyes wide as she stared at the stunned expression on his face.

"I had to silence you somehow," she said softly, sucking in a deep breath, and stepped back. Alex released her. She'd thrown his words from a week ago right back at him. His fingers grabbed for the shirt at her waist, and he tugged until she had no choice but to step toward him. His other hand reached up, and he brushed the hair from her face, his fingers lingering against her soft cheek.

The muscles along his jaw clenched and unclenched in rapid succession, and his eyes roamed her face, looking for a reason for her unexpected action.

"Don't ever do that again," he said, his voice a low rumble.

Evelyn's mouth fell open. She blinked, then her eyes narrowed. "So it's fine for you to kiss me, but I can't kiss you first?"

Alex's forehead wrinkled, his brows pulling together. She'd misunderstood. "Not that, you insufferable woman. Don't ever scare the tar out of me like that again. Ever."

CHAPTER ELEVEN

With shaking hands, Evelyn rummaged in her pack for the length of muslin Alex had given to her while they were still at rendezvous. She hadn't had a chance to cut the material and begin sewing a dress. She tore off several wide strips at one end. There was so much of the material, she could probably make two dresses from it. She certainly had enough to make bandages for Alex and Yancey. Her heart had finally slowed to its normal pace after that experience with the bear.

Laurent hadn't allowed her to see Yancey, whom he'd moved under the lean-to, but he had assured her that the impulsive easterner would live. She had no idea how badly he'd been hurt. Soft moans came from under the lean-to as Laurent hovered over his charge.

The bear had wandered into camp, obviously attracted to the meat from the deer that Alex had brought from his hunt the evening before. Yancey had spent many hours cutting it into large strips, which he had then hung to dry from some nearby tree branches. He had dashed for his rifle when he saw the imposing predator.

Evelyn had begged him not to shoot at the animal, advising him that if they remained quiet, the bear might leave. It wasn't worth risking their lives over a few pieces of meat, but Yancey hadn't listened. His shot had merely enraged the massive beast, and it had charged, one swipe of its huge claws sending Yancey to the ground. The bear would have lunged for Yancey if she hadn't startled the creature momentarily by yelling and waving her hands in the air. She'd darted for Yancey's rifle, even though she knew it would be useless. Her conscience wouldn't allow her to simply let the bear kill the man on the ground

Alex's fight with the bear replayed in her mind. Fearlessly, he had thrown himself at the mighty predator without any thought to his own safety. Evelyn could only watch in silent horror while the man she loved battled the giant monster to the death. She raked her teeth across her lower lip. She loved Alex. It was the one thought that came to her mind as she watched helplessly while he threw himself in harm's way to shield her. There was no doubt in her mind that she would be dead at this very moment if Alex hadn't come to the rescue.

Evelyn fingered the cotton material in her hand. Alex Walker was the most perplexing man she had ever met. One minute he behaved in ways that sent her temper soaring, and the next his thoughtful actions left her breathless. Shaking her head to clear her mind, she tried to focus on the task at hand. She had caught a glimpse of the torn flesh on Alex's arm where the bear had raked him with its claws. Alex had dismissed it as a minor wound when she noticed it while he held her after her impulsive kiss. She could sense he wanted to kiss her again, had seen the longing in his eyes even as he scolded her and called her insufferable.

"I'll tell you who's insufferable," Evelyn had voiced loudly, staring at Alex's torn and bloodied shirt. "It's you, Alex

Walker, and your damn stubbornness." She'd pulled away from him, and pointed a finger at his chest. "I may not have the skills and knowledge of a healer, but I do know a wound when I see one, and yours needs to be treated. At the very least, allow me to clean it and wrap it, and perhaps it won't fester." She hadn't given him a chance at a rebuttal, and rushed off to find her leather pouch that held her meager belongings. Her most treasured item was the length of muslin.

Evelyn peered over her shoulder. Alex hadn't argued, and headed for the creek that flowed at the edge of their camp. He unbuckled his belt from around his waist and pulled his shirt up and over his head. Even from a distance, several wide, angry-looking red gashes visibly slashed across his upper left arm where the bear had clawed him. Evelyn hoped the wounds weren't too deep. She didn't have Aimee Osborne's skills to treat Alex's injuries.

With a will of their own, Evelyn's eyes remained fixed on Alex's profile. Heat slowly crept up her neck, and into her cheeks. Well-sculpted, corded arms hung from wide shoulders. He knelt at the creek's bank, splashing water on his face with his good hand, giving her a pleasing view of his broad and chiseled back. Fascinated, she watched the play of muscles along either side of his spine bunch and relax. He clearly favored his injured arm by letting it dangle at his side. Without having to see the front of him, she envisioned an equally solid and firm chest and abdomen. The skin on her back tingled with the memory of pressing up against him during the night, his strong arms shielding her from the cold.

Alex chose that moment to look up and glance in her direction. Evelyn whipped her head around. Her cheeks flamed in embarrassment at having been caught staring. Her pulse pounded at her temples, and the sensation of drowning took hold in her. She drew in a deep breath of air to fuel her deprived lungs. Had she been holding her breath while admiring his physique?

Raising her chin, she swallowed back the lump in her throat. She swiped some hair away from her face that had come loose of the confines of her braid, and gathered the strips of muslin. Evelyn pushed herself up off the ground, and with a determined set of her mouth headed in Alex's direction. With each step she took, her heart sped up.

Good grief, Evie! It's not like you've never seen a man's nude torso before.

Her father and Henry had often removed their shirts in the summer months when coming in from the fields, but neither her father nor her brother looked like Alex. His lean body and sculpted muscles exuded strength. The memory of his strong arms holding her gave testament to that fact. Evelyn shook her head to clear her mind.

"Are you in a lot of pain?" she asked, hoping her voice sounded normal. There was no need to give Alex a glimpse of what she was thinking.

"It stings a little," he said, his eyes on her. Evelyn hesitated for a moment, then sank to her knees beside him. Her nose caught a trace of his distinct male scent of sweat and rawhide, and her heart fluttered again.

She dipped one of the cotton rags in the cold water, resisting the impulse to use the wet muslin to cool her own face and neck. Instead, she wrung out the excess water and dabbed gingerly around Alex's wounds to clean away the dried blood. She repeated her actions over and over, until finally the area was free of blood. He remained motionless while she worked, and Evelyn raised her head to find him watching her intently. She couldn't tear her eyes from his at that moment if her life depended on it. An intense gleam shone in the depths of his stare, and she swallowed the lump in her throat. Extreme longing smoldered in his eyes, along with regret and uncertainty.

Give him time, Laurent had told her. *He is afraid he will become his father.*

"I think a bandage to keep the wound clean should suffice to allow it to heal." The words barely escaped her dry mouth. If she could make time stand still, this was a moment she wanted to hold on to. To divert her attention away from Alex's stare, she grabbed for another swath of muslin. Gently, she wrapped the material around his arm to cover his wound.

Evelyn tied off the end of the bandage in a knot, and pulled her hands back. She adjusted her knees on the hard ground, intent on standing up. Before she could move, Alex reached out, and his calloused fingers grazed against her cheek with a feather light touch. Heat seared through her body at his tender gesture. Wide-eyed, she glanced at his face. His mouth curved upward at the corners. Slowly, he leaned forward.

Evelyn closed her eyes, and she held her breath. Her lips parted and tingled in anticipation of what she knew was to come. Alex's hand slid behind her head, cupping the back of her neck. He pulled her toward him, and just when she thought he wouldn't kiss her after all, his lips brushed against hers. Her hands reached out to brace against his chest. The feel of his warm skin against her hand, the strong beating of his heart, and the solid strength beneath her fingers sent ripples of some unknown need racing through her. Just when she thought she would drown in the sensation, Alex pulled away, ending his gentle kiss much too soon. His fingers lingered just a moment longer against her cheek, then he broke off all contact with her. Evelyn's eyes flew open, and she fought for a breath of air.

"I'll ask Laurent to take you back to St. Louis," Alex said, and stood. Avoiding her eyes, he reached for his torn shirt lying in the grass, and then turned his back, his gaze fixed across the water at the distant snow-capped mountains. Evelyn stared in stunned disbelief. It was the last thing she expected him to say. The muscles in his shoulders and back tensed.

"I don't understand," Evelyn said quietly. Dumbfounded, she reached up to touch his arm.

"He should have never brought you here," Alex said firmly. He turned his head, and his mouth was set in a firm line. "You need a husband who will take care of you, not someone like me."

"Alex, I don't think—"

"No arguments. I free you of your ties to me. You're going back."

"And what if I refuse to go back?" Evelyn moved around him to stand in front of him, and glared at his face. It was time to put her foot down. All her life, someone else had made decisions on her behalf, telling her what was best for her. "What would you have me do in St. Charles, Alex? Marry the man who killed my parents?"

Alex faced her fully. "A week ago you thought you were already married to that man." He scoffed.

"And I've changed my mind," she said. "I realize I was wrong about you, Alex." Evelyn stepped closer, inches from him. The heat coming off his body seeped right through the fabric of her shirt. "Perhaps it's time that you come to the same conclusion," she whispered. Hesitating for only a second, she placed her palm on his chest over his heart. Alex's jaw clenched.

"Same conclusion?" His eyebrows scrunched together. "I know I didn't kill your folks."

Evelyn laughed quickly, and shook her head. "You really are as dumb as a warthog, Alex Walker. When will you realize you are wrong about yourself?" She shook her head. What did she have to do or say to prove to him that he wasn't like his father? "Why I am even in lo—"

"Hello the camp," someone called loudly from the direction of the woods, and Evelyn spun around before she could complete her thought. A lone trapper rode into view, two mules laden with supplies following closely on the heels of his horse.

* * *

Alex stepped in front of Evie at the sound of a man's voice calling the customary greeting when riding into someone's camp. Her soft palm left a searing scorch mark on his chest as if she had branded him. No words could describe the way her tender touch affected him when she cleansed his wounds. Intense desire had rippled through him along with the urge to protect this woman from harm, which meant he had to protect her from himself. He cursed under his breath. He would have thought Evie would be happy to go back to St. Louis. Why was she arguing with him? What had she meant by he was wrong about himself? This wasn't the time to ponder her words, nor the look in her eyes. Or the kiss they had shared.

Alex forced his focus to the visitor riding into their camp. He recognized the trapper instantly. He held up his hand in greeting, and stepped away from Evie to meet him.

"Jasper Williams, what a surprise." Alex approached the man's horse, and reached his hand up. The trapper leaned forward and over his saddle, and firmly clasped Alex's hand and arm.

"Wal, ah'll be et by a tater. If it ain't Shadow Walker," he nodded with a wide-eyed smile. He pushed the fox fur cap he wore away from his forehead. "Thought you'd be up in that hole of yers by now, buildin' that cabin."

"Heading there now. Didn't see you at rendezvous this summer. Get off your horse and have some coffee."

The trapper nodded, and dismounted. Holding firmly to his rifle, he pointed to the dead bear.

"That'll make a nice meal," he grunted. "Didn't know ya was huntin' bar."

Alex laughed. "He didn't give me much choice."

"I remember when ya was just a green pup, tryin' to get yerself kilt by Ole' Ephraim up on the Madison." He chuckled, and spit tobacco on the ground. "Yer green shore is weared off now. Heard ya was no longer a company man."

"I've learned a thing or two over the years. And, yeah, I joined the free trappers."

Laurent had left Yancey's side and came walking up to them, a wide smile on his face. "Jasper Williams. I believed you to be dead." He grabbed the trapper's hand and pumped his arm up and down.

"I's feelin' right pert, ya crazy voyageur. Ain't gone under yet."

"Why did we not see you at rendezvous?" Laurent added coffee grounds to the pot in the fire, and headed for the creek with it without waiting for a reply. A low moan came from under the lean-to.

Jasper Williams' eyes darted in the direction of the sound, his bushy brown eyebrows raised.

"A flatlander who Laurent insisted on bringing along," Alex said in answer to the man's unspoken question. "Thought he'd try and prove himself against the bear and lost."

"Sounds summat like you, Walker," Jasper chuckled, and slapped Alex on the back.

"Yeah, well, at least I was alone, and didn't put someone else's life in danger," Alex argued, resisting the urge to glance over his shoulder. He knew the loner was referring to Alex's first year in the mountains, when he had tried to prove himself by foolishly shooting at a grizzly. He'd almost paid with his life that day. Lucky for him the incident had happened far to the north of here along the Madison River. Daniel Osborne, the man who would become his friend and mentor had saved his life that day. Anger seethed through him again, thinking about the danger Yancey had put Evelyn in by shooting at the grizzly.

Jasper Williams grunted, and scratched at the stubble on his jaw. He glanced around camp, and his eyes widened with a look of disbelief. There was only one reason for the man's reaction. He must have directed his attention on Evie. That the trapper hadn't noticed her before was a surprise. Alex turned to see her standing by the creek where he'd left her. Uncertainty was etched on her face. He couldn't blame her. She hadn't met many friendly trappers, and it was wise of her to be cautious.

"That ain't no Injun squaw," Williams proclaimed, his eyes volleying between her and Alex. A wide grin spread across his face. "I'll be," he said, and slapped Alex on the back again. "Ya got yerself a woman, Walker. And a fine lookin' one at that. How'd ya get so fortunate'n get a white woman to come to the mountains with ya? I thought only Dan'l Osborne was that lucky."

Jasper stepped around Alex before he had a chance to respond, the thick buffalo-hide robe he wore making him appear twice as wide as he really was. Without hesitation, he strode up to Evelyn and appraised her from top to bottom. Alex followed quickly on his heels. If he remembered Jasper Williams correctly, the man didn't have the best manners, even though he was completely harmless.

"She shore shines, Walker. No question. She shore shines. Looks like she's got a lot of pluck, too."

Evelyn narrowed her eyes, and Alex couldn't help but grin. She probably had no idea that the trapper was complimenting her appearance. The look of annoyance she shot him and the other trapper grew with each second.

"Evie, this is a friend, Jasper Williams," he said, and took hold of her hand. He gave it a reassuring squeeze. Evie remained stiff for a moment, then, to his utter surprise, the annoyance vanished and she flashed the other man a radiant smile.

"It's a pleasure, Mr. Williams," she said, extracting her hand from Alex's, and reached to offer it to Jasper. The man's bushy eyebrows widened, then his hand swallowed up Evelyn's. He chuckled heartily.

"Ya shore is a purty little thing," he said. "Walker got hisself a fine woman, an ya got yerself one fine man, there. Walker is brave as a buffler bull in spring, ya mark my words. He'll do right by ya, no question."

"Thank you, Mr. Williams," Evie said sweetly, and slowly pulled her hand from the trapper's grip. She turned to Alex and favored him with a smile that sent his pulse racing. She inched up next to him and slipped her hand back in his. What the hell was she doing? Alex gripped her hand and stared at her. The same warm glow shone in her eyes as what he'd seen that morning, before he left camp. Before he left Evie with that no-good greenhorn, which almost got her killed. It was the same look she favored him with while tending to his wounds. His gut clenched, and he tore his eyes away from her.

"Go and fix some food, Evie. I'm sure Jasper is hungry." He had to get her away from him. She would surely drive him mad. Alex released her hand, and the warmth in her eyes cooled almost immediately when he spoke his harsh words, and he instantly regretted it. She visibly inhaled a deep breath and held up her chin. Nodding silently, she turned to leave. Alex's hand reached out and grazed her arm. "I'd be much obliged," he said quietly, silently calling himself every vile name he could think of.

"Of course, Alex," Evie said, and she smiled softly, but the hurt was evident in her eyes.

"Wouldn't mind eatin' some of that there bar," Jasper said, running a hand across his lips.

"I'll have to ask Laurent about how to cook that," Evie said, glancing from him to the trapper. "I've never prepared bear before." She turned quickly and scurried off toward the fire where Laurent was busy with the coffeepot. Alex stared after her. So did Williams.

"Yessir, ya got a good woman," Jasper said again, nodding in approval and appreciation of Evie. "Shore makes me miss my Molly."

Alex raised his brows. "Molly?" he asked.

"My wife," Jasper answered, and adjusted the furry hat on his head.

"I didn't know you were married." Alex was certain that Williams had never mentioned a wife. Everyone he knew, and who knew Jasper, assumed he lived a solitary life.

"Yep. Left'er back in St. Louie."

Alex chuckled. "You never spoke of a wife before."

"Cause talkin' 'bout 'er would be plumb hurtful," Jasper said quietly, looking right at Alex. "Yer a lucky man, Walker. Yer gal is here with ya. Mine didn't wanna come. I shore miss her summat fierce when I'm in these here mountains. This's my last season. Come next spring, I's goin' home fer good. My Molly needs me, an' I need her." He pulled his hat off his head and held it to his chest. Then he pointed a finger at Alex. "Ya be sure an' do right by that gal, Walker. I can see the love shinin' in her eyes for ya. There ain't nothin' more powerful'n a woman lovin' ya, and it's a lucky man who can lay claim to such a woman. I thought them mountains was more important than my wife, but over the last year, I come to realize it ain't so. You hold on to that gal, and don't let 'er go."

The mountain man ran his hand over his face, and turned away from Alex. Alex stared at Evie. She squatted by the cooking fire, poked at the coals and added some wood. She laughed at something Laurent said, just before her gaze darted to him. The laughter froze on her face when their eyes met. Alex held his breath.

Jasper's words echoed in his mind. *I can see the love shinin' in her eyes for ya.* Was that what he himself had seen in her eyes earlier today, and just before he sent her away to cook a meal? Impossible. Evie couldn't be in love with him. He hadn't done anything to win her favor. Alex looked away. He couldn't allow her to see how much she affected him, how much he wanted her to love him. Sending her back to St. Louis would be bad enough. After listening to Jasper talk, he wasn't sure he could go through with it and let her go.

CHAPTER TWELVE

Evelyn gave the cloth in her hand a hard twist to wring the excess water from it. Kneeling beside Byron Yancey under the lean-to, she gently dabbed the cool rag against his forehead. His eyelids fluttered open and his unfocused gaze settled on her face. She offered a reassuring smile.

"How are you feeling?" she asked quietly, and wiped at his whiskered cheeks, taking care to avoid the gash along the side of his jaw that ran from his lip up into his scalp. Laurent had done his best to sew the man's skin together using the hair from his horse's tail, but the ugly jagged wound would no doubt leave a visible scar.

"I feel like I've been mauled by a bear," Yancey groaned, and tried to smile. Evelyn frowned at his apparent attempt at humor. Shifting his weight, he raised his head. "Where are we?"

"Still in camp," Evelyn answered, turning her head to cast a fleeting look over her shoulder. Crickets chirped loudly in the evening air. It would be dark soon. Laurent, Alex, and Jasper Williams sat around the campfire, the lone trapper telling boisterous tales of his travels. Evelyn understood only a few words of what the mountain man said. After serving a supper of bear paw meat and corn cakes to the men, she had excused herself to tend to Yancey.

"You saved my life, Miss Evelyn," Yancey said, his eyes wide as he struggled to raise himself to a sitting position. His hand flew to his head and he groaned again.

"You might want to lie back." Evelyn focused her attention back to the injured man and pushed against his chest to discourage him from doing more harm to his injuries. "And don't thank me. If not for Alex, we would both be dead."

"I did a stupid thing." He reached for her hand, and Evelyn squeezed his.

"I put your life in danger. If anything had happened to you, Walker would have finished me off for sure."

Evelyn cleared her throat. Apparently everyone was under the notion that Alex cared for her. Even she had started to believe it, but then why had he told her he was sending her back to St. Louis? Gritting her teeth, she didn't know what to believe anymore. His tender kisses and those looks of longing in his eyes spoke of something more than casual affection for a friend's sister.

Frustrated, she leaned back, and turned her head again to watch the men at the fire. Alex smiled broadly at something Jasper said, and her heart fluttered in her chest. Damn the man for being such a stubborn oaf! If he thought he could simply send her away, he was sorely mistaken.

For six long years, she had believed he was lost to her. Why she had allowed Charles Richardson to feed her and Henry a bunch of lies that Alex had killed her parents was beyond her scope of comprehension now. The only reason she planned to return to St. Louis some day was to bring the true murderer to justice.

"How bad am I hurt?" Yancey's raspy voice forced her attention back to him. His eyes glazed over with pain. Evelyn wished she wasn't so helpless and knew what to do to comfort him. She couldn't lie to him.

"The bear tore the side of your face. You will always have a scar, but Laurent stitched it up as best as he could. The bear clawed you fairly deep along your ribs on your left side, as well as on your thigh. Laurent assured me that you would mend." Evelyn met his stoic stare, and a look of acceptance washed over him.

"Let me bring you some broth. Alex wants to head out in the morning. You'll need all your strength."

Yancey nodded, and Evelyn pushed herself up off the ground. Silently she wondered how he could possibly travel with his injuries. By the fire, Alex stared in her direction, his lips drawn in a tight line. Squaring her shoulders, she strode toward the men.

"I need a bowl to bring Yancey some food," she said, meeting Alex's stare head on. The man was as unreadable as a stone statue. Laurent handed her a cup, and she leaned toward the kettle hanging over the fire to dip it into the hot broth that simmered within. Alex stood and took the cup from her.

"Laurent can bring it to him," he said quietly. "You've done enough today." His penetrating gaze locked onto her eyes, and for a second that look of longing that sent her heart racing emerged.

Evelyn tore her eyes away, and glanced from Laurent to Jasper, who had stopped talking when she approached. He seemed to find great interest in the lacings of his tobacco pouch that hung from around his neck. Laurent stood and relieved Alex of the cup.

"I will see to our young *jeunot*." He dipped the cup in the kettle, and headed for the lean-to.

"Walk with me," Alex said, and took hold of her hand. Evelyn's pulse increased. He pulled her along with him away from camp toward the creek. A loud chorus of crickets and frogs greeted them, and swarms of insects fluttered above the water in the twilight. A lone coyote barked nearby, and a soft golden glow shimmered along the snow-capped mountain range in the distance.

Evelyn dared not speak first, and waited for Alex to say something. A soft breeze grazed against her cheeks, and she shivered involuntarily.

"Are you cold? We can go back." Alex stopped walking, and turned to face her.

She shook her head, unable to speak. Her mouth went dry, and she ached for his embrace. Disappointment flooded her when Alex released her hand. She stiffened her back and glared at him. It was time to set some things straight.

"I'm not going back to St. Louis," she stated firmly. "Why all of a sudden are you so eager to be rid of me, Alex? We had an agreement. You promised to protect me. You can't do that if I'm in St. Louis, and you're here in these mountains."

Alex's eyes narrowed. "By sending you back, I am protecting you," he said. "Can't you understand that, woman?" His arms clenched at his sides.

"Protecting me, or yourself?" Evelyn challenged, and stepped closer. She reached out and touched his uninjured arm. The muscles beneath his shirt bunched taut.

"What the hell is that supposed to mean?" His eyes blazed, but Evelyn refused to back away.

"I'm not afraid of you, Alex. You can continue to push me away, but I'm not leaving. Six years ago, you broke the heart of a thirteen-year-old girl when you left St. Charles. I'm no longer a little girl. Now that we're here, together, I'm not letting you break my heart a second time." Her heart pounded as she whispered the words. How would he react to such a confession?

Alex pulled away from her and ran his hand over his face. He wheeled to turn around.

"I'm no good for you, Evelyn," he said, his voice strained as he stared off at the distant mountains. "I'm sorry for what happened to your folks and Henry, and that you ended up here. I made a mistake when I decided to take you further into the mountains with me. I didn't know what to do at the time when I . . . when I bartered for you." He paused, and glanced at her before turning his head back toward the mountains. "I'll make sure you're taken care of in St. Louis." His jaw muscles clenched and unclenched.

Evelyn stepped around him, and stared up into his hardened face. She reached up and touched his cheek, forcing him to look at her.

"What if I want you to be the one to take care of me?" she whispered. "As you've reminded me before, according to the law of the land, you're my husband. I see it in your eyes that you have feelings for me. I can feel it in the way you kiss me."

Alex's chest heaved. "It doesn't matter what I might feel for you, Evie. Don't you understand?" His words sounded forced. "Your safety is more important to me than what I want." He pried her hand away from him, and held on to her wrist.

"Alex Walker, you are making no sense."

"I hurt you once, Evie. Remember?" He lifted her wrist to her eye level. "I don't ever want to hurt you like that again."

"Then don't," she said in a sultry voice.

"Evelyn . . ." His voice trailed off, and he shook his head, avoiding her eyes.

Evelyn yanked her arm free of his grip, and fisted her hands at her hips. "Don't be a warthog, Alex Walker."

Alex's head shot up, and his eyebrows furrowed. For a moment he just stood glaring at her. He sighed audibly. His eyes roamed her face, and Evelyn held her breath. The firm set of his jaw tensed even more. Abruptly, he stepped away from her. "Time to get back to camp. It's getting dark."

Without another glance at her, he turned and headed toward the glow of the campfire. Evelyn stood in stunned disbelief.

"I'm not going back to St. Louis. You hear?" She stomped her foot and yelled after him. "Damn you for the stubborn mule that you are." With her hands still on her hips, she stared after him. Her vision blurred, and she sniffed. Had she been mistaken about him after all? She'd almost declared her feelings for the one and only man she ever loved. Perhaps she was just being naïve, and he truly didn't care about her.

Evelyn listened to the crickets chirp and the soft gurgle of the water as it flowed past. She didn't know how long she stood at the creek's edge, but something was different all of a sudden. The frogs stopped their chorus.

Her head shot up just in time to see Alex in the distance wheel around and pull his pistol from his belt. He was almost back at the campfire. It all seemed to happen in slow motion. He called her name, but it sounded like a faraway echo, just before a firm hand clamped over her mouth, and someone dragged her away from the creek. She tried to kick out at her assailant, but a steely hand slapped her across the cheek, making her head snap to the side. She blinked away the pain and darkness before her eyes, and a firm arm wrapped around her middle. The breath left her lungs when she was thrown over someone's shoulder. She tried to call Alex's name, but no words escaped her lips. Her captor ran through the brush and into the forest as the sounds of gunshots reverberated all around her.

* * *

Alex realized something was wrong the instant it

happened. The crickets and frogs ceased their loud noise for a brief moment. The hair at the back of his neck stood on end, and by pure reflex he pulled his pistol from his belt. At camp, Laurent and Jasper both shouted at the same time. Several horses whinnied, and shots rang out.

Evelyn!

Everything seemed to happen at once. With his pistol in one hand, he yanked his knife from his belt. A scream filled the air; the scream of the woman he cherished above everything else. He wheeled around, his pistol cocked and ready to fire.

Evelyn struggled against the hold a Blackfoot warrior had on her arms. He backhanded her across her face, and her head snapped to the side. Rage like a wildfire out of control consumed Alex. Visions of his father hitting his mother flashed before him. He raised his pistol and took aim. Just as he was about to pull the trigger, the warrior threw Evie over his shoulder and took off into the thicket. Alex cursed loudly. He couldn't fire his weapon for fear of hitting her. He charged after the Indian, determined to overtake the savage. His fingers gripped the knife tighter. The Injun would pay with his life for touching her.

"Evelyn," he shouted, wanting her to know that he was coming for her. An arrow whirred through the air, narrowly missing his chest. Alex twisted to the left, raised his gun, and fired in the direction the arrow had come from. With a small sense of satisfaction, his target fell to the ground. Instantly, he bolted forward again to renew his pursuit. A loud war cry and the pounding of horses' hooves behind him alerted him to another attack.

Alex spun around, his knife raised. He tossed his useless pistol to the ground, and yanked a tomahawk from his belt. A warrior on horseback charged at him. The Indian held his war club above his head with the obvious intent to strike him down. Rather than avoid the charge, Alex stood his ground. The Indian swung his arm back, and Alex lunged forward at the same time, blocking the warrior's blow. His forward momentum pulled the Indian off of his horse's back, and he landed with a loud thud in the dirt as his animal kept running.

Alex ran toward his opponent, and kicked the weapon from his hand. The Blackfoot pulled his knife and sprang to his feet. Alex leapt back, and widened his stance. He waited for the warrior to make the next move. Leaning forward, he gripped the knife in one hand, the tomahawk in the other. He cursed under his breath. He was losing precious time while the savage who carried Evie off was getting away.

His opponent bared his teeth, and lunged. Alex held his stance. Moments before the Indian reached him, a shot rang through the air and the warrior fell forward, and dropped to the ground. He didn't move to get up. Blood ran freely from a bullet hole in his back. Alex's head shot up to see Jasper grinning broadly. He tipped his fingers to his fur cap and raised his rifle.

Alex spun around. The warrior who carried Evie away was nowhere to be seen.

"We run 'em off, Walker," Jasper shouted. "They's all hightailin' it outta here like a buncha squaws. Damn Blackfoot."

Alex raced toward camp. "Where the hell's my rifle?" he shouted, his eyes darting frantically around camp.

Laurent rushed to him, tossing his rifle at him. "It is freshly loaded, *mon amie*, but I do not believe we will need it. Jasper and I killed four of them, and there were six more who thought it best to retreat."

"They took Evelyn," Alex called loudly. Blinding rage consumed him. He had to get her back. He would get her back. The warrior who had hit her was as good as dead.

"*Mon dieu!*" Laurent exclaimed.

No sooner had the Frenchman exclaimed his words, when a war cry resonated across the meadow. A lone Indian on his horse far across the creek raised his war lance high in the air. Alex recognized the man who took Evie, but something else looked familiar about him, even though his face was painted black with a broad white stripe below his eyes. Where the hell had the bastard taken her?

"You steal my horses, Shadow Walker, I take your woman," the warrior hollered in his native tongue. He yanked on the reins and pulled his horse's neck around, kicking it into a gallop, whooping loudly as he raced away.

Comprehension dawned on Alex as to why this warrior looked so familiar. He was the Blackfoot whose horses he took the night he stole back his own animals.

"Goddammit," Alex cursed. The rider was too far away to shoot at. Without a second thought, he ran for where his horses stood tethered and hobbled. With one swift motion, he cut through the leather thongs that bound his saddle horse's front legs together, and untied the bridle from the picket line. He swung up onto his mount's bare back.

"Where are you going?" Laurent shouted, running at him, his eyes wide.

Alex circled his excited mount. The animal's muscles bunched up underneath him while it pranced in place, as if sensing Alex's urgency.

"To get my wife back," Alex retorted between clenched teeth.

"Don't be a fool. Wait for us to come with you," Laurent implored frantically. "It is suicide to give chase by yourself."

"They'll kill her, and you know it. I don't have time to waste." Alex glared at Laurent, who had no response. He eased up on the reins and kneed his horse in the sides. The gelding sprang forward. Alex raced his mount toward the creek, and the animal plunged through the water, sending up jets of cold spray. He gave his horse its head and leaned low over its neck, racing in the direction the warrior had taken. His heart pounded fiercely in tune with his horse's hoof beats. Visions of the terrified look in Evie's eyes as the warrior slung her over his shoulder spurred him on.

The setting sun cast a golden glow in the western horizon, the last of the light disappearing quickly behind the mountains. It would be completely dark soon. Alex pressed his thighs against his gelding's sides, urging the horse to go faster. If he lost the trail in the impending darkness, he'd never get Evie back alive. Clenching his jaw as the cool evening air whipped around his face, Alex was well aware of the fate a white captive encountered among the Blackfoot. No man had ever escaped with his life. The Blackfoot enjoyed toying with and slowly torturing their captives. What would they do to a white woman?

Blinding fury tore through his heart. Had it really only been minutes since he told Evie that she was better off in St. Louis so she'd be safe from him? If he hadn't walked away from her by the creek, her life wouldn't be in danger at this very second. Alex growled in frustration.

The trail the Indians left behind cut through a small swath of forest, only to return to more open terrain of sagebrush and willow. The freshly trampled grasses made for an easy trail to follow.

The fresh tracks once again entered a section of forest that wasn't very dense, but would certainly hinder his pursuit. Alex pulled back on his horse's reins to slow his mount's speed. The animal beneath him apparently had other ideas. The horse grabbed hold of the bit, and tossed its head forward, refusing to alter its pace. Racing amongst the trees, the gelding leapt over downed logs as if its hooves had taken on wings. All Alex could do was grab hold of the animal's mane and guide its head in the right direction.

When the forest opened up to another clearing, excited shouts ahead alerted him that he had caught up with his enemies. In the dim light, he saw six riders stopped at the far end of the clearing, their horses dancing nervously beneath them. One horse carried two riders, one of whom was struggling wildly. He spotted the warrior who had taunted him earlier, the white stripe of warpaint across his face distinguishing his from the others. Alex didn't hesitate. Images of the man striking Evie merged with images of his father hitting his mother. He pointed his rifle between his mount's ears, then took aim and fired.

A shot rang out, and the warrior dropped from his horse. Loud war cries hung in the air. Alex yanked his tomahawk from his belt. His horse galloped wildly toward the small group, its ears pinned back as if it knew what the stakes were. Alex fumbled with the flapping reins, and by the time he regained control of his charging mount, his horse had reached the raiding party. Among loud whoops and surprised hollers from the Indians, Evelyn's high-pitched voice screamed his name. The sound of her pleas drove him into the midst of the group of warriors.

"No one steals Shadow Walker's woman," he roared in the language of the Blackfoot. He raised his ax, and charged among the startled Indians, close to another rider. He swung his arm back and to the side, and knocked the warrior from his horse with a well-aimed blow to the man's abdomen. Quickly, he yanked his horse's neck around, and kicked the gelding forward. The smell of blood and sweaty horses hung in the air. Again, he raised his tomahawk, ready for an attack. Gunshots rang out behind him, and Alex recognized Laurent's whoops and hollers. Three of the four remaining wide-eyed Blackfeet wheeled their horses away from him and kicked their mounts into a run. The final warrior dropped Evelyn to the ground just before his horse bolted forward in pursuit of his kinsmen.

Alex's eyes darted around the clearing. Evelyn scrambled to her feet where seconds before a warrior's horse pranced. His pulse quickened, and relief enveloped him like a glowing fire on a cold day. He swung his right leg over his horse's neck and leapt to the ground. For a second he couldn't move. He simply stood by his horse, staring at her. Most of her hair had come loose from the confines of her braid, falling in disheveled waves over her shoulders and down her back. Alex swallowed back the lump in his throat. She had never looked more beautiful. His knees went weak all of a sudden while his heart pumped furiously in his chest. He took a step forward, then another, overcome with relief that she was safe.

"Alex," Evelyn cried, and she ran toward him. With a loud sob, she fell into his waiting arms.

CHAPTER THIRTEEN

"Evie," Alex whispered. He wrapped his arms around her and lifted her off the ground in a fierce embrace, unable to get her close enough to him. She threw her arms around his neck and sobbed against his cheek.

Trembling, he held her close. He never wanted to let her go. The terrifying thought that he almost lost her twice in one day consumed him. He inhaled deeply, catching the faint flowery scent of the soap in her hair that he'd come to associate with the woman he loved.

"Alex, I can't breathe," Evie gasped. Startled, Alex eased his tight grip on her. He set her on the ground, and clasped her face between his hands.

"I'm sorry, Evie," he stammered, clenching his jaw.

Darkness surrounded them, and he had to strain his vision to make out her features. Wide eyes stared back at him, shimmering with relief, trust, and . . .

"I knew you'd come for me. I love you, Alex," Evelyn whispered. Her words sent a jolt of adrenaline searing through him, and Alex was sure his heart would burst. He drew in a deep breath, the heaviness in his chest gone and replaced by a feeling of lightness. His thumbs lightly stroked her cheeks.

"I love you Evelyn. God help me, but I love you." Slowly, he brought his mouth down on hers. Evie sighed when his lips made contact with hers, and she wrapped her arms around his middle and pressed up against him. Her mouth parted slightly in response to his kiss, and he slanted his lips across hers, a sudden fire igniting deep within him. Her eager response sent his mind spinning out of control. His arms trembled, and he curbed the urge to pull her closer. Instead, he eased his head back, and inhaled several deep breaths.

"I waited six years to hear you say those words to me, Alex." Evelyn's arms tightened around his back, and her hands reached up to grip his shoulders from behind.

"Well, Jasper, I believe we are not needed here." Laurent's loud voice boomed from behind him.

"Reckon not, ya crazy voyageur. Better git back'n see if that no-good greenhorn needs ya ta wipe his nose."

Evie smiled, her eyes never wavering from Alex's gaze. He paid no attention to his comrades' laughter. Nothing mattered at that moment but the woman before him. An indescribable feeling of peace and calm enveloped him, and he gently coiled his arms around her waist, drawing her close. Fear of possibly losing her suddenly overshadowed everything else.

"Thank you for saving my life again," Evie whispered, and the warmth of complete trust in her eyes as she stared wide-eyed up at him reached deep into his heart. He couldn't recall ever having such an absolute feeling of contentment as what washed over him at this very moment. Jasper's words from earlier in the day echoed in his mind. *There ain't nothin' more powerful'n a woman lovin' ya, and it's a lucky man who can lay claim to such a woman.*

Evie drew in a deep relaxed sigh, and her heart beat softly against his chest.

Alex cleared his throat and pressed his lips to her forehead. Crickets chirped and his horse snorted a short distance away, the soothing sounds adding to his feeling of peace.

"I don't know how I ever thought I could let you go," he whispered, his gaze locked on hers. He brought his hand up to her face, and his rough fingers caressed her soft skin. The sudden wetness on Evie's cheek sent a jolt of dread through his heart.

"Are you hurt? Did I hurt you?" He immediately released her and took a step back, and a sinking feeling jolted his gut.

Evie reached out and grabbed hold of his arms. She laughed softly. "Alex Walker, you are an impossible man. You understand bears and beavers, but you have a lot to learn about me." She stepped up to him, and stood on her toes. "I'm happy because I love you. Because you told me you love me." She pressed her lips to his, and wound her arms around his neck.

Alex pulled her close again and accepted her invitation. His hands slid up and down her back, loving the feel of her soft feminine body pressed up against him. It still seemed unreal that she cared for him, loved him. He kissed her long and slow, his lips trailing along her jaw and down her neck. Her soft moans would surely drive him mad. She'd told him adamantly that she would not share his bed after he informed her that she was his wife, and her fearful reaction to him when he came to her blankets the previous night begged for caution. With great difficulty, Alex eased his head back. Her reaction communicated the opposite of what she'd said.

Evie was right, though. He did know how to read the signs of the animals and the Injuns better than he understood her. He needed to tread lightly and learn her language.

Daniel Osborne had told him once that in order to survive in the wilderness a man had to understand her first. The same had to be true with a woman. He suddenly wished he had his mentor nearby to ask for advice. A fierce desire to learn all he could about the woman in his arms took hold in him.

He inhaled a deep breath, hoping his racing heart would slow. He couldn't get enough of simply holding her close to him. How could a man hurt something as precious as what he held in his arms? He shook off the vision of his father's face. Laurent had been right all along. He was not like his father. He would be different. He had to believe that. An intense love for the woman in his embrace began to slowly burn away the fears and doubts that had haunted him all his life.

"Alex?" Evelyn's softly spoken question pulled him from his thoughts. He smiled, not sure how much she could see in the darkness that had finally swallowed them up.

"Time to head back to camp, or Laurent might believe the Blackfeet came back." Reluctantly, he unwrapped his arms from around her.

"That was either the bravest or the most foolish thing I've ever seen, even coming from you," Evie said lightly. Alex noted the laughter in her voice.

"What?"

"The way you came galloping headlong into the group of those Indians."

Alex chuckled. "It may not be wise of me to admit this, but I had no choice in the matter. I lost control of my horse."

"Oh." Evelyn giggled softly. "It was still a brave thing to do."

Alex reached for her hand and led her to where his horse stood grazing behind him.

"I would have charged into a war party of a hundred Blackfeet to get you back," he said with more force than he had intended. Fresh anger consumed him, thinking about what might have happened to Evie if he hadn't caught up with the warriors.

"I know you would have, Alex. I'll never be afraid of anything while I'm with you."

Alex clenched his jaw. Pushing his negative thoughts aside, he lifted Evie onto his horse's back, then leapt up behind her. The faint light from an almost full moon guided their way back toward camp. She leaned back against his chest, and he wrapped one arm around her middle, holding her close to him. He allowed his horse to pick its way through the forest, listening for any unusual sounds.

Evie seemed content to ride in silence for a while, allowing his mind to wander. More eager than ever to reach the valley at the base of the Teewinots, he envisioned the cabin he would build. It would have to be bigger than what he first planned on. He could never offer her a house like what she was used to growing up in St. Charles. And he wasn't going back to live the life of a farmer, except . . .

"I still plan to take you to St. Louis." Alex broke the silence between them. Evie stiffened against him, and turned her head.

"What?" she gasped. "Why? I don't want to leave you."

Alex's hold on her tightened. He couldn't help but smile. "Not the way you're thinking. I'm going to find out what happened to your folks, and bring the person responsible to justice. If Charlie killed your parents, I want him to pay for what he did."

Evie remained silent for a moment. "It's what I wanted, too, when Henry decided to come to the wilderness to bring you to justice. And look what happened to him." She spoke barely above a whisper, but her voice cracked nevertheless.

Alex inhaled deeply. "I'm sorry about Henry, Evie. He was

my best friend. But he was also foolish to try and come here. He had no experience."

Evie nodded, but didn't respond. Alex hoped he hadn't said the wrong thing to her again. He enjoyed his new closeness with her, and didn't want to jeopardize ruffling her feathers again.

"Yancey is occupying the lean-to," he said to change the subject. "I'd like you to sleep under my blankets tonight. And every night from now on."

* * *

"I'll take first watch," Alex told Laurent, and reached for his rifle. "Those Blackfeet might decide to come back."

The orange glow of the campfire cast eerie shadows on the men's faces as they sat around the fire. Yancey was asleep under the lean-to. Evelyn listened quietly, her eyes on Alex. They had arrived in camp a short time ago, and she already missed her time alone with him. After lifting her off his horse, he'd kissed her quickly on the cheek, then led her to where Laurent and Jasper waited with smug looks on their faces.

"You, ah, sure you would not want me to take first watch?" Laurent asked, and darted glances from Alex to her. Evelyn's face flushed hot, and she hoped no one could see. Laurent and Jasper had seen her and Alex kiss. It shouldn't matter what they thought.

"I'll wake you in a couple hours," Alex replied, looking at Laurent, then stood. He reached for Evelyn's hand, and pulled her up off the ground.

He led her to where his bedroll was laid out on the ground, just beyond the glow of the fire. "Get some sleep."

Releasing her hand, he was about to turn. Evelyn reached into the darkness and caught hold of his shirtsleeve. She moved closer, not about to let him walk away from her so easily.

"I love you, Alex," she whispered, and lifted her hand to his face. His warm hand covered hers, and he inhaled a deep breath. Leaning forward and up, she touched her lips to his. Alex grasped her hand for a moment and returned her soft kiss, then quickly released her.

"I'll bring some more blankets for you. You won't be cold." He stepped away from her and disappeared into the darkness.

Evelyn inhaled a deep breath and blew the air out from between parted lips. She didn't want more blankets to keep her warm. If memory served her right from the night before, Alex was more than capable of making sure she wouldn't be cold. Had he deliberately decided to take first watch to avoid her? Was it something she was doing wrong? Was she being too forward?

The most exhilarating feeling had swept through her after Alex told her he wanted her to share his blankets. She would truly be his wife in all ways now. He told her he loved her. His kisses and embrace spoke louder than his words. Evelyn was giddy with happiness up until they rode into camp, and Alex seemed to close up again. She wasn't sure how she should react, or whether her forward behavior would be considered inappropriate. She had no experience in these matters. Everything she'd always heard was that in a marriage, the man was to be in charge and lead in the matters of intimacy.

Alex reappeared with a pile of furs and blankets, and laid them out on top of what was already there.

"I'll be nearby. Don't worry about anything." He pulled her into his arms, and Evelyn melted against him.

"I told you already, I'm not afraid when you're near," she said huskily, and wrapped her arms around his middle. His chest heaved, then he lowered his mouth to hers. Evelyn parted her lips, hoping he'd kiss her again the way he'd done before they returned to camp.

"Ya sure ya don't want Laurent or me to take first watch?" Jasper's voice came out of the darkness. He chuckled loudly.

"Go," Evelyn whispered, resigning herself to the fate of a cold bed. She didn't want to appear as a wanton, although she would have much rather held Alex back and begged him to stay with her. Silently, she conceded that being in such close proximity of the other men would not be a good way to share intimate moments with her husband.

My husband! For the first time, Evelyn truly thought of Alex as her husband. Her heart swelled, and she couldn't wait to begin the rest of her life with him. She had a lot to learn about living in the wilderness, but she had no doubt she would be happy. Just as Aimee Osborne was happy and raised a family alongside her husband, she could do the same. Aimee had even told her that she saw her as capable of living here.

Alex left her side in silence after his hands lingered at her waist. Evelyn sank to her knees on the pile of furs and untied the leather thong in her hair. A slight shiver ran down her spine, not from the cold, but from anticipation of Alex returning in a few hours. Her skin tingled from the memory of him holding her in a protective embrace while they rode back to camp.

After working her fingers through the knots in her hair, she quickly re-braided it and coiled the leather around the end. She crawled under the thick buffalo robe, and stared wide-eyed up at the stars twinkling high above. Minutes later, she rolled to her side and punched her hand against the blanket that served as her pillow.

Unable to sleep, she pulled her knees up to her belly and listened to the soft cracking and popping sounds of the fire.

An owl hooted in a nearby tree, and the crickets and frogs kept up their loud cadenced chorus. The day's events raced through her mind. Evelyn suddenly realized how close to death she had come not once, but twice in one day. And both times, Alex had been there to rescue her, just like he'd rescued her from a mob of eager trappers, and many years ago when he defended her against Charlie. Evelyn inhaled a deep breath, and blinked away the tears that pooled in her eyes. She couldn't dwell on the past. Her family was gone, but she had a husband who loved her and protected her, and she had to move on.

Loud snores from the opposite side of the campfire mixed with the sounds of the night. Evelyn squeezed her eyes shut, and the more she wished for sleep to overtake her, the more awake she became. Memories of Alex kissing her, holding her, telling her that he loved her wouldn't allow her mind any rest. When Laurent grunted and stirred under his blankets, and muffled voices reached her ear, her heart pounded in her chest. Had she lain awake for two hours already? Would Alex come to her now and expect his rights as her husband?

Evelyn bit her lower lip. *It's what you want. You want to be his wife in all ways.* She wouldn't refuse him. She was ready for him this time, unlike the previous night when he'd startled her awake. Her heart raced with anticipation of what was to come. She only hoped that she wouldn't disappoint him.

The covers behind her lifted slightly, and Evelyn held her breath. She hadn't even heard Alex approach. Every nerve ending on her skin snapped to awareness of the man who slid under the covers next to her. Perspiration beaded on her forehead, and she wished she wasn't under the heavy buffalo robe. It had become much too hot all of a sudden.

Evelyn exhaled slowly. She scarcely dared to breathe.

Nothing happened. Alex remained immobile a few inches from her. His body heat burned right into her. He rolled to his side, facing away from her, and sudden tears spilled from her eyes. Crying silently, she swallowed her disappointment, and stared into the darkness. As exhausted as she was from the day's events, sleep would be a long time coming.

CHAPTER FOURTEEN

The horses splashed cautiously through the water, picking their way slowly over the abundant rocks that lined the river bottom. Evelyn held tight to the horn of her saddle, keeping her focus on the mountains ahead. She tried to let their beauty sweep away the apprehension in her mind. Laurent had called this the Snake River, and it was the widest body of water they had to cross so far. The uneven, rocky footing gave her cause for alarm, even if the water level wasn't all that high. All it took was one slip of a hoof, and one of the animals could take a fall.

The majestic mountain range of the Teewinots loomed ever closer. For three days, they had traveled toward the towering snow-capped peaks. Evelyn gazed in amazement at nature's splendor before her. She was used to seeing mountains, but foothills and lower outlying hills usually preceded the taller ranges. These mountains rose abruptly out of the ground before them, as if some invisible force had lifted them in this location. No wonder the trappers chose to congregate here. It was the perfect landmark to draw men from hundreds of miles away.

Evelyn's horse took an abrupt misstep, its head bobbing to catch its balance, which launched her forward in the saddle. An involuntary squeal escaped her mouth, and her hands tightened around the saddle horn as if it would prevent the animal from collapsing completely. Recovering its footing, the horse scrambled on. Up ahead of her, Alex's upper body rotated in the saddle, and he shot a worried glance her way. He halted his mount mid-stream, and his two packhorses came to a stop beside him.

"You all right?" he called.

Evelyn nodded vigorously. Determined to prove herself capable of traveling with the men, she wasn't about to show her apprehension. Laurent's horse moved past her, and he offered a smile of encouragement. Yancey guided his own horse awkwardly behind the Frenchman's set of mules, his upper body hanging stooped-over in the saddle. Evelyn wondered how much longer he could remain in the saddle before he dropped from his horse's back. Laurent had built a travois for the injured easterner, on which Yancey had ridden since they left the camp where the bear had nearly mauled him to death. Today was the first time he was back in the saddle. Everyone had agreed that a travois could not be pulled through this wide river.

Alex waited for Evelyn's horse to reach him, then he guided his own mount close to her.

"We're almost across," he said, concern etched on his face. "It's not as far as it looks. I should have stayed beside you." His eyes roamed her face.

Evelyn glanced up at him briefly, then forced a smile. "I know," she said, and eased her tight grip on the saddle. "The horse stumbled and it was unexpected. I'm all right."

Alex reached out and touched her arm, letting his hand slide from her shoulder to her elbow. Evelyn pressed her lips together, and tried to avoid the renewed jolt of adrenaline that rushed through her. This time it had nothing to do with fear of falling from her horse into the frigid water. It was a familiar reaction whenever Alex touched her. A sudden burst of annoyance swept over her, and she nudged her horse in the ribs with her heels, determined to reach the opposite riverbank on her own.

Since his declaration of love, Alex had been nothing but the perfect gentleman. Evelyn imagined that even a properly courting couple back in St. Louis would touch and kiss more than what she and the man who called himself her husband were doing. Every night, he sent her to their common sleeping area, bid her goodnight with a light kiss, and stood watch for hours before waking Laurent or Jasper to take a turn. He'd crawl under their blanket and roll to his side, facing away from her, leaving her to stare into the darkness until sleep finally claimed her.

True, he watched over her like a hawk, and saw to her every need, but he made no move to claim her as his wife in every sense of the word. The few times she caught him far enough away from camp to do more than hold casual conversations, he'd pulled her into his arms and kissed her with such tender restraint, Evelyn thought she would go mad with need. Once, she'd tried to prolong their kiss by wrapping her arms tightly around his neck, and just when she thought he would answer her unspoken request, Alex had pulled away abruptly and declared they needed to return to camp.

Evelyn's horse finally reached the safety of dry land, and she inhaled a deep breath of relief. Her frustration with Alex grew, however, when he rode past her and resumed his position at the head of the group.

Jasper parted ways with them after crossing a wide open

sedge-covered meadow several hours later. He tipped his furry hat at her, then slapped Alex on the back.

"Take good care a that wife a yer's, Walker," he said loudly as his parting words, and raised his arm in the air in a departing wave.

"Why does he travel by himself?" Evelyn whispered to Laurent.

"He prefers the solitude, I believe. Some men would much rather be alone than in the company of others."

Evelyn shot a quick glance at Alex's back. Was he a man who preferred the solitude? Was she merely a burden to him? He'd already told her that here in the mountains he had no one to answer to. He told her that he loved her, but did he truly want her to be with him?

You have to find a way to make him see you as his wife. Was she bold enough to try seducing her husband? Evelyn absently licked her lips. She didn't know the first thing about seducing a man. She knew she enjoyed his strong arms around her. His kisses made her go weak in the knees and her heart race in her chest. What did Alex like? It had taken a kidnapping to get him to finally admit that he loved her. What would it take for him to truly see her as a woman? She nudged her horse in the sides to catch up to him. What did she have to lose? If she failed, perhaps nothing would change. If she somehow succeeded . . .

Alex's head turned her way when she rode up beside him. The corners of his mouth curved in a soft grin, and his eyes roamed her face appreciatively. Evelyn smiled brightly at him, and Alex's eyebrows rose.

"You seem more at ease now that the river is behind us." He cleared his throat, and focused his attention straight ahead again. "I didn't know you were afraid of water."

Was that a hint of teasing in his tone? Evelyn's heart sped

up. He was usually so reserved and serious. Encouraged, she guided her horse closer to his. Her lower leg brushed up against his, and Alex shot her another quick look, then glanced down at their legs.

"You should know I'm not afraid of water," she said. She raised her chin and shook some lose strands of hair from her face, and stared straight ahead.

"How would I know that?"

"Remember the summer you and Henry hung that rope over that big sycamore tree down by Willow Creek? It was a really hot day, and you were both nude from the waist up, and Henry suggested you should remove all your clothing, and . . ." Evelyn glanced to the side at him. Her face flamed. Alex looked straight at her, and the smile vanished from his face. His eyes locked onto hers, and Evelyn thought she might drown in their blue depths. Swallowing the lump in her throat, she laughed.

"You were spying on us?" he asked, his eyes wide.

"No." She quickly shook her head in denial. "I was . . . ah . . . merely coming to the creek for a drink of water, and I overheard. I left immediately." Evelyn wished she had a cool glass of water available to her at this very moment. Her attempt at seduction wasn't going so well.

"Is that why I saw you sitting by the creek in that same spot later that day in only your shift?"

Evelyn's head snapped to the side. Her mouth fell open. "Alex Walker," she feigned outrage. "Now who's the one who was spying? Besides, I know you were watching me."

Alex grinned broadly, and Evelyn thought her heart would melt. She hadn't seen such a devilish smile on his face, ever. Abruptly, he leaned over toward her, and his hand reached for the back of her head. He pulled her toward him, and kissed her softly on the mouth. Evelyn stopped breathing. When had the tables been turned on her? She didn't even have the chance to try her hand at a game of seduction, and Alex had managed to seduce her. Not that he needed to.

"Relax, Evie," he whispered. "You were, what, twelve years old at the time? Not much to look at . . . I mean, unlike now." He pulled away from her, averting his eyes. "Ah, hell," he growled, and kicked his horse into a faster pace.

Evelyn stared after him, her mouth open. Had he just told her she was attractive? His annoying habit of walking away from her was getting . . . well, annoying. "You're not running away this time," she said under her breath, and urged her horse forward. Finally, he'd shown her a side of him that wasn't dark and moody, and she would not allow him to clam up again.

Alex looked surprised when she pulled her horse up alongside him a second time. His forehead wrinkled, and a frown marred his handsome face.

"How much longer until we make camp?" she asked, glancing at the sky. It had to be getting close to early evening. The sun reached far into the western horizon, already casting shadows along the snow-tipped peaks of the mountains.

"See those woods up ahead?" Alex nodded toward the forest. "Nestled amongst the trees, just at the base of the mountains, is a series of small lakes." He turned to look at her. "It's where I plan to build my . . . our cabin. We'll be there within the hour."

Evelyn stared at him. *Our cabin.* Her lips parted in a wide smile. "Why didn't you like--"

A loud thump and a groan interrupted what she was about to say. Alex reined in his horse and twisted his body to look behind him. Evelyn did the same.

"Oh dear God! Yancey," she called.

Laurent jumped from his horse and ran to where Yancey had fallen from his mount. He groaned again, in obvious pain. Laurent looked up, his eyes darting from Evelyn to Alex.

"He cannot go on today," Laurent said, concern etched on his face. "He and I will rest here. You and *Madame* Evelyn go ahead. I know you are eager to reach your destination. I will tend to this greenhorn and catch up with you in the morning."

Alex dismounted his horse, and knelt beside Yancey. He glanced at Laurent. "Are you sure?"

"We will be fine," the Frenchman answered. Alex nodded, and squeezed Yancey's arm. "I was counting on your help to build my cabin before winter," he said. Evelyn was glad to see Alex smile at the injured man.

"I'll be good as new in the morning," Yancey answered weakly, his face glistening with perspiration.

Alex stood, and exchanged a look with Laurent that she couldn't interpret, then remounted his horse.

"Will they be all right here?" Evelyn glanced around. While there were tall shrubs that could serve as shelter, there was no water that she could see.

"They'll be fine. Laurent will see Yancey through the night, and they'll be along in the morning. If we hurry, we'll get to the lake before dusk." Without waiting for a reply, he kicked his horse into a fast trot.

* * *

Evelyn gaped at the crystal clear waters of the narrow lake nestled between tall lodgepole pines. She had to tilt her head back to see the tips of the Teewinots through the dense conifers. They had reached the forest about an hour ago, and

Alex led the way along the shores of an azure alpine lake. The rocky banks of the lake were too steep in most areas to get near the water, but Evelyn enjoyed the serene view. Several eagles soared above the water, looking for their next meal.

After riding around nearly half of the lake's perimeter, Alex guided his horse away from the shore and followed what looked to be a fast-flowing inlet. Heading upstream, the waters became much calmer, and the stream widened into a narrow lake that appeared to be rather shallow. Every rock and every fish was visible beneath the crystal clear water. The snowy mountain peaks and the surrounding trees reflected artistically off the water like a mirror image.

"We'll set up camp here tonight," Alex said, halting his horse and pack animals near the sandy shore of the lake. Birds chirped loudly in the tree branches above, and a soft rustling of the breeze completed the peaceful atmosphere.

"This is a beautiful area," Evelyn said, and waited for Alex to help her off her horse. It suddenly occurred to her that they were completely alone, and her pulse quickened. Alex held her at the waist while she dismounted, the warmth of his hands seeping through her clothing. She turned to face him, and grabbed hold of his upper arms, afraid he would walk away after setting her on the ground.

Alex flinched. Startled, she realized she had touched the area on his arm where the bear had clawed him.

"I should look at those wounds," she said quickly. "You need a fresh bandage."

To her surprise, he didn't argue. "I'll get camp set up first and the horses taken care of."

Evelyn nodded. Butterflies churned in her stomach. Would he be distant with her this night like all the others? With no one else to disturb them, this might be her best opportunity to attract his attention.

She rummaged in her leather pouch for a swath of muslin

while Alex hobbled the horses and started a fire. She spread out their bedding, and filled the iron kettle with water from the lake. After a simple meal of leftover corn cakes and venison, eaten in awkward silence, Alex headed for the lakeshore. Evelyn remained by the fire, wringing her sweaty palms in her lap. She studied the flickering orange flames that danced upward, envisioning her insides burning up like the fire before her.

"You can see to my wounds now," Alex called, his voice echoing in the serene stillness. Her head shot up, and she inhaled sharply. He stood at the water's edge, his back turned to her. When had he removed his shirt? Her mouth suddenly went dry, and she scrambled to her feet. Warmth spread from her insides to her extremities and back, making her limbs tingly and weak. Carefully, she walked toward her husband, her eyes on his broad shoulders, watching the slight play of muscles along either side of his spine.

"I brought a fresh bandage," she managed to whisper when she reached his side. He turned slightly toward her. Evelyn forced her eyes upward, past his lean and sculpted torso and chest. A smoldering look greeted her, more heated than the fire blazing at their camp. Her heart leapt up into her throat and pounded in her ears. Alex had once again managed to turn the tables on her. How could she possibly attempt to seduce her husband when he stared at her with such intensity? Was it even necessary to try?

With trembling hands, she reached for the bandage on Alex's arm and fumbled with the knot. His jaw clenched tight, and the rock hard muscles on his arm tensed. Evelyn's fingers wouldn't cooperate. She would need a knife to slice through the bandage in order to remove it.

To avoid his burning stare, she concentrated on his arm. With a will of their own, her fingers slid up past the bandage, up along his shoulder, and across his chest. A slight shudder passed through Alex, and his chest heaved. Emboldened by his reaction, Evelyn stepped closer, and placed her other palm in the middle of his upper body. His masculine scent penetrated her senses, and a renewed longing lodged itself firmly in her lower abdomen. His chest moved in faster succession beneath her palms, and she ran the tips of her fingers along the smooth contours of his skin.

"Evie," Alex rasped, and his hands clamped around her waist. He clutched her hips and drew her up against him. The breath left her lungs, and she dared to look up and seek out his eyes. The hunger expressed there was unmistakable, and Evelyn's knees went weak.

"Please kiss me, Alex," she whispered, and leaned up toward him. Her hands gripped at his shoulders. His response to her request was immediate. Like a starved man, his mouth descended on hers. One hand reached up and cupped the back of her head, drawing her closer. Evelyn wrapped her arms around his neck, and moaned as pleasure so intense she thought she might faint rushed through her. Alex wrapped his other arm around her waist, pressing her tightly to him. His lips slanted across hers, then left her mouth to trail hot kisses along her jaw and neck. He nuzzled the sensitive spot behind her ear, and Evelyn gasped as a new wave of intense heat flushed through her. She raked her fingers through his hair and clung to him as if her life depended on it. His mouth returned to cover hers again, and she parted her lips in response.

Without breaking the kiss, Alex scooped his arm behind her knees and lifted her to his chest. He left the shore of the lake and carried her up the embankment toward their camp. Evelyn's head spun dizzily. She was no longer aware of what direction they were headed. The only thing that mattered, the only thing her body and senses were in tune with was the man holding her, kissing her. Anticipation raced through her, and she wrapped her arms more firmly around his neck.

Abruptly, Alex broke his heated kiss. His body tensed against hers, and he stopped walking. Evelyn tried to shake her euphoric feeling, sensing that something wasn't right.

"Hello, Shadow Walker. I see you have returned," a soft and feminine voice spoke in broken English.

CHAPTER FIFTEEN

Evelyn's head snapped around at the sound of a woman's voice. An audible groan escaped Alex's throat, and he slowly set her on her feet. "What the hell," he mumbled under his breath.

She turned to come face to face with the most beautiful woman she had ever seen. Long ebony hair framed her delicate bronze face, and fell loosely to nearly her waist. She wore a simple buckskin dress adorned at the shoulders with shells and intricate bead patterns.

Evelyn's mind raced. This woman obviously knew Alex. Her almond eyes glowed with quiet appreciation as her gaze traveled over his nude torso. Evelyn glanced nervously from Alex to the young woman. His eyes were locked on the Indian, looking at her appreciatively. The way she smiled warmly up at him spoke of more than a casual acquaintance.

Hurt, jealousy, and disappointment flooded her. Why had he never mentioned that he had an Indian woman waiting for him? What other secrets was he hiding from her? She swallowed the sudden lump in her throat, and tried to blink away the burning sensation in her eyes. Her body still sizzled from Alex's kisses and the way he touched her. There was no doubt in her mind that he would have made love to her if not for this woman's arrival. She glanced at the Indian woman. Had he . . . had the two of them . . ?

Alex cleared his throat behind her. "Evie, this is Whispering Waters. She's a friend."

The woman studied her with keen interest. Evelyn had the distinct impression that she was being assessed from head to toe.

"What sort of *friend*, Alex?" Evelyn couldn't disguise the hurt in her question. She turned to face him. The intense look of desire from a moment ago was gone, replaced by a hard set to his jaw. His eyes no longer smoldered with want, but held an impassive appearance. A deep sense of insecurity and inadequacy in the presence of this pretty Indian woman washed over her.

Alex stared down at her after her question was out, and his eyebrows drew together.

"We've known each other for some years," he said slowly, as if choosing his words carefully.

The Indian girl spoke again, this time in a language that Evelyn didn't understand. Alex answered her, his own words foreign to her. He said her name, but the rest of the words were in the Indian's gibberish. She felt like an intruder standing there while the two conversed. The girl nodded slowly, the smile vanishing from her pretty face. She stared at Evelyn, but her expression was as unreadable as Alex's.

The girl strode up to Alex, and for a split-second, Evelyn thought she was going to push her out of the way. The Indian reached for Alex's arm, touching the bandage there. She spoke again, and he answered. Evelyn caught the quick look the girl threw in her direction, then she untied the knot and removed the wrapping, exposing three slash marks that had torn the muscle in Alex's arm.

After another quick exchange of words, the girl nodded to Evelyn, and a hint of a smile formed on her lips. Evelyn wasn't sure if it was a friendly gesture or if the Indian was mocking her. Abruptly, she moved past her and Alex, and disappeared into the trees away from their camp.

Evelyn swallowed and stared up at him. "Who is she, Alex?"

Alex drew his eyebrows together, and met her gaze. "I already told you. I've traded with her people for years. She came to tell me that her father and uncle found Laurent and Yancey, and their healer is taking care of Yancey's wounds."

Evelyn blinked several times, and she swallowed back her apprehension. Alex hadn't answered her question at all. If he had nothing to hide, why would he be so evasive about the girl?

"I told her to stay here for the night," Alex continued.

"You what?" Evelyn blurted. Her heart sank. As if a gust of icy wind had hit her, the last flickering flame of passion and desire extinguished within her.

"It's not a good idea for her to head back to her people in the dark. I wouldn't want to be responsible if something happened to her. That's why I offered her a place to stay for the night."

"And where's she going to sleep, Alex? Do you plan to share your blankets with her, too?" Evelyn turned on her heels. She wished the ground would swallow her up. Suddenly she was glad the girl had shown up when she did. If she found out about Alex's *friend* after . . . after giving herself to him, her humiliation would be much greater.

"What the hell's gotten into you?" Alex's hands cupped her shoulders, and he applied pressure to turn her around to face him. Evelyn ducked away from his grip. She chewed her lower lip, and resisted the urge to turn around to stare him in the eye. How could he not see what he was doing to her?

By having this woman here in camp? He was obviously unaffected that she was here. Or perhaps he was glad she'd shown up.

Unwilling to start an argument in the presence of the Indian girl, Evelyn inhaled a deep breath, then said, "I'm feeling rather tired, Alex. It's been a long day. Enjoy your company." Blinking back the tears in her eyes, she stumbled to where she had lain out their furs and blankets earlier. If not for the woman, she would be lying here right now, in Alex's arms . . .

"Evie." He called to her, exasperation in his voice. She scrambled under the covers, and pulled them up over her head. The tears flowed freely down her cheeks. If he came after her, she'd crumble. Perhaps she could face him later, but at the moment, the thought of Alex in the arms of another woman was too much to think about.

The girl's melodious voice drifted to her. She'd obviously returned from wherever it was that she'd gone off to. Evelyn strained her ears to listen, not that she understood anything of what was said. Curiosity got the better of her, and she slowly lowered the covers to see what was going on. Almost too dark now to see much, she squinted to where Alex sat on the ground where she left him. The girl sat beside him, pressing something to his arm. They conversed in hushed tones, and the woman wrapped a strip of leather around Alex's arm.

Evelyn turned her back on the scene. She squeezed her eyes shut. Countless thoughts raced through her mind. Had Alex taken an Indian wife? She'd heard the men talk about it while she was still a captive with the river pirates. Even Laurent had mentioned that he planned to go to the father of an Indian woman and ask for her in marriage. Several of the trappers had boasted that they had Indian wives from various different tribes in the mountains, and a white wife when they returned to the city, and none of the women knew about the others.

He told you he loves you. Perhaps she shouldn't be so rash to judge. Maybe it would be best to hear Alex out. Yes, that's what she would do, but she'd wait until morning. She would wait until she could talk to him alone, not in the presence of this other woman. Clearly she knew some English. Fresh tears pooled in her eyes, thinking about what almost happened between her and Alex. What if he did have an Indian wife? She could never share the man she loved with someone else. Evelyn pressed her hand to her chest. A knife slicing through her heart couldn't be any worse than the thought of Alex with another woman. Would it be too late to ask Laurent to take her back to St. Louis?

The covers lifted behind her, and Evelyn held her breath. Her heart sped up, and she bit her lower lip. Alex slipped under the covers, and inched up behind her.

"I know you're not asleep," he whispered in her ear, sending chills racing down her back. He held his hand at her hip, and a renewed wave of desire spread through her. Would she always react this way from a mere touch of his hand? Even when she was angry with him, all it took was one simple touch from him and she melted.

"I . . . I'm feeling rather poorly, Alex. I would like to get some sleep." Every cell in her body screamed to turn and face him, and ask him to hold her close. Having this woman in camp made it impossible.

Alex stiffened beside her, and his hand dropped away. "Good night, Evie," he said after a long pause, then he rolled to his other side, facing away from her as he had done every night since she started sharing his bed.

* * *

Alex lay awake, and tried to listen to the sounds of the night. No matter how much he willed himself to focus on these things, his mind and body had other ideas. For nearly a week, he'd slept next to Evie, or tried to sleep. Having her so close without touching her proved to be more agonizing than the worst form of torture the Blackfeet could conjure up. Repeatedly, he convinced himself that she needed time; that he shouldn't ask for something she wasn't ready to give. He'd agreed to those terms before they left rendezvous.

Each day it became harder to uphold that agreement. Tonight, having her all to himself, he'd finally given in to his desires. He recognized the same longing in her eyes as what he'd been feeling for weeks, and he hoped to show her how much he loved her and finally claim her as his wife in all ways.

Seeing Whispering Waters, Alex's first impulse was to run the Bannock woman out of camp, but it wouldn't be wise to anger her people. Over the years, he'd established good trade relations with them, and treating the daughter of the chief with anything but respect was certainly not a wise thing to do. She'd made it clear to him in the past that she wanted to be his wife, but Alex had always been direct with her that he had no interest in her. Now that Evelyn had entered his life, he was even more convinced that he'd made the right choice.

Admittedly, Whispering Waters was a beautiful woman, and Laurent would be a lucky man to have her for his wife. But where Whispering Waters was quiet, Evie was feisty and outspoken. Alex loved the sparks that flew from her emerald eyes when she got her feathers ruffled, and how the sun reflected in her auburn hair, turning it a deep bronze. While some men preferred a demure and obedient wife, he enjoyed her independent spirit and that she spoke her mind.

"I see you have made your choice, Walker. I've always known your heart would never belong to me, but I had hoped," Whispering Waters told him when he introduced Evelyn as his wife.

"I believe my heart has always belonged to this woman. Even as children, although I didn't see it until now."

"I see she cares for you deeply." She had smiled in quiet acceptance, then said, "I must tell you that your friend, the Frenchman Laurent Berard has approached my father. If you were not so pleasing to look at, Walker, he would have caught my eye sooner. I came here to tell you that I have consented to become his wife."

Alex smiled inwardly. So, Laurent had finally found the courage to ask for the woman he'd been in love with for years.

"He will be a good husband, and he is a lucky man to have you as his wife."

Whispering Waters had smiled softly. She finished applying the herbal poultice to his arm, and wrapped a piece of leather around it, then looked up at him.

"I will leave at dawn. Your wife does not want me to be here. You would do well to put her mind at ease about us, Shadow Walker." Her smile widened. "For a white man, you are a good hunter and tracker, and you are observant of all things around you. All things but what is right before you." She'd stood, and accepted the buffalo robe Alex offered her, then chose a spot near the fire and laid down to sleep.

Alex pondered her words. Kicking himself mentally, he suddenly understood Evelyn's reaction. She'd made an assumption about him and the Bannock woman, and although it was the wrong assumption, it was his fault for not putting her mind at ease immediately. Would he ever learn to communicate effectively with her to avoid misunderstandings in the future?

Evelyn stirred next to him, and he clenched his hands into tight fists and ground his teeth. Every cell in his body screamed for him to reach for her, pull her to him, and hold her close. Not acting on his impulse required every ounce of self-control he possessed. He'd startled her out of her sleep once before, and he wasn't about to make that mistake a second time. He never wanted to see fear of him in her eyes ever again. He closed his eyes, and allowed the memories of Evie's passionate kisses and soft curves to overrun his mind.

CHAPTER SIXTEEN

Alex moved and startled awake. When had he fallen asleep? Sweat trickled from his forehead, and he breathed heavily. The gray sky of predawn greeted him. He was instantly alert. A quick glance across camp told him Whispering Waters had already left. The disturbing dream that woke him began to fade. His heart pounded in his chest, and adrenaline rushed through him. Evelyn had left him. In his dream, she'd told him she couldn't be with him. She thought he was in love with Whispering Waters. He rolled over and reached for her. He had to feel her, convince himself that she was still here. His hand touched only cold furs and blankets next to him.

Alex bolted upright. Evie was gone! He flung the covers aside, ignoring the cold rush of air that hit his bare torso, and leapt to his feet. How could he have slept so soundly that he wouldn't have noticed her get out from under the covers? He grabbed his rifle lying on the ground next to his blankets, and scanned his surroundings. Nothing seemed out of the ordinary. The first birds awake in the morning chirped loudly in the branches above. There was no breeze in the air.

A quiet splash and soft humming reached his ears, and Alex headed toward the sound.

Evelyn's shirt and britches lay on the sandy ground at the shore of the lake. Soft white vapors rose into the air as the warmer water met with the early morning chill. Near a large boulder protruding out of the lake, Evie splashed in the water. Alex's mouth went dry. Any attempt to swallow became futile. Like a lithe cat, she moved her arms through the water. Even from a distance, he could see that she wore her shift, but she might as well not be wearing anything. The white cotton became all but invisible, and clung to every curve and contour of her wet body.

Time stood still. He couldn't tear his eyes away even if a war party of Blackfeet were to descend on him at this moment. Evie rubbed her hands up and down her glistening arms, her hair falling in wet strands down her back. Her eyes were half-way closed as she hummed her soft tune, a look of pure contentment on her face. Would she ever gaze upon him with such pleasure and serenity?

Alex's actions were no longer his own. He set his rifle on the ground and bent down to remove his moccasins, then untied the leather laces of his britches, letting them fall to the ground. He hadn't bothered putting on his shirt the night before. Slowly, he waded into the lake. Shallow and heated by the previous day's sun, the temperature was not as frigid as some of the other mountain lakes in the area. By the time he reached the rocks, the water lapped around his waist. Evelyn continued her dreamlike humming, and Alex relaxed to the sound of her soft melody. He shouldn't be here, disturbing her bath, but it was too late for that. She drew him to her by some invisible rope, and he could no longer stay away. Reaching out, his hand touched her lightly on her wet shoulder.

"Evie," he said quietly.

Evelyn spun around with a loud splash. A startled gasp escaped her open mouth, and she almost lost her footing. She stood before him, water drops running down her face, her lips glistening wet. There was no fear in her eyes, only surprise, and . . . longing. Alex took another step toward her. His gut clenched painfully, and he sucked in a deep breath of air. One hand reached out and slid along her neck, his thumb caressing her jaw. He leaned forward and covered her mouth with his, sipping at the moisture on her lips. He slowly wrapped his other arm around her waist, pulling her fully up against him. A low moan rumbled in her chest, and she wound her arms around his middle.

Surprised by her reaction, Alex pulled his head back, and smiled down at her. Wide-eyed, she stared up at him.

"Evie," he whispered, and cleared his throat.

"Your friend left," she said quietly. "She told me I was lucky to have you, and hopes you and I can be present when she marries the man who asked for her." The corners of her mouth raised in a slow smile.

A great weight seemed to lift from his shoulders. "Whispering Waters means nothing to me, Evie. She never has. Only one woman has ever caught my eye, and she's right here, in my arms, where she belongs." His thumb stroked slowly back and forth along her jaw.

Evie's eyes widened even more, and Alex wasn't sure if the wetness on her cheeks was water or tears. He swiped wet strands of hair from her face with a slow sweep of his hand, and studied her expressive eyes, her full lips, and tried to burn every little detail of her into his memory.

He swallowed, and tightened his hold around her, drawing her even closer. The slow-burning fire inside him ignited fully, and his pulse raced through his veins. She had to be aware of how she affected him.

"Evie, I can't uphold my end of our agreement," he said slowly, searching for the right words.

Her forehead wrinkled, and her eyes clouded with confusion. "You plan to return me to St. Louis?" she whispered, the hurt loud and clear in her voice. A slight shiver passed through her.

Alex chuckled, and smiled slowly. He caressed her cheek, while his other hand gripped her waist. "No," he said in a low voice. "That's not the part I'm talking about." He inhaled deeply, then stared into her eyes. "I . . . I don't want you as my wife for appearances only. I want to touch you, and hold you, and make love to you."

"Alex," Evie sobbed. She gripped his shoulders and pressed closer. "How many nights have I waited for you to hold me, and . . . and come to me as my husband," she whispered. "I was starting to believe you didn't like me."

Alex's chest exploded with such raw emotion, he couldn't put a name to it. All he knew was that he loved Evie, and she just told him that she wanted to be his. Another shiver passed through her, and he quickly scooped her in his arms, just as he'd done the night before. Water poured off her body, and he waded back to shore. Evelyn wrapped her arms tightly around his neck.

"Time to warm you up," he said, and grinned. "No interruptions."

Alex's heart pounded fiercely in his chest. The cold early morning air felt good against his heated skin, but Evelyn shivered in his arms. She clung to his neck, and he hurried to their pile of furs and blankets. Laying her on top of a thick buffalo robe, he knelt beside her and reached for a blanket.

Evie's gaze of unmistakable love and trust took his breath away. She lifted her arms up to him. His eyes roamed first her face, then traveled lower. The white cotton of her undergarment hid none of her feminine beauty. Alex forced air into his lungs. He lowered himself next to her, and Evie rolled to the side and wrapped her arms around his neck.

"You won't warm up in your wet underclothes," he whispered as he nuzzled her ear. His hand slid along the curves of her hips until he met with the end of the fabric, then back up, sliding the damp material upward. He pulled it over her head, and once she was free of the garment, wrapped her in his arms.

"Come here," he said huskily. "I want to feel you next to me, all of you."

"I love you, Alex," Evie murmured, and pressed her lips to his. Alex moaned, and rolled her to her back. He claimed her mouth unhurriedly, wanting to make every exquisite first moment with her last. His hands explored her curves, loving the feel of her soft breasts against his chest.

"No more misunderstandings," Alex mumbled as his lips grazed along her neck. "I'll never lay a hand on you, Evie. I swear it." He wanted to make sure she understood that she had nothing to fear from him.

Evie's hands gripped his shoulders. A wide smile formed on her face. Then she started to giggle. "Then what do you call what you're doing right now, Alex Walker?" She leaned her head forward, glancing to where one of his hands rested on her hip. Slowly, she raised her leg and ran her foot along his thigh. "I like having your hands on me," she whispered huskily.

Alex groaned. Heat coursed through him, and his stomach tightened almost painfully.

"I love you, Evelyn." He brought his mouth down on hers, and crushed her to him. She breathed heavily against his lips, and her hands ran up and down his back, scorching his skin wherever she touched him.

He kissed her long and slow, until Evelyn began to squirm beneath him.

"Alex," she gasped.

He knew what she was asking, and that there was no easy way the first time.

"Evie, I might hurt you," he whispered against her neck. Apprehension filled him.

"You'll never hurt me, Alex," she panted. "Haven't you realized that by now?" She held her hand to his cheek, a trusting smile on her face. Her eyes smoldered with passion, and Alex swallowed. It was too late to turn back. He couldn't wait any longer. Slowly, he eased her legs apart. He settled between her thighs, and slowly pushed past the barrier that told him she was his, and only his. His heart raced in his chest, and warmth rushed through him. She gasped when he entered her fully, and he waited until her body relaxed beneath him.

"This is the last time I'll ever hurt you, Evie, I swear it," he breathed against her neck.

Evie's gasps and moans of pleasure when he moved inside her drove him onward. She wrapped her legs around his back, and cried his name when her body began to convulse. He shuddered against her in his own release, and their bodies, slick with sweat, melted together in a heap of dangling limbs and blankets.

Alex rolled to his back and drew her up close to him. He wrapped her in his arms, waiting for his breathing to slow. Holding her tightly to him, he would always remember the feeling of her heart beating against his chest. He gazed down at her, and caught her staring up at him, a soft smile on her face. She touched her hand to his damp chest, and a warm sense of peace and contentment flowed through him. Words eluded him. He tucked some strands of her tousled hair behind her ear, and kissed her forehead.

Evie rested her head in the crook of his arm and sighed. His heart nearly burst with love for her; with the knowledge that she felt safe with him. Alex ran his fingers through her damp hair, the tension that he'd lived with for so many years slowly melting away in the arms of the woman who had become his entire world. The thought of ever losing her was unthinkable. They lay together in silence, and watched the sun rise over the tallest of the Teton peaks. A golden glow spread along the mountains to match the glow in his heart.

CHAPTER SEVENTEEN

⁂

Evelyn stirred awake, and her eyelids fluttered open. A soft smile spread across her lips and she arched her back in a languid stretch, moaning softly. Warm and relaxed, her bare leg draped over Alex's hard thigh.

"Mornin'," he murmured, and leaned over her. His calloused hand ran along her neck and behind her head, just before his mouth covered hers. Her body ignited instantly as ripples of desire spread through her. She wrapped her arms around her husband's neck and welcomed him to her.

For the last week, this was how her days started and ended, and she had never been happier. Alex doted on her almost to the point that she had to tell him to find something else to do besides hover over her. It didn't matter if Laurent, Yancey, or a small gathering of Indians stood nearby. At every opportunity throughout the day, he'd find a reason to be near her and touch her. He'd often pull her into his arms and kiss her to the point that she wished for night to come quickly.

Work had begun on their cabin. Alex cleared an area a

short distance from the lake where they had first consummated their marriage, and used the lodgepoles he felled to build the framework of their home. He constantly asked for her opinion and input on matters such as where the door should go, or the window, the hearth, and the bedroom. Rather than a simple one-room trapper cabin, he planned to build a two-room home for her, even after she insisted she didn't need such an elaborate dwelling. He'd used her protests as an excuse to pull her into the bushes, and by the time they re-emerged, she was willing to tell him anything he wanted to hear.

Lying in his arms now, Evelyn listened to the sound of the slight breeze that flapped against the deerskin covering of the tent Alex had erected at the edge of the Indian camp. Until their cabin was finished, this would be their home. Outside, horses whinnied and people's voices drifted in. A thin ribbon of bright light streamed down through the small opening at the top of the conical structure, a sure indication that a new day was well underway.

Evelyn had little trouble blocking out the noise. Her entire focus centered on the man in her arms, making love to her with such tender devotion that it took her breath away. She trailed kisses along his shoulder and chest, her fingers tracing the outline of the fresh scar from the bullet he received at the hand of Charlie Richardson.

"He could have killed you," Evelyn whispered against his neck. Alex rolled to the side and wrapped his arms around her.

"Who?" His forehead wrinkled. He caressed her shoulder, his hand traveling slowly along the contours of her body and over the curve of her hips with practiced familiarity.

"Charlie," Evelyn clarified, and kissed the scar.

Alex scoffed. "I'll deal with him next spring when we return to St. Charles."

Evelyn's head shot up to look up at him. "What are you planning to do?"

A wide grin formed on Alex's face. "I'm going to marry you in a church, for starters."

Evelyn's pulse quickened. Startled, she shook her head. "I don't need a church wedding to feel married to you, Alex. I don't want you getting in trouble with the law. Everyone in St. Charles thinks you killed my parents. If you're recognized, they'll hang you. They won't ask questions."

"Your folks were always good to me, Evie. Your ma bandaged me up every time I stopped by with some new injury, and remember how they let me stay for days at a time when I didn't want to go home?" Alex's face sobered, and his jaw clenched. "I won't stand by and allow their murder to go unpunished." His body tensed, and he drew her more firmly to him.

Evelyn clasped his face between her hands. She studied the pained expression in his eyes. "I never realized how hard it was for you, growing up. I know that he . . . hit you and your mother, and everyone always turned a blind eye."

Alex's gaze roamed her face. His blue eyes, which had smoldered with passion a moment ago, were now iced over in anger. "I wish the old bastard were still alive, so I could kill him myself for what he did to my mother," he said, his voice taking on a menacing tone.

"You're not a killer, Alex. You're not like him." Evelyn stroked his jawline, and leaned up to kiss his lips.

He scoffed. "I've killed my share of men." His voice matched the chill in the air.

Evelyn ran her fingers along his rough cheek. "I would wager that every man whose life you've taken would have killed you first if you hadn't acted. You had plenty of chances to kill your father, but you walked away instead. Let him go."

Alex nodded slowly, and held her tight. His facial features

softened, and a slow grin spread across his lips. He nuzzled her neck, sending ripples of pleasure racing along her spine. She purred as Alex methodically worked his magic on her with his mouth and hands.

"I don't know how I will get our cabin built before winter," he growled softly in her ear. "You are the most delectable distraction."

Evelyn wound her arms around his neck, giving herself over completely to the pleasurable sensations his touch evoked. Without him, she no longer felt whole.

"Remind me to thank Laurent again for bringing you to me," he said huskily.

"Laurent!" Evelyn exclaimed, and she pushed against Alex's chest. The mention of his friend suddenly reminded her of something important.

Alex's hand froze against her thigh, and he raised his torso away from her. His forehead wrinkled and a perplexed look washed over his face. The corner of his lips twitched into a smile.

"If that's the reaction I get for mentioning his name, I'll never utter it again," Alex mumbled. "Especially not at times like this." He lowered his head back to hers. Evelyn pushed harder against him to prevent his intended kiss. Although she could never deny her husband, and would much rather lie in his arms all day, a sudden thought entered her mind.

Alex's smile turned into a slight frown. Evelyn reached her hand up to touch his cheek. Her fingers softly outlined his lips.

"Don't you know what today is?" she asked. Alex's brows drew together in confusion. Clearly, he didn't remember.

"Laurent and Whispering Waters' wedding ceremony." She'd almost forgotten it herself. Whispering Waters had asked Evelyn to be with her today while she prepared for her union with the Frenchman. After their initial encounter, she had taken an immediate liking to the soft-spoken Indian woman, and she was glad for the friendship that slowly developed between them. She'd missed not having another woman to talk to, and Whispering Waters' grasp on English was good enough for most conversations.

Alex hesitated, then inhaled a dramatic breath of air before he rolled off of her and onto his back. Evelyn threw back the fur covers, shivering as a blast of cold air hit her bare skin. She sat up and reached for the newly-sewn muslin dress that lay in a tangled heap next to the pallet of furs. Alex's warm palm stroked along her lower back, and sent a completely different chill racing down her spine.

"And that's the reason you're leaving our bed?" he asked. "It's much warmer under the covers." Evelyn glanced over her shoulder at him, meeting the pleading look in his eyes, and the wide grin that spread on his face.

"I promised I'd help with the festivities. Besides, who was it that complained about not getting a cabin built?" She raised her brows at him, and hoped her stern look had the desired effect. Apparently it didn't. In one fast move that Evelyn would have missed had she blinked, Alex grabbed her upper arms and hauled her backwards. She squealed and giggled as he rolled her over, and pulled her on top of him.

"What if I refuse to let you go?" He cupped the back of her head and brought her face down toward him. His mouth covered hers, and Evelyn parted her lips in an unspoken answer to his question. The ceremony wasn't until later in the day. Perhaps a few more minutes with Alex couldn't hurt.

* * *

Alex pushed the carcass of the buck he'd shot off of his

horse's withers, and it fell to the ground with a loud thud. He swung his leg over the gelding's neck and landed lightly beside the deer. Spotting Laurent standing near the chief's tent, talking to his future father-in-law, Alex led his mount toward them.

"*Mon ami*, you have returned in time to witness the wedding." Laurent rushed toward him, his arms spread wide to match the smile on his face.

Alex grinned and clasped his friend's shoulders. "Wouldn't miss it." He turned his head to study the Frenchman. "It appears we both require a woman in our lives to remind us to get cleaned up."

Laurent's shoulder-length brown hair, which he normally kept tied back with a leather thong, shone in the afternoon sun. His beard looked freshly trimmed, and he wore a clean wool shirt.

"I had no choice, Walker," Laurent said, combing his fingers through his mustache. "The shaman came with a bowl of water, and insisted he wash my hair. It is tradition for the ceremony."

"So I've heard." Alex sniggered. "I brought meat for a feast after the ceremony." He pointed behind him to the deer on the ground.

Laurent's smile widened even more. "My bride and I may not stay for a feast. We have our own celebrating to do. I do not plan to wait as long as you did to claim my bride." He straightened and puffed out his chest. A wide, unabashed grin spread across his face.

Alex laughed, and slapped Laurent on the back. "I understand," he said. How well he understood. He could have saved himself and Evelyn weeks of misery if he had only known how to communicate with her. Laurent certainly didn't suffer from that particular deficiency.

His eyes scoured the camp. He hadn't seen Evie since she

left their tent this morning, insisting on helping Whispering Waters with her wedding preparations. His insides warmed just thinking about his own bride. Not an hour went by in a day that he didn't think about her. In fact, she was constantly on his mind. He was slowly making progress in reading her thoughts and moods by watching for subtle clues in her body language.

When the corners of her eyes twitched, it was a sure sign she was about to speak her mind, just like when her pert little nose rose higher in the air. Often, these subtleties were accompanied by a more obvious sign of annoyance when she fisted her hands at her hips. Luckily, he hadn't been the recipient of those gestures lately. Hopefully it meant that he was doing something right.

Alex's mouth curved in a slow smile. Thoughts of her soft sighs when he held her in his arms, and the way her green eyes shimmered with love and need sent his heart galloping in his chest. How well he'd learned those signs. She was probably not even aware of how much her coy glances in his direction, the way she licked her lips, or her discreet smiles affected him and made him forget the world around him.

Evie's most difficult mood to interpret was when something upset her enough to cry. Wide and round eyes most often preceded her tears, and she fidgeted with her hands in front of her. He'd failed to recognize this particular warning sign a few days ago when he'd finished for the day at the site of the cabin. Tired and hungry, he'd walked into their camp, eager for a hearty meal followed by his wife in his arms. When he'd casually mentioned that he was famished, her eyes had pooled with tears.

"What's wrong?" He'd pulled her into his arms, alarmed by her behavior. He wondered silently what he had done to cause her distress.

Evie lowered her chin. "I'm sorry, Alex," she sobbed. "I . . .

I burned supper." She pulled away from him, and buried her face in her hands. He could barely understand her muffled words. "Time slipped away from me while I was sewing my dress, and I forgot that I had the biscuits in the fire. The meat is charred as well. I know how hard you work on the cabin all day, and you must be hungry."

Alex had stood there silently. When she raised her head slightly and peered at him from between her fingers, he burst out laughing.

"You're crying because you burned some biscuits?" he asked, and scooped to lift her into his arms. "I have another hunger that needs to be satisfied, wife," he murmured against her neck. "The burnt biscuits can wait."

Alex sucked in a deep breath, and his gut clenched, remembering the pleasant incident.

Another memory crept into his mind, leaving a sour taste in his mouth. He recalled an incident when his mother had prepared a supper that angered his father. Alex couldn't have been more than eight years old at the time, when the bread pudding she'd prepared was a bit too dark on the bottom for his father's liking. She'd received a beating that left her eye swollen shut for days.

Alex pushed the memory from his mind. Not even for a second had he thought to react in anger when Evie told him about the ruined meal. He smiled softly. After he thoroughly put her mind at ease that he wasn't upset with her about the food, he'd eaten every last biscuit, and the charred meat as well. The look on Evie's face, the pure love that sparkled in her eyes for him, made every distasteful bite worth it.

He couldn't imagine a life without her anymore. She made him happy no matter what she did. He took pleasure in simply watching her perform even the most mundane tasks throughout the day, and the tension he'd felt in his body for most of his life melted away in her arms.

"It is time, my friend," Laurent said excitedly, and rubbed his hands together. Alex blinked. He hadn't even realized he'd been deeply absorbed in thought. Looking up, Whispering Waters stood outside her parents' lodge, a red blanket draped around her shoulders. The clan's shaman stood next to her, and beckoned Laurent to him.

"Go on, Laurent. Go wed up with your bride." Alex gave him a hasty shove, but his attention was on the woman who emerged from the lodge behind Whispering Waters. Evie looked around until her gaze met his. A wide smile spread across her face, and she rushed to him. Alex pulled her into his arms, and kissed her like he'd wanted to do all day.

"Doesn't she look beautiful?" Evie beamed and turned to glance at Whispering Waters. Laurent now stood before her, and held her hands.

"Not nearly as beautiful as you," he whispered, and drew her fully up against him. Evie lowered her head and smiled coyly. She held up her hand, and revealed a leather-wrapped bundle.

"The shaman gave this to me," she said. "I am supposed to bury it somewhere, and not tell anyone. It's hair from Laurent and Whispering Waters that he tied together."

Alex nodded. "It signifies their union," he explained. "If they ever want to part ways, they can only do so if they find this bundle. So make sure you hide it well." He grinned. "Laurent isn't about to let go of his new wife easily."

The shaman draped the blanket Whispering Waters wore around her and Laurent, and spoke a few words that Alex didn't hear. He knew their union was now complete. He reached for Evie's hand and waited for her to look at him.

"Well, I don't think we'll see them for a few days," Alex said and chuckled. He nodded toward the happy newlyweds. Laurent held his bride's hand, pulling her away from the small group of well-wishers and family members. Those who stood by to watch the informal ceremony dispersed to go about their daily business.

"I just hope Laurent remembers to visit and say goodbye when he leaves for St. Louis."

Evelyn's head snapped up. "Why is he going to St. Louis?" Her forehead wrinkled.

"He has business there. Remember that he is looking for information about the people behind the raids on the Rocky Mountain Fur Company's supply boats. He has to meet Oliver Sabin and his men. We probably won't see him again before spring."

Evelyn tensed, and her eyes widened. Alex wrapped his arms firmly around her. He shouldn't have mentioned Sabin's name.

"And Whispering Waters?" she asked tentatively, leaning into him.

"She'll remain with her people while he is gone, I believe." He couldn't imagine being away from Evie for any length of time.

"How awful," Evie scoffed. "They just got married, and now they're going to be apart all winter?"

Alex gazed down at her. "I'm sorry you didn't have a real wedding, Evie. I want to give that to you. Next spring." He caressed her soft cheek. She favored him with one of those smiles that left him breathless, and wrapped her arms around his neck.

"I know you think I've turned into a savage," he said, grinning. "But I still remember a few things about living among civilized people. Here in the mountains, you're my wife because of the customs of the people, but when we go to St Louis, I want there to be no doubt that you are legally wed to me."

"I love you, Alex," Evie whispered against his lips. "I can't imagine anything or anyone doubting our union. There isn't a person on this earth who's going to take me away from you."

Warmth spread through him like the hot sun on a July afternoon. Alex lifted her into his arms and carried her to their own tent at the edge of the small village, intent on doing some celebrating of their own.

CHAPTER EIGHTEEN

"Close your eyes."

Alex's deep voice resonated behind her, and his warm breath against her ear sent shivers of anticipation rushing down Evelyn's spine. She leaned into the warm hand at her waist, and glanced over her shoulder. They followed the well-worn path from their tent to where the newly finished cabin stood. Evelyn's steps were light and bouncy. She felt giddy like a little girl on the morning of her birthday.

"Do I have to close my eyes?" she asked, feigning a pout. "You haven't allowed me a single peek inside the cabin in almost a week."

"If I did, it wouldn't be a surprise. And since you're being difficult, I suppose we'll have to do this the hard way."

Before Evelyn had a chance to react to what he'd said, Alex quickly wrapped a strip of cloth around her head, covering her eyes. Then he swept her up in his arms. She squealed in delight at the game he played, and instinctively, her arms flew around his neck.

"I've seen the inside of the cabin, Alex," she reminded him, smiling. "I helped you build it, remember?"

For weeks, they'd worked side by side, laying the stones that now formed the large hearth and chimney that took up most of one wall in the main room. Yancey, who was almost recovered from his near-death encounter with the grizzly, came to help erect the roof more than a week ago. His deeper wounds still hadn't healed completely. He walked with a noticeable limp, and he would always have a large scar that ran from the left side of his face up into his scalp. He had elected to stay the winter at Laurent's unoccupied cabin, which was about an hour's ride away.

"Do you miss your family back east?" Evelyn had asked Yancey one day when he stayed for supper.

The polite and refined easterner shook his head. "My father wants me to help run the family clothing and textile business back home. He is one of the major exporters of beaver fur to England. I thought it would be a good idea to learn all about the fur trade, and I told him I would be in the mountains for a few years, learning the ways of the trappers. I don't see myself returning home anytime soon."

An easy smile passed between Yancey and Alex. "Your husband plans to take me trapping, too, so that I can perhaps earn a few beaver pelts for Laurent over the winter while he's gone." Yancey beamed.

Evelyn had raised her brows at Alex. The change in him over the last few months astounded her nearly every day. He was no longer the dark and serious man who had bartered for her several months ago. He laughed easily now, and talked to her about most things that were on his mind. He'd even taken a liking to Yancey. She loved him more with each passing day, and couldn't imagine ever returning to her life in St. Charles.

Never in her wildest dreams had she believed that someday she would be content to live an isolated life in uncharted wilderness. Or that her home would be a small cabin at the base of a spectacular mountain range. Most mornings, the new day greeted her with a beautiful display of gold and orange colors as the sun rose beyond the peaks of the Teewinots. Although she sometimes wished for female company, she was never lonely in Alex's arms, and she knew that Whispering Waters would return by next spring.

The hinges creaked as Alex pushed the door open to their new home. The scent of fresh cut pine filled her senses, and she inhaled deeply of the rich aroma.

Alex carried her into the dark interior of the cabin. He set her on her feet, but didn't remove the binding covering her eyes.

"When do I get to see the surprise?" she asked when he didn't speak. She reached out her hand and grabbed hold of the first thing that she came in contact with. It happened to be Alex's hand which he apparently held out for her to find.

Silently, Alex led her further into the cabin, and Evelyn tried to tune her senses to where they were heading. To the right should be a small crude table and a pair of chairs that Alex had fashioned just a few days ago. It would feel good to sit down for a meal at a real table again. Alex guided her to the left, which would be the direction of their bedroom, which was no more than a little side addition to the main room of the cabin. If she moved further forward in a straight line, she would bump into the stone hearth that lined most of the opposite wall. She stepped slowly and carefully so she wouldn't trip over something on the dirt floor. Someday she wanted a wooden floor, but that would have to wait, just like the glass windows she wished for. For now, the two windows in the cabin would have to be boarded up in cold weather. Alex had promised her real windows next spring.

Evelyn's senses told her that she now stood at the entrance of their doorless bedroom.

"Now you can look," Alex whispered in her ear. His breath against her neck sent shivers down her back. He brushed the hair away from the back of her neck and kissed her softly where her pulse beat strongly under her jaw, while his fingers worked the knot in the cloth that covered her eyes. A pleasant shiver passed down her spine, and she moaned softly.

Evelyn blinked when her eyes were no longer covered, and she squinted to adjust her sight to the dim light. A candle flickered in the corner on a small crudely built table, but her eyes fell to the bed that took up most of the space.

"Alex!" Evelyn gasped, and her hands flew to her mouth. A wooden bedframe made from pine logs and piled high with furs and blankets stood in the center of the space. A week ago, this had been an empty room. The frame wasn't what caught her attention, however. In one step, she reached the edge of the bed and ran her fingers over the smoothly carved headboard. On closer inspection, the flat pieces of wood held a carving of the mountain peaks that had become so familiar to her, with a sun shining high above. She traced every contour of the wood with her fingers, marveling at the attention to detail in the carving.

"I know this isn't what a true sunrise looks like, but I wanted the sun over the mountains to show the start of a new day. With each sunrise, I want to celebrate the beginning of a new day with you, for the rest of our lives."

Evelyn turned and stared at Alex in stunned silence. Tears pooled in her eyes. For the quiet man that he was, he suddenly spouted words that would rival the most gifted poet.

Alex's brows drew together. "You don't like it?"

Evelyn smiled broadly. "Like it? I love it, Alex. You've left me speechless." She wrapped her arms around his neck, and kissed him soundly on the lips.

He grinned. "That would be a first." He pulled her into a tight embrace, the love reflecting in the depths of his eyes.

"When did you do this? It's stunning." Evelyn looked over her shoulder at the headboard. She'd never seen anything more beautiful.

Alex shrugged. "Over the last few days."

"I can't wait to move in today. I can't wait to spend the rest of my life here, with you," she murmured against his lips. In one swift motion, Alex lifted her to the bed.

* * *

"I don't like leaving you alone for such a long stretch of time," Alex said quietly, and pulled Evelyn into his arms.

"It's no different than being alone for part of the day," she argued. Smiling up at him, she pushed him to the door of the cabin. "I'll have plenty of things to occupy me while you're off setting traps with Yancey."

Alex nodded. He released her, and reached for the rifle propped by the door. He held it up in front of her.

"You remember everything I taught you about firing this, and reloading?"

Evelyn nodded.

"If you notice anything unusual, you bolt the door and windows. I have not seen any sign of Blackfeet, but that doesn't mean there aren't any nearby. Yancey and I will hear if you fire the rifle. We won't be more than a few miles away."

"I'll be all right, Alex," Evelyn assured him again.

"I would still prefer that you come with us." He ran the back of his hand across her cheek, his eyes filled with worry.

Evelyn inhaled a deep breath. She'd argued with him already about his trapping excursion with Yancey. He didn't want to leave her alone, and she was adamant that nothing would happen in his absence. She hadn't told him that the idea of smelling the horrible odor of beaver musk that he used on his traps would make her already nauseated stomach roil even more.

You have to tell him soon.

She'd been fairly certain for some time that she was in the family way, but she had put off telling Alex until she could be absolutely sure. Feeling ill each morning, she'd hidden her delicate condition from him as best as she could. He hadn't given any indication that he suspected anything.

Looking up at the clouds that blanketed the tops of the mountains, she wrapped her arms around her middle and shivered.

"Besides, it looks like we might be in for some bad weather. I'd rather stay home and dry than get a drenching out there." She nodded toward the forest.

Alex frowned, but nodded in agreement. "All right. We'll be back before dark." He bent and kissed her gently on the lips, then turned to where Yancey waited, already mounted on his horse. Alex picked up the reins to his own mount, and swung onto the animal's back. The steel traps and chains hanging off the back of the saddle clanked and rattled against each other.

"I love you," Evelyn called, and waved from the door. "Be safe." She smiled brightly, belying the turmoil inside her. She knew that Alex had work to do, but it wasn't easy to watch him ride away.

Alex stared at her for a moment, then turned his horse away from the cabin and led the way into the trees. Evelyn watched until they disappeared, then rushed around the outside of the cabin. Emptying her stomach contents, she covered the mess with dirt. She rinsed her mouth with water from the lake, and stood to catch her breath. Slowly, she walked back to the cabin.

"Mama always gave me mint leaves to chew on when I

had an upset stomach," she spoke out loud. Perhaps it would settle her stomach now, too. She had seen mint growing somewhere near the shores of the river that connected their small lake with a larger one further to the north.

Reaching for Alex's wool capote that hung on a peg by the door, she pulled it on over her head. The thick material would keep her warm and dry if she encountered rain. She slung Alex's spare bullet pouch and powder horn around her neck, and picked up the rifle on her way out the door.

Evelyn followed a path along the lake to where it narrowed and finally became a river channel that connected it to a larger lake less than a mile further upstream. The water rushed loudly over the many rocks and boulders, drowning out the serene sounds of the forest. She cautiously stepped over the rocks that created a natural bridge over the water, and safely reached the other side of the shallow river.

Not seeing any mint grow along the edges of the water, she headed away from the river and further toward the base of the mountains. The narrow trail she followed became steep in some areas, and she stopped to catch her breath and to allow her stomach to settle again. She was sure that she had seen mint growing in some shady patches where the soil was moist.

Alex had brought her this way on a few occasions, and they had explored the base of the mountains and surrounding small lakes, and even bathed under a towering waterfall after a somewhat steep climb at the opposite shore of one of the larger lakes. She hadn't planned to come this far on her own, and a slight tingle of apprehension passed through her.

Evelyn stopped and sat to rest on a large boulder. Swallowing back the nausea, she placed a hand over her abdomen and smiled softly. She was carrying Alex's child. Nothing, not even her unsettled stomach, deterred her from her happiness. Tonight, she would tell him he would be a father. She had kept the news to herself long enough.

She removed the capote, and swiped her palm across her damp forehead. The somewhat strenuous uphill trail left her flushed and sweaty under the thick material. Leaning back, Evelyn closed her eyes and allowed her mind to wander. She thought of the years ahead, and the family she and Alex would raise. The subject of children had never come up, but she had no doubt that Alex would be a wonderful father, just as he was a loving husband to her.

For a moment, she wondered how he would react to the news. Would he be overjoyed, or would he remember his own childhood, and doubt his abilities again? He hadn't spoken of his father, nor had he given any indication that he still thought he might turn into the same abusive man as Silas Walker had been. It appeared as if he had completely laid that demon to rest.

Evelyn hoped that by the time her child arrived, Whispering Waters would be back. She would surely want female company during the time of the birth.

Early spring! Her baby would be born in early spring, right here beneath the mountains that she'd fallen in love with.

Suddenly eager to see Alex and tell him the news, Evelyn stood. She would search just a little further up the mountain for the mint, and then head back. If she didn't find any now, she would ask Alex if he knew where to look. She'd been gone from the cabin longer than she planned.

Reaching for the rifle and wool capote, the sound of gravel rolling downhill startled her, and she spun around on her heels. Wide-eyed, her hands flew to cover her mouth, and her heart leapt up into her throat.

"Hello, Evie," the man who stood several paces away from her said in a low even voice, a smile forming on his lips.

CHAPTER NINETEEN

"Oh my goodness! Henry!"
Evelyn's heart hammered in her chest, and her knees went weak. She inhaled sharply, trying to recover from the shock of seeing her brother stand right before her. All these months, she had believed him to be dead. Evelyn stumbled toward him on shaky legs. She threw her arms around his neck and hugged him close, sobbing against his shoulder.

Henry stood stiffly, and patted her back.

"I thought you were dead," Evelyn cried, and her voice cracked. "I saw that horrible man stab you, and you . . . fell overboard."

"I survived," Henry said dryly. There was no warmth to his voice. With his hands at her waist, he peeled her away from him.

Evelyn wiped at the tears in her eyes. "How?" she asked, shaking her head slightly. Her eyebrows pulled together.

"Some Indians found me, and pulled me from the water," he said hastily. Henry avoided her stare. "After I recovered, I've been looking for you."

Evelyn smiled warmly at her brother. She touched his

cheek just to make sure he was even real, then squeezed his hands. Joy flooded through her like a ray of sunshine. Could her life get any better? She was married to the man of her dreams, she was carrying his child, and Henry was alive!

Her eyes roamed over him, her mind still not quite comprehending that she hadn't lost the only remaining member of her family after all. Dressed in wool trousers and shirt, with a wide brimmed hat on his head, he looked as out of place in this wilderness as he had when he stood next to that bunch of river pirates. Evelyn shuddered involuntarily. One man's dark and menacing face flashed before her eyes, and her heart leapt nervously in her chest. She hoped she never had to cross Oliver Sabin's path again.

"How did you find me?" Evelyn asked. Her lips quivered, overwhelmed at seeing her brother alive. She looked past Henry's shoulder to see if anyone else was with him, but he appeared to be alone. Her eyebrows drew together slightly. "And here on this trail, of all places."

"I came up on that little cabin in the woods by the lake, and saw you in the distance. I couldn't believe my eyes at first, and I wanted to make sure it was really you before I made my presence known."

"I have so much to tell you, Henry. So much has happened, but I want to hear all about you first." She smiled brightly, and squeezed her brother's arm.

Henry studied her in silence. He pulled his hand from her grip, and turned away from her. In the back of Evelyn's mind, something about his behavior nagged at her. He didn't seem to be happy at all to see her.

"We can talk back at the cabin, Henry," she said, and stepped around him. "We can catch up on everything there. Alex will be so happy to see you."

Henry glared at her. "Alex?" The name slipped coldly from his mouth.

"We were both wrong about him," Evelyn said hastily, and reached for Henry's arm. "He didn't kill our parents, Henry. I'm convinced of it. I think Charlie lied to you that day. I think he's the one who murdered them."

Henry's eyes widened, the shock and surprise at what she'd said written clearly in his eyes. He removed his hat and ran his hand through his hair.

"I see you're still starry-eyed for Alex," he said slowly. "How did he manage to convince you of his innocence?"

Evelyn averted her eyes momentarily. She stared down at her feet, then squared her shoulders and raised her chin. Henry should be glad his longtime friend was innocent of any crimes.

"Alex and I are married, Henry." She studied his face for a reaction.

Henry grabbed her arm. "You what?" he sputtered. "How can that be possible? Here, in this awful wilderness?" He swept his arm toward the mountains.

"He saved my life," Evelyn said, taken aback. "He's a good man."

"You can't be serious, Evie? Have you lost all of your Christian values? A heathen marriage isn't a marriage. Besides, he's a ruthless killer. The Indians told me he is known as Shadow Walker, a man who kills without mercy. One of these days he'll kill you, too."

Evelyn stared wide-eyed at her brother. The man before her was not the man she had known all her life. A stranger stood before her now. What had happened to Henry to make him so cold?

"I would be dead if not for the man who protected me from those thugs you hired. The ones who tried to kill you. If not for Laurent –"

"Laurent Berard?" Henry's head snapped up, and a murderous gleam sparked in his eyes.

Evelyn took an involuntary step back. She stumbled on a loose rock, and nearly lost her footing. Her hand shot out, and Henry grabbed for it, pulling her roughly toward him.

Evelyn stared into her brother's cold eyes. "Yes, he's become a good friend. He kept me safe from men like Oliver Sabin, and brought me to Alex. He's not one of those criminals. In fact, he's been trying to uncover who they work for."

Henry's eyes narrowed. "Is that right?" he mumbled. His eyes darted around the hillside before his gaze settled on her again. His grip on her arm tightened, and his jaw tensed.

"Evie, you're coming back with me. I'm getting you out of this wilderness. You're going back to St. Charles, and you will marry Charlie like we planned."

Evelyn yanked her arm from his grip. She shook her head vigorously. "I'm not going back, Henry. I'm married to Alex. My life is here now. If you would only hear me out, then—"

In an unexpected move, Henry forcefully grabbed her upper arms and shook her. The gleam and hate in his eyes sent a jolt of dread down her spine.

"You'll come with me willingly, Evie, and marry Charlie, or I will hand you over to Oliver Sabin."

Evelyn's jaw dropped, and she couldn't suppress a gasp. "He's the man who tried to kill you," she sputtered.

Henry laughed coldly. "By the time he's through with you, not even your precious Alex will want you."

Evelyn's mind raced. Comprehension and words failed her. Why would Henry offer her up to a killer? Why was he so unwilling to listen to her. She struggled against her brother's tight grip. Fear flooded her. Fear of her own brother. Her eyes darted to where her rifle lay on the ground a few feet away.

"Let go of me, Henry. I don't know what's come over you, but you can't make me do something against my will."

Henry released one of her arms, only to strike her forcefully across the face. Her head snapped to the side, and she gasped for air. Blackness swirled before her eyes, and she blinked to try and clear her head. Her knees buckled, and she struggled to remain standing. Henry yanked at her arm.

"Why?" she stammered, staring into the cold and cruel eyes of her brother.

"Let's go, Evie," he said callously, and shoved her in front of him. Evelyn dug in her heels, and twisted her body.

"Don't make me hit you again," he warned. "You've always had to make everything difficult, haven't you?" he spat. "I had the perfect plan. I was even going to take care of you, give you a good life in St. Charles, but you had to ruin everything when you couldn't do what you were told and had to follow me." With every word, Henry's voice grew louder and angrier.

"I don't know what you're talking about," Evelyn retorted. "What plans?" She had to keep her brother talking. She had to buy some time so she could figure out what to do. How long had she been gone from the cabin? Alex would surely come looking for her when he returned. But that wouldn't be for many hours yet. There was no telling what Henry was capable of in his deranged mental state.

Henry laughed again. "Do you really think I was going to spend my entire life breaking my back on that farm?" He shoved her again, jabbing his fist into her lower back. She flinched, and took a reluctant step forward. Evelyn couldn't believe what she was hearing. Suddenly she realized that the brother she had loved all her life was someone she didn't know at all.

"I told Father I didn't want to be a farmer. I wanted to go on an adventure in the wilderness with Alex, but he wouldn't allow it. He needed me to work the farm. I was no better than a slave to him."

"What on earth are you talking about?" Evelyn twisted to

look back at her brother. "Papa gave you the best of everything. The best he could afford. We all worked hard. After everything I've seen and witnessed here in these mountains, I don't think this sort of life would have suited you any better."

Henry bared his teeth at her, hate and anger spewing from his eyes. He laughed again. "You are so naïve, Evie. The fur trade is going to make me rich, and I don't so much as have to lift a finger. I wouldn't even be here if you had simply married Charlie, but you forced me to come looking for you, and bring you back."

A sick feeling washed over Evelyn. She didn't want to believe the terrible thought that entered her mind. She stopped and faced her brother.

"What have you done, Henry?" she whispered, afraid she already knew the answer. Blinding fear for her unborn child raced through her, and she stood still.

An evil smile spread across his face. Bile rose in her throat, and she recoiled from his sinister stare.

"If you don't cooperate, dearest sister, I'll—"

A sudden loud explosive boom jolted the serene stillness of the mountain, and the ground shook, cutting off Henry's words. They both stopped and stared. A low rumble coming from deep beneath the earth suddenly gained in intensity, and rocks broke free from the terrain. First gravel, then smaller stones, then larger rocks rolled down the trail, stirring up dust and debris. Trees and bushes began to sway, even though there was no wind.

"Henry, what's happening?" Evelyn shouted, trying to steady her feet. She leaned against him, wondering if she would lose her balance and fall. The earth beneath her feet continued to shake and rumble, as if she were standing in a bouncy buggy. Only, this ride gave her no sense of control. Fear raced through her, and she realized they were at the mercy of an unexplainable force of nature.

"Come on," Henry yelled, and pulled her along with him. Dodging rocks and debris, he ushered her down the hill. She nearly fell to her knees when a large crack in the ground opened right before her, and just barely managed to dodge around it. Faster and faster they ran. A tree uprooted right in front of them, falling to the ground with a loud groan and thud, and Evelyn screamed.

Henry held firm to her arm, leading her away from the direction that should take her back to the river and her home. The loud rush of water reached her ear, and she glanced swiftly toward the river. Like a flash flood, water raged in a muddy torrent where a crystal clear stream had flowed peacefully earlier in the day. It would be impossible to cross now.

Thoughts of Alex entered her mind. Was he safe? He was most certainly along some stream or riverbed, laying his traps. Would a flash flood sweep him away? Tears streamed freely from her eyes. Her beautiful world was literally crashing down right in front of her. After a couple of minutes that seemed like hours, the ground stopped rolling. Rocks and boulders continued to tumble down the hillside, and the air was thick with dust.

"Henry, look out!" Evelyn shouted when another tree creaked and groaned, then toppled before them. Henry yanked viciously at her arm, but it was too late. A large branch snapped across her back like a whip, and she fell forward. She gulped for air, and her free hand flailed out instinctively to block her fall. Her head hit the ground, and blackness claimed her.

* * *

Alex pulled back on his horse's reins, bringing the gelding to a skidding halt in front of the cabin. A quick glance in all directions told him that the shaking of the earth hadn't done any damage at his home site. The trees all stood, and except for the whitecaps and murky water of the usually pristine lake, nothing else seemed out of the ordinary.

"Evelyn," he called. He swung his leg over his horse's neck to dismount in a hurry. His gelding trotted off. Alex darted to the door, and pushed down on the wooden latch. The newly fashioned door swung open with a creak, and Alex stepped into the dark interior.

"Evie?" The eerie quiet, and the coals smoldering in the hearth sent an icy chill of foreboding down his back. "Evie," he called, more loudly. He reached their bedroom in a few hurried strides. Nothing looked out of place. The only thing missing was his wife.

Alex spun around, and headed for the door. He noticed immediately that the rifle was gone, and the wool capote he'd hung on the back of the door was missing, too. Where had she gone? His heart pounded in his chest, and he raced around the side of the cabin. Repeatedly, he called her name. Cold sweat beaded his forehead and trickled down his back, even in the chill of the early afternoon.

Cursing under his breath, he found his horse grazing near the water's edge. He pulled his rifle from the saddle, and scoured the area for tracks. A million thoughts raced through his mind. There were no signs that Blackfeet or any other Indians had been here.

When the earth had started shaking, Alex's first thought had been of Evie alone at the cabin. He'd heard of earth tremors before, through legends from the Indians. Never had he imagined he would experience one. The usually calm waters in the stream he waded in had sloshed over their banks like bathwater in a wooden tub, and dust swirled in the air. Nearby trees swayed with the movement of the earth, and loud rumbling and crashing of rocks and boulders that loosened from the mountains reached his ears. Yancey shot him a startled look. He grabbed for their horses, whose ears twitched nervously back and forth. Not more than a few minutes passed and the shaking stopped. Alex hadn't wasted any time, and leapt onto his horse.

As he galloped his mount toward home, visions of Evie, alone and most likely scared, raced through Alex's mind. Had his cabin withstood the tremors? He shouldn't have left her today. He should have insisted she go along. Clenching his jaw, he conceded that he had no choice but to head out and set his traps. From now on he would insist that she accompany him.

Alex spotted fresh footprints close to the shore of the lake, and followed them toward the inlet. Debris covered some of the prints, indicating that they had to have been made before the ground started shaking. Where was Evelyn headed this morning? She hadn't told him she had plans to leave the cabin. The further along the river he walked, following her trail, the greater his sense of dread took hold in him. When the tracks ended abruptly at the edge of the churning water, Alex stared across the river. Why had she headed out into the mountains? He couldn't think of one good reason that would send her this way alone.

Alex scanned the area across the heavily wooded opposite bank of the river. The well-traveled deer trail on the other side looked disturbed by uprooted trees and boulders that had crashed down the side of the mountain.

"Evie," he called repeatedly, his voice reverberating through the air. There was no answering call.

Alex pushed the dreadful thought that something had happened to her from his mind. He stepped into the water and, using the butt end of his rifle, steadied himself as he navigated his way through the current. The river wasn't deep, reaching only to his mid-thigh, but the current was strong and the invisible bottom slick and dangerous. Once safely across, he sprinted up the trail, skirting around boulders and debris.

A massive landslide of huge rocks and large boulders that the earth's shaking had no doubt broken loose finally blocked his way. His heart hammered in his chest. Facing down a grizzly, or fifty Blackfeet warriors could never produce the kind of fear he experienced at this moment. His eyes scanned the hillside, and he climbed on top of the massive heap. Nothing. Not a sound, not a footprint, nothing.

Ravens circled the air, their harsh caws drawing his attention. Alex's gaze followed their movement. The presence of ravens was not a good sign. They were often the first at the scene of a dead animal or . . . *No!* He wouldn't allow himself to think it. He swallowed back the sudden nausea, and his stomach clenched as if someone had punched him in the gut. Ignoring the sensation, he climbed further up and over large rocks and boulders blocking his way, then stopped abruptly. A sudden movement on the ground drew his attention. His eyes fell to the space where two large rocks had collided. A familiar red piece of wool fluttered in the breeze, stuck between the large boulders.

"Evelyn!" His breath left his lungs, and his heart must have stopped beating. A cold numbness washed over him from head to toe, and for a moment he couldn't move. Then he rushed to where the tip of his capote stuck out from under one of the countless rocks that had piled up here in the slide.

Alex dropped to his knees. He pushed against the stone with his shoulder, leaning his entire weight into the massive object, grunting in frustration. It wouldn't budge. Frantically, he dug at the dirt around the rock with his bare hands. His fingertips and knuckles soon tainted the ground with his blood, scraped raw from the hard ground. The pain only drove him to greater effort. It was no use. The earth below the boulder was hard and packed down.

Alex panted, and his chest heaved in painful spasms. He barely managed to scrape away several inches of dirt. Defeated, he sank to the ground, drawing his knees up to his chest.

"Evie," he murmured. Abruptly, he turned and pounded his fists against the rock. "Evelyn," he roared, his voice reverberating off the mountains. The sights and sounds around him ceased to exist. He slumped against the hard earth, pounding his fist repeatedly against the gravelly ground.

"I love you, Evie. You made me whole." His voice cracked, whispering her name over and over. He cursed the Creator and everything around him, but most of all, he cursed himself. His life held no meaning. Everything he lived for lay buried under the rock he leaned against.

CHAPTER TWENTY

Laurent strained against the leather binding his hands behind his back. Discreetly, his eyes scanned the camp. Leaning against the trunk of a lodgepole pine, he slowly worked his wrists up and down along the rough bark of the tree. For several hours, he'd sat here already, and his efforts seemed to produce some favorable results. The ties didn't bite quite as painfully into his flesh, and he hoped to work his hand through one of the loops very shortly. Breaking through the leather would be impossible. The pain was a small price to pay in order to be free.

Quietly, he listened to the three men sitting around the campfire a short distance away. Oliver Sabin tilted his head back, taking a long drink from the leather bag in his hand. Soon, these men would be drunk enough to fall asleep. Or so Laurent hoped. Sabin had made a grave mistake when he boasted that he wanted to keep Laurent alive to prolong his death. Apparently the man still held a grudge for not handing Evelyn over to him.

Although it had been unfortunate that he had been found out as a spy against the American Fur Company, Laurent had gained valuable information in the process. Two days ago, he had met with a couple of the men who considered him one of their own. It hadn't been until Oliver Sabin showed up in their camp that his cover had been revealed. Without warning, Sabin had pointed a pistol at his head, and ordered the other men to disarm and bind him. How had Sabin known that he was a spy?

Laurent shook his head. No matter now. He would get his answers. Whiskey quickly loosened a man's tongue. He only needed to ask, and Sabin was all too eager to boast, and share his information with him.

"Laurent, you French bastard, the very person you tried to keep from me is the one who gave you away," Sabin had slurred, waving the pistol in front of his face. "That sweet little morsel that you bartered away at rendezvous told her dear brother." He laughed. "She was supposed to be mine," he shouted, spittle drooling from his mouth. "Henry Lewis told me I could have her, after I staged his death. And then I was supposed to kill her."

Laurent quickly processed the information in his mind. Henry Lewis was alive? He was the man behind the cargo thefts against the Rocky Mountain Fur Company? Anger surged through him. Evelyn had grieved for him. He would have handed his own sister over to men like Sabin.

"*Mademoiselle* Evelyn, she was in on the plan, no?" he asked with narrowed eyes, hoping Sabin would supply him with more answers. The man laughed scornfully.

"Of course not. Stupid Lewis tried to marry her off back in St. Charles to be rid of her. A few weeks ago, after I met up with him, I finally thought I'd get my chance at her, but he refused." He swayed back and forth, taking another swig from the whiskey bag. He leered at Laurent. "Damn big wig told me he was taking her back to St. Charles. The man she was supposed to marry threatened to expose Henry to Jed

Smith's outfit if she doesn't, so he had to come back to find her."

Sabin leaned toward Laurent. The smell of whiskey and foul breath nearly choked him. "Lewis sent me here to kill you, Laurent. We can't have you exposing the operation. Soon, I'll take care of that corncracker in St. Charles, and then that trapper's whore will be mine." His ugly sneer gaped at him.

"What about Walker?" Laurent asked, ignoring Sabin's threats. "He bartered for her. Did he simply let her go with her brother?"

Sabin shrugged. "He didn't come after her. Bastard probably got tired of her and is glad to be rid of her. Always heard he was a loner."

Silently, Laurent wondered how Henry Lewis had managed to find his sister. Not many people knew of Alex's plans about his cabin. It didn't matter now. He was certain that Evelyn wouldn't leave Alex of her own free will, and Alex would certainly not allow his wife to return to St. Charles to marry another. The answers to these questions would have to wait. Once he was free of his bindings, and away from these men, he would head back into the mountains and seek out his friend. The thought that he would see his wife again sooner than he had thought brought a smile to his face.

"What's so funny, Laurent?" Sabin demanded, his speech slurred. He raised his pistol again, and held it to Laurent's forehead with an unsteady hand. He laughed coldly. "I could just put this bullet between your eyeballs right now. But I learned a trick or two from the Paiutes. They know how to make a man live for a long time, writhing in pain so great, you'll beg for a merciful death."

Laurent had no plans to find out if Sabin was well versed in Paiute torture methods firsthand or not. He pulled against the leather thongs wrapped around his wrists. The binding sliced into his skin, and he gritted his teeth against the pain. His hand finally slipped through the loop. In one swift move, he swung his fisted hand forward, knocking the pistol from Sabin's grip. He grabbed the surprised man by the neck with his other hand and shoved him to the ground. Picking up the pistol, he fired it at one of the men who'd turned his head at the commotion. Before the other man even had a chance to react, Laurent pulled the tomahawk and knife from Sabin's belt, aimed, and threw the ax. The weapon lodged itself in the trapper's chest, and he fell to the ground. Sabin staggered to his feet, and bared his teeth.

"You sonofabitch," he snarled. His unfocused eyes darted from Laurent to his dead companions.

"You will die, too, *mon amie*," Laurent said calmly, holding the knife out in front of him.

With a savage roar, Sabin charged. Laurent sidestepped, and raised the knife. The toe of Sabin's boot caught on a protruding root. He stumbled forward, and collided against Laurent. A scream of anguish reverberated through the forest. Laurent pulled the knife back, and Sabin clutched his hand over his face, blood running in rivulets between his fingers. Laurent stepped back. He realized the weapon had stabbed Sabin in the eye.

Like a rabid dog, the river pirate screamed, breaking the stillness of the forest. Then he ran between the trees into the thicket. Laurent watched him disappear. His chest heaved as he drew in a deep breath. He could just follow Sabin and kill him, but nature would do the job for him. The evil man deserved a slow death. He rushed for his horse and pulled the reins free of the picket line. Without a backward glance, he leapt into the saddle and kicked his horse into a run. It would take several weeks to reach Alex. There was already snow in some of the passes, but he had to find out why his friend hadn't gone after his wife. He dreaded what he might find when he reached the cabin.

***

Muffled voices reached Alex's ears from outside the cabin. He ignored the sound, hoping it was only Yancey talking to himself. The bitter wind that had howled all day had finally ceased. A few days ago, several feet of snow had fallen, blanketing his cabin and everything around him in a dusting of white powder. Evelyn would have loved the way the morning sun sparkled off the ice hanging from the cabin's roof or from the tree branches nearby.

They would have sat by a roaring fire, listening to the wind howl outside. He'd wrap her in his arms, and they'd kiss and touch under a blanket, and talk about nothing important. Instead, he sat alone in a dark corner of his cabin, the fire dead in the hearth, and the windows boarded up. Unable to look at the bed he'd built for her, and the memories it sparked, he hadn't set foot inside the bedroom since the day of her death.

Yancey had arrived earlier in the day, bringing fresh meat. Not that he had much of an appetite these days. He wished the greenhorn would just go away. He had served his purpose when Alex asked him to bring him Laurent's stash of whiskey from his cabin several days ago. At first, Yancey had refused, but a quick threat with a knife held to the coward's throat had changed his attitude. His old man had always preferred to drown his troubles in liquor. Maybe it was time he gave it a try. Nothing else he'd done seemed to take away his pain.

Days had dragged into weeks, and weeks into several months since Evie's death. He'd tried to immerse himself in his work, felling trees and chopping wood for hours at a time that would see him through two winters. He left his cabin for days, sometimes even a week, to wander the streams and tributaries of the Snake River, setting his traps, and hunting game. A strong blizzard finally forced him back to his cabin. Nothing seemed important anymore. Nothing held any meaning. He fingered the cork on the whiskey pouch in his hand, and slowly pulled it open. The strong scent of alcohol filled his senses.

You are not like your father.

The softly spoken words of the woman he loved above everything else echoed in his mind. Only those faint words had prevented him from uncorking the pouch before now. Would he betray her love, her memory, if he took a drink?

The hinges on the cabin door creaked, followed quickly by an icy blast of air.

"He's over there, Laurent. It's good that you're back."

"*Mon dieu*! I thought I could warm up by a fire. It is no warmer in here than it is outside."

"I'll get one lit," Yancey said. He shuffled toward the hearth. "He prefers to sit in the cold."

"Well, we will have to change his attitude, no?"

Alex cursed under his breath. Why the hell was Laurent here? It couldn't be spring already. He had lost track of time, for sure, but not that much time had passed for Laurent to have been to St. Louis and back. He held the tip of the whiskey pouch to his lips.

"Shouldn't you be with your wife, Laurent?" he grumbled, and tilted his head back. The taste of whiskey on his tongue nauseated him.

Laurent reached for the bag and yanked it from Alex's hands before he could even swallow. Spitting out the small amount in his mouth, Alex shot to his feet, and grabbed the Frenchman by the front of his shirt. Baring his teeth, he glared at his friend.

"You will not waste my good whiskey to drown your misery, *mon amie*," Laurent said without flinching, and stared him in the eyes.

"Leave me the hell alone, Laurent, and mind your own business." Alex released his hold on the Frenchman's shirt and shoved him away. He ran a trembling hand through the coarse hairs on his face. He hadn't shaved in weeks.

"Get the hell out of my cabin. Both of you," he roared. Yancey dropped the flint in his hand, and stumbled to his feet. Wide-eyed, he stared from Alex to Laurent, uncertainty in his eyes.

Laurent advance on Alex, and placed a heavy hand on his shoulder, tightening his grip when Alex tried step to the side.

"I told you to leave me alone. Go and be with your wife, Laurent. Enjoy the time you have with her."

"I will do that, *mon amie*," Laurent said lightly. "But I think it is you who should be with your wife, also."

Alex blinked. Pain jabbed his heart. Perhaps Laurent was right. Maybe he should go and be with Evie up on that mountain. "My wife is dead and buried, Laurent. I suppose I should go join her."

Laurent's bushy brows drew together. "Dead and buried? That is not what I was told."

Alex stared blankly. Moments passed in silence.

"Evelyn is alive and well, I presume, in St. Charles, my friend." Laurent finally released his arm.

"What the hell are you talking about?" Alex scoffed. Why would he tell such a lie?

"Henry Lewis is not dead. He came for her, and took her. I didn't know why you would not fight for her. I thought perhaps I might find you dead. Young Yancey here has told me what has happened."

Alex tried to absorb what he had just heard. Henry was

alive? Evie went with him? Why would she do that? Who lay buried under those rocks at the base of the mountain?

"Who told you this?" Alex asked slowly, the air leaving his lungs. His chest tightened, and a tiny spark of hope ignited in his heart. A tingling sensation replaced the emptiness inside him all these weeks. Was there a chance Evie was alive? He stared at Laurent.

"There is a lot more to tell, my friend." Laurent pulled out one of the chairs from under the table, and sat. He took a quick drink from the whiskey bag he still held in his hand. "I will tell you what I know, and then you must decide what you wish to do."

CHAPTER TWENTY-ONE

St. Charles, Missouri, Spring 1829

Alex guided his exhausted horse down the main street along the Missouri River. The gelding sloshed through puddles of mud from a recent spring rain, and carried his head low. Discreetly, Alex glanced through weary eyes at the hustle and bustle around him. Laurent's equally tired horse prodded along next to his own. Boatmen moved along the docks, shouting orders and cursing. Some exchanged heated words with one another. Alex already longed for the solitude of the mountains.

He observed the people around him. Men, and some women, of all shapes, sizes, and colors milled about among the busy throng along the banks of the Missouri. Vagrant Indians loitered along the streets, some Frenchmen sang loud songs, and even a few hunters and trappers in buckskins mingled with the rest of the crowd. The smell of liquor and fish mingled with the cleaner scent of honeysuckle blooming in early spring. Had it been a year already since he'd last been to St. Charles? Since he caught his first glimpse of Evelyn as a grown woman? The image of her, as he remembered her when he first saw her, blended with the image of the woman who had become more important to him than his own life.

"It has been a long journey, my friend, but soon you will be reunited with your wife," Laurent said, guiding his horse closer to Alex. The smile on the Frenchman's face lacked his usual exuberance. Alex nodded imperceptibly. His pulse increased despite his fatigue. Long journey was an understatement. Three months of navigating snow-packed mountain passes that others had said were impossible to traverse had taken their toll on both of them and their horses. The rigorous journey didn't matter. He hadn't seen Evie in nearly five months. The ache to hold her in his arms had become unbearable at times, and the need to feel her had driven him beyond human endurance.

How many blizzards and bitter cold nights had he suffered on his near-impossible trek through the mountains these past months to reach St. Louis, and finally St. Charles? The few mountain men he and Laurent had encountered had told him they'd never survive the trip. Sometimes days or even a week had gone by when they'd been forced to hole up somewhere when a mountain blizzard made travel impossible.

Visions of Evelyn kept him going. The emptiness in his heart, and the unbearable yearning to see her smiling face and to touch her drove him to attempt the impossible. Even Laurent had suggested it might be better to wait until the spring thaw. Alex refused to listen to reason. The moment Laurent's words had sunk in that Evie wasn't dead, he'd sprung into action. The next morning, he'd left Yancey in charge of his cabin, and mounted his horse. Laurent had insisted on going with him, and Alex was grateful to his friend for the company.

To the best of his estimate, it was October the day the earth shook and she disappeared. Since she'd come into his life at the summer rendezvous in early June, he'd barely had five months with her. No matter how much time had passed, her face remained etched as clearly into his memory as if she stood before him. During those horrible months when he thought she was lost to him forever, her soft voice and delicate feminine scent had remained imprinted on his mind.

His fingers tingled, and he gripped the reins tighter. If Henry had harmed her in any way, the bastard would pay with his life. Alex's jaw clenched. His father's farm was just a few miles outside of town. The closer he came, the stronger the anger and rage coursed through him, as if his old man held some kind of power over him now that he was back. He shook the unpleasant feeling aside. Anger at Henry had nothing to do with his father. Any man in love would react the same way if his wife had been kidnapped.

Nagging thoughts had consumed him during those cold and lonely weeks of trekking over frozen mountain passes. What if Evie had married Charlie? He knew without a doubt that she would never consent to marry him of her own free will, but Henry could have easily forced her. She had no proof that she was already married. Alex shifted in the saddle. The ways of the mountain men were not honored in St. Louis. She had no proof that she was already a married woman. If she was legally wed to another man, what recourse did he have? Pushing the unpleasant thought from his mind for now, he nudged his gelding forward.

After leaving the last buildings of town behind, Alex led the way along the narrow dirt road that followed a shallow stream. Recollections from his childhood rushed back to him. How often had he walked this road as a young boy, running errands for his mother or simply to escape his father's temper? He glanced toward the creek. A vague memory of a young girl arguing with a boy seeped into his mind. Alex pulled his horse to a stop.

"Let's rest here for a moment," he called to Laurent, who shot him a grateful look. As eager as he was to find Evelyn, he didn't want to show up at her doorstep looking and smelling like the man she'd first met in the mountains. Although he was sure that she would receive him without distain and animosity this time, he ignored the urgency to reach the farm so that he could clean up before seeing her again.

Dismounting his horse, he pulled a shirt from a pouch tied to his saddle, and headed for the creek. He could clearly see Evie, a sassy young girl, punching Charlie Richardson in the nose. He'd laughed silently, hiding in the bushes that day. When Charlie grabbed her and pushed her into the creek, anger had exploded inside him. He hadn't thought twice about coming to her aid, and punching Charlie as hard as he could. The look of gratitude in her eyes that day had sent his young heart fluttering, and he'd run off like a coward. From that day, he'd avoided Henry's sister as best as he could. A slow smile spread across his face.

You've been drawn to her since that day, and you never even realized it.

Quickly, he finished shaving the beard from his face that he'd let grow over the months, and slipped into his clean shirt. Impatient to find Evelyn, he strode to his horse, which was eagerly grazing the green grass along the creek bank.

"I will catch up with you, *mon amie*," Laurent said. He leaned up against a wide sycamore tree. "I will give my horse a little more time to rest. You go and be reunited with your wife."

Alex nodded, and climbed into the saddle. He patted his horse's neck. "A little further, and then you'll get some much deserved rest."

Guiding his horse along the road, his gaze scanned into the distance. If he took the cutoff to the left, he'd reach the farm where he'd grown up. Alex had no desire to see the place. He didn't care what became of it. He nudged his mount with his heels, and continued on his way to the Lewis farm.

Only a few more miles. His heart pounded with apprehension and eagerness in his chest. That he'd have to confront Charlie went without question. What he didn't know was the reception he'd receive from Evie. Did she think he'd forgotten about her when he didn't come looking for her? Perhaps she had thought that he was dead, just as he had presumed about her.

A man walking behind a team of oxen in a field stopped to watch him ride by. The smell of freshly tilled soil mingled with the pungent scent of cows; scents he'd grown up with but long ago forgotten. He'd traded those smells for the musky scent of beaver. Soon, the familiar house and outbuildings of the Lewis farm came into view. A dirt yard separated the simple farmhouse from the much larger barn. Chickens cackled and scratched at the ground in the yard. He pulled his horse to a stop in front of a small corral. A shaggy brown dog came running from around the other side of the barn, barking loudly and scattering the chickens.

Alex turned his head slowly, taking in the well-kept house and barn. This property was vastly different from his cabin in the remote Teton Mountains. He suddenly felt strange and out of place here. His mountains called to him. What if Evie didn't want to go back with him? He couldn't offer her what she had here. There was no constant threat of hostile Indians or wild animals to endanger her life. Slowly, he brought his leg over his horse's neck and hopped to the ground. The dog continued to bark at him, but kept a safe distance away.

The front door of the farmhouse opened, and a man

stepped outside. Alex dropped his horse's reins. His jaw clenched, and anger rushed through him. Charlie Richardson, the man who had put a bullet in his chest a year ago. The man who had killed Evie's parents.

Holding a rifle in his hand, Charlie pointed it at Alex.

"I see you haven't changed, Charlie. Gonna try and finish what you couldn't do last spring?" Alex glared at him, his eyes unwavering.

"Henry Lewis warned me you might show up here one day," Charlie said, and stepped further into the yard. Alex noted the slight hesitation in his step, and the unsteadiness in Charlie's hold on his weapon.

"Is that right," Alex said casually, his hand slowly inching toward the tomahawk hanging from his belt. He stepped away from his horse, a few paces toward the farmer. "Then I suppose you must know why I'm here."

"Leave, Walker. You have no business here," Charlie called across the space that separated them. He continued to step away from the house, pointing his rifle at Alex's chest. "Go back to where you came from."

Alex's lips parted in a sneer. " I'll leave, as soon as I get what I came here for."

"There's nothing here that concerns you," Charlie said hastily.

Alex inhaled deeply. "Where is Evelyn," he demanded, tired of beating around the bush.

"She doesn't concern you. You need to leave."

"Like hell she doesn't—"

A muffled cry came from inside the house, and Charlie's head whipped around toward the sound. A woman's cry of pain jolted Alex to the chore. Evie! What was happening to her inside that house? Cold sweat and fear raced down Alex's back. It sounded as if someone was torturing Evie inside. His first thought was of Henry. He seized on the diversion, ignoring the rush of panic to his own heart, and charged at Charlie. Grabbing the rifle from the distracted man's hands, disarming him proved rather easy. Charlie was a farmer, not some Crow or Blackfoot warrior out to kill him. Alex tossed the weapon to the ground, and pulled his knife from his belt, holding it to Charlie's throat.

"Where's my wife?" he snarled.

Charlie backed up. His eyes widened in panic, and he swallowed repeatedly. Sweat beaded his forehead. He shook his head vigorously from side to side.

"She's—"

Alex grabbed Charlie by the shirt, and slammed his fist against the man's jaw, sending him to the ground. He rushed toward the house, kicked the door open, and held his knife out in front of him. Quickly, he scanned the large central room. A fire blazed in the hearth, and everything looked neat and tidy. Muffled voices and strange sounds came from a room down the narrow hallway to the left.

"Evie?" Alex roared. He sprang in the direction of the sound, his heart pounding in his chest.

A woman wearing a bloodstained apron and holding a thick bundle of white cloth in her arms emerged from the room that Alex vaguely remembered had been Evie's childhood bedroom. She stared at him, her mouth set in a firm line, her eyes shooting daggers at him.

"What is the meaning of this?" she demanded. "Who are you? Where's Mr. Richardson?"

Alex glowered at the woman, his focus on the door behind her. He stepped closer when she didn't move aside, guarding the entrance to the bedroom with the fierceness of a mother grizzly.

"Where's Evelyn?" he demanded.

"She's resting at the moment. You can't go in there."

"Alex?"

Evie's weak and muted voice jolted him to the core. An arrow to the chest from a Blackfoot warrior couldn't have made a greater impact.

"Like hell I can't," Alex growled, and pushed past the woman. He ripped the door open amid her adamant protests. The sight before him stopped him in his tracks. The pounding of his heart in his ears seemed to drown out all sound, and the air rushed from his lungs. A quick scan of the room revealed bloody linens tossed on the ground. A washbasin stood near the foot of the bed. It looked as if something had been butchered in this room.

CHAPTER TWENTY-TWO

Alex's eyes fell to the figure on the bed along the wall in the center of the room. His heart lurched in his chest.

"Alex? Oh my God, Alex?" Evelyn cried, struggling to lift herself up from the bed.

Dressed in a long white cotton nightgown, Evelyn sat half-reclined on the mattress. She braced her hands on either side of her to slide her body to a more upright position. Her eyes grew wide, and tears rolled down her cheeks. Her face looked ashen and matched the color of the sheets. Sweat-soaked hair clung to her forehead. She held her arm out toward him, beckoning him to her. He didn't need any further encouragement.

In two strides, Alex reached her side and dropped to his knees beside the bed. His palm cupped her clammy cheek, and he swiped away the damp strands of hair. Something was terribly wrong. She looked ill and exhausted, but a quick scan down the length of her revealed that she seemed otherwise unharmed. Where had all the blood come from?

"You came. You really came," Evie sobbed. "I hoped and prayed that you would come." She reached for him, and he leaned forward. Her body shook as she wrapped her arms around his neck, and weakly pulled him toward her. Alex cautiously gathered her to him, unsure where she was hurt and afraid to do more harm. Slowly, he moved from the floor and sat at the edge of the bed.

"Evie," he whispered against her neck, stroking her back. "I thought I'd lost you." His voice cracked, and he could do no more but hold her in his embrace. The long months of misery, of thinking that she was dead vanished, and happiness replaced the anguish in his heart. He inhaled long and slow, savoring her sweet feminine scent. His arms trembled, and her upper body quivered in his embrace. She continued to sob.

"What did Charlie do to you?" he murmured, cradling the back of her head.

He kissed her forehead, then brushed his lips against her mouth. His muscles tensed, anger at Henry and Charlie exploding inside him. They would pay for what they had done to her. A loud wail pierced the stillness of the room, followed by the harsh words of the woman he had encountered in the hall.

"What is the meaning of this?"

Alex ground his teeth at the stern voice of the irritating woman behind him. The shrill cries of what sounded like a newly born mountain goat nearly drowned out her words. Reluctantly, he pulled away from Evie, and turned his upper body to stare at the woman standing in the middle of the room. His eyes dropped to the bundle in her arms that he had mistaken for a wad of linen material a few moments ago. A tiny human hand poked from between the layers of cloth, bunched in a tight little fist. The baby's wails grew in intensity with each second that passed.

Comprehension failed him. Why was this annoying woman bringing her child into Evie's room? He needed to be alone with her. His irritation with her grew, and he stood from the bed to face her.

The woman's eyes narrowed on Alex before she glared at Evie. "I don't know what's going on here. Where is Mr. Richardson?"

"Probably still lying in the dirt outside," Alex said loudly over the baby's cries. "I ain't leaving this room, but I suggest you do."

Evie's hand grabbed for his arm. "Alex, I have to tell you—"

"Your infant requires his first feeding." The woman's face turned red, and she puffed out her cheeks. She marched toward the bed, and Alex straightened to his full height. She held out the bundle, and Evie reached for it with trembling arms. Alex's brows scrunched together, his mind struggling for comprehension.

The woman stepped back, her hands on her hips. "This is outrageous," she screeched, glaring at Alex. "This man can't be in here while you feed your child."

The blood drained from Alex's head, down his arms and chest and into his legs, and seemed to ooze right into the floorboards. He stepped back for fear that he might fall on his unsteady legs.

Evie's child?

Alex swallowed. He gaped at Evie. His mind went numb. She cooed at the little infant, whose cries had lessened in her arms. She fumbled with the buttons on her nightdress, and Alex stood rooted to the spot.

"Mrs. Kirk, may I have some privacy?" she said, glancing up briefly. Then her eyes met Alex's.

"Well, I never," the woman huffed, and wheeled around. "Mr. Lewis and Mr. Richardson will hear about this." She stormed from the room.

Alex's eyes remained fixed on the baby, and on Evie. She

parted the nightgown, exposing first her shoulder then her breast, which was fuller than what he remembered. The baby latched on to her nipple after several unsuccessful tries, and Evie continued her soft coos. Then she glanced up at him, and smiled wearily. If this was Evie's baby, then . . . He counted back the months in his head. A force greater than a horse's kick to the gut jolted him.

"Sit, Alex," she whispered. "Come and meet your son."

Alex stared at her. He swallowed repeatedly, trying to force down the hard lump that had formed in his throat. His heart pounded in his ears.

"My son?" He barely produced a sound. His mouth went dry, and his chest tightened. He stared at the dark-haired infant at Evie's breast, and warmth flooded his chest, wrapping around him like a warm cocoon.

"I hadn't told you. I'm so sorry, Alex. I should have told you right away when I suspected, but I waited. That's the reason I left the cabin that morning. I wanted to find mint for my unsettled stomach."

Alex eased himself onto the mattress. His eyes never left the tiny human in Evie's arms. *He had a son.* And he'd missed all those months of watching Evie swell with a baby growing inside her. What if he'd never found out she was alive? The thought sickened him, and a new wave of anger at Henry slammed his gut.

"Henry showed up, and that's when the earth started shaking that day," Evie continued. He grabbed me and we ran." Fresh tears spilled from her eyes, and her gaze lifted to him. "He threatened me, Alex. I had no choice but to do what he wanted. I was afraid for our baby."

"I thought you were buried under a pile of rocks up on the mountain." He ran a shaky hand over his face, trying to disguise the crack in his voice.

Evelyn gripped his arm. "I'm sorry, Alex. I should have

stayed at the cabin that day. I should have told you I was with child. Please forgive me."

"Forgive you?" Alex's eyes widened, and he sucked in a deep breath. He cupped her face in his palm, and she leaned into his touch. "Evie. There is nothing to forgive. I'm sorry I failed to protect you. I should never have left you alone that day." His thumb swiped at the tears running down her cheek. "I love you. You're alive, and safe, and . . . the mother of my son." He glanced at the baby, a soft smile forming on his face. He still couldn't comprehend that he was now a father. Forgotten were the months of bitter cold and hardship as he forged his way over impenetrable mountains. Love for his son and the baby's mother flowed freely through him like a river during spring thaw. He would endure it all again, and more, if he had to.

He touched a tentative finger to the baby's head, surprised at the softness of his skin, and the downy feeling of his hair. Leaning forward, he touched his lips to Evie's mouth. Then he pulled back, a sudden thought nagging at him.

"Are you . . . married to Charlie?" His eyes sought hers for the truth, afraid of what her answer would be.

Wide-eyed, Evie quickly shook her head. "No. I refused to marry him until after the baby was born. Henry told everyone in town that Charlie and I were wed to keep up appearances after I told them I was with child." She paused, and reached for his hand. Alex held his breath and waited for her to continue.

"I knew I couldn't find my way back to you carrying a child. I had hoped you would come for me."

Alex clenched his jaw, and the air left his lungs.

"I told him and Henry that I'd cooperate for the sake of our baby."

Alex clutched her hand. "My God, Evie. For two months, I

wanted nothing more than to join you up on that mountain. If I had known you were alive . . . you know I would have come after you. I found a piece of the capote sticking out from under a boulder. I thought . . . I thought it was you."

"I wasn't wearing it when Henry found me." She reached her hand up to touch his face. "I never gave up hope that you would come. If not, I was prepared to find my way back to you. One way or the other, I knew we'd be together again."

The infant stirred, and Evie lifted him to her shoulder. Alex drank in the tranquil scene. He couldn't get enough of just looking at her and the baby that had been born of their love. A fierce protectiveness grabbed hold of him, something to rival the fiercest predator watching over its young.

"Henry is going to be sorry he ever took you from me." Alex's jaw muscles tightened. He stood from the bed. "I'm still not clear why."

Evelyn's eyes widened. "Alex," she whispered, and he stared at her, waiting. Her eyes filled with renewed tears. He sat beside her again, and held her hand.

"What is it?" he asked, alarmed by the sudden anguish on her face.

She swallowed, and gripped his hand, her arm trembling. "Charlie didn't kill my parents," she continued. Each word sounded forced from her mouth. His eyebrows scrunched together. If Charlie hadn't killed them, then who . . .

Comprehension dawned, and his heart sank to his stomach. He ran a hand over his face. "Why would Henry murder his own parents?" he asked between clenched teeth. The question left a bitter taste in his mouth.

"To be free of the farm, and so he could finance his smuggling operation against the fur company you worked for. The one Laurent is spying for."

"How does Charlie fit into all that?" Alex asked. He had to know what he was up against.

"Charlie saw Henry leave the house right after the murder. Henry convinced him to keep his mouth shut, and promised him a part of the profits in exchange for his silence. The farm and I were part of the bargain." She paused, and looked at him before continuing. "When they saw you heading toward the farm, Henry realized quickly that he could kill you and blame you for the murder, so he told Charlie to shoot you. He never meant to come after you. It was the story he told me. He had only planned to head upriver with the men until the cargo was stolen. He didn't count on me refusing to marry Charlie, or following him, and so he told Oliver Sabin to stage his death, and then Sabin could kill me." Evelyn gulped for air, and a shudder passed through her.

"Why did he come for you all these months later?"

"Because Charlie apparently still wanted Henry to uphold the agreement that I would marry him for his silence. He threatened to go to the authorities."

"If Henry is capable of all this, what would stop him from killing you and Charlie now?"

"Good question indeed, old friend."

Evelyn gasped, and Alex leapt from his seat at the edge of the bed. Henry stood in the doorway to the room, pointing a pistol at him. Alex slowly moved to stand in front of the bed, blocking Evie from her brother's aim.

"Oliver Sabin was supposed to kill you, Alex," Henry smirked. "Right after he took care of that French spy."

An easy smile formed on Alex's face. His hand slowly reached for the knife at his belt. "From what Laurent tells me, Sabin won't be doing any more killing."

Henry stared, his lip twitching in a sneer.

"And neither will you," Alex added as an afterthought.

"Don't be so sure about that, Alex," Henry retorted coldly. He laughed. "I've realized that too many people know my secret now. I always figured Charlie was too much of a coward to go to the authorities. If I handed you to him, dear sister, he would keep his mouth shut. But I see you're not going to stay quiet. I wish I had killed you up in those mountains. I honestly thought I'd find you eager to return home. I've underestimated you, and I've given it a lot of thought. I can't let you live. Either of you." His eyes met Alex's hard stare.

Alex stepped toward Henry, taking a calculated risk. Just as he'd hoped, Henry pointed the pistol at him. He took another step to the side. He had to draw Henry's attention away from Evelyn and the baby. Henry only had one shot. It was best the pistol was aimed at him.

If he was going to act, it had to be now. With practiced speed, he pulled his knife from his belt, and threw it, while at the same time he rolled to the ground. Henry cried out when the knife struck his hand, and the pistol fired, the bullet sending splinters of wood in the air from where it hit the floorboard. Evelyn screamed, and the baby began to cry. Alex sprang up from the ground, and ran toward Henry. He rammed into him, and slammed him into the wall. Grabbing him by the shirt, he nearly lifted him off the ground.

"Today is the last time you'll ever threaten me, or my wife and family again," he growled, his face inches from Henry's. Shocked and wide-eyed, his former friend stared back at him, then suddenly began to laugh.

"Go ahead, Alex. Kill me. I know it's what you want to do."

Alex sneered. "I'd like nothing more than beat you into the ground," he growled.

"Then why don't you? Isn't that what your old man loved to do?"

"I'm not my father," Alex said between clenched teeth. He yanked Henry away from the wall, and pushed him toward the door, and out into the hall. He caught a glimpse of Charlie rushing toward them from the main room. He held a pistol in his hand, and aimed. Before Alex realized what he intended, Charlie fired, and Henry slumped to the ground. Alex stared. Nothing made sense any more.

"This time my aim was true. This is the man I should have shot a year ago," Charlie said. His chest heaved, a fierce gleam in his eye.

"Alex?" Evelyn called frantically from inside the room. Alex turned his head in her direction.

"I'll be right there," he answered to ease her worry, then directed his gaze back at Charlie.

"I love her," Charlie said quietly, looking at Alex. "Since Henry brought her back, it's become clear that I'll never win her heart. You have always been in possession of that. Make sure you treat her well." Charlie met Alex's stare for a moment, then bent down to grab hold of Henry's lifeless body. "I'll take care of him."

"Charlie," Alex called. He held out his hand. Charlie glanced at it, then reached forward and shook it. "My father owned 125 acres of good farm land. I don't know what shape the house is in, but combined with this place, you'll have quite a nice spread. It's yours, if you agree to let Evelyn remain here until she is recovered from the birth."

Charlie nodded slowly. "You're welcome to stay as long as you need."

A silent understanding passed between the two. Charlie reached down once again, and grabbed hold of Henry's legs, dragging his lifeless body down the hall and out of the house.

Alex turned on his heels and rushed back into the room. Evie struggled to sit up, and console the crying infant in her arms.

"Is he . . . is Henry . . .?"

Alex nodded, not letting her finish her thought. "I'm

sorry, Evie. I didn't want it to end like this. Henry was your brother, after all." He sat at the edge of the bed. His eyes searched her weary face, and silent tears rolled down her cheeks.

"He's someone I didn't know anymore, Alex," she said barely above a whisper. "I can't help but think he would have always tried to find a way to hurt us."

"I want to wrap you in my arms and hold you," he said as quietly as he could and still be heard above the baby's cries. Evie sniffed, and smiled.

"Perhaps you should hold your son instead." She held the swaddled infant toward him, and a jolt of apprehension rushed through him. He swallowed, and tentatively held out his arms. Bending forward, he gathered the bundle to his chest. An intense feeling of love and pride rushed through him, and he gazed down into his son's red and angry face. Alex stood and moved around the room, slowly swaying his arms back and forth while holding the bundle close to his heart. What if he held him too tight? What if he dropped him?

The baby suddenly stopped crying, and his little lips quivered and puckered. His eyes closed, and he appeared to be content.

Alex looked toward Evie, who watched him intently. A smile spread across her face. "I knew you'd be a great father," she said. Alex grinned back at her.

"What should I do now?" he asked.

"His bassinet is ready for him." She pointed to a wicker basket that Alex hadn't noticed before, on the other side of the bed. Slowly, Alex walked around the bed. He didn't want to let go of his son, but he also wanted to hold the child's mother in his arms. Carefully, he placed the infant in the basket, and straightened. Observing his sleeping son for another moment, he tore his eyes away and turned toward Evie. He sat on the bed, and gathered her into his arms.

"Tomorrow, I'm calling for the preacher. It won't be a church wedding, but I refuse to spend another day without a piece of paper that says you're my wife."

Evie hugged him tight, then pulled away to kiss his lips. "I love you, Alex Walker, and I've told you before, I don't need a piece of paper to know I'm married to you."

"This is one argument you're not going to win, Evie," he said. "No one is ever going to take you from me again. And as soon as you're well enough, I'm taking you and my son home so I can uphold my promise to you."

"What promise?" Evie's eyebrows raised.

He hugged her close and whispered in her ear, "That you will wake up each morning to watch the sun rise above the Tetons."

EPILOGUE

⚜

F*ive years later*

"Did you find anything?"

Evie glanced up from watching her two-year-old son, Lucas, play in the dirt and throw pebbles at his five-year-old brother, Joseph.

Alex had just emerged from the trail that led from their cabin into the woods. He carried his flintlock cradled in his arm, and a dissatisfied look on his face.

"No. He's gone. He doesn't want to be found."

Evie met her husband as he approached. She wrapped her arms around his middle, and offered a soft smile.

"Yancey learned from the best. If he doesn't want to be found, he won't be."

Alex frowned. "He should have stayed with us. We could have protected him, and the little girl."

Evie leaned her head against Alex's chest. "He didn't want to bring danger to us, Alex. I think he thought he was doing what Laurent asked him to do. He took Sophia and is heading to Boston with her to hide her away from Sabin. That evil man is capable of anything." A tear fell down her face. "He proved that when . . . when he murdered them."

The grim thought that their two good friends, Laurent and Whispering Waters were dead tore at Evie's insides. The news of their deaths still hadn't completely sunk in, even days after Yancey had come to their cabin, carrying the couple's two-year-old daughter in his arms, and frantically telling them what Sabin had done.

"Sabin knows I'm looking for him," Alex growled. "And he knows what will happened if I find him. The coward probably left the territory. I'm not leaving you or the boys unprotected, or I would hunt him down."

Lucas came running toward her and Alex, holding out his hand. With a wide smile, he opened his fist and held up a wriggling worm. Alex chuckled.

"Your son is going to be trouble," Evie said. She sniffled, and wiped at her eyes. "Laurent always said he would be a handful."

Alex's hold around her waist tightened. He smiled, but he couldn't conceal the sadness in his eyes. He leaned forward to take the worm from Lucas' hand.

"I'll take you fishing in a while," he told his son.

"Fish," Lucas said, then ran back toward his older brother, who sat quietly on the ground, holding his toy bow and arrows.

"Sophia always followed poor Joseph around so much, he had to hide each time they were together." Evie laughed softly, wiping at her nose. "Lucas and she are of the same age, but for some reason she took a liking to Joseph. I remember the day Whispering Waters told me she was expecting. She was beside herself with happiness."

The birth of Laurent and Whispering Waters' daughter,

Sophia, who was known as Little Raven among her mother's people, had been nothing short of a miracle. For the first two years of their marriage, they had tried for a baby. Evie remembered how Whispering Waters had blamed herself, saying she was barren and useless as a wife.

She'd been fond of Evie's young son, Joseph, never showing her deep sorrow and perhaps even jealously that her friend was a mother. When Evie and Alex had announced another pregnancy, Whispering Waters had cried for days, according to Laurent. Nothing he'd tried to do had snapped her out of her sorrow, until one day she'd come to him, and announced that she was expecting.

"Perhaps our beautiful daughter will marry Joseph someday," Laurent had predicted.

Whispering Waters had laughed at her husband whenever he spoke of it. "She will have to behave more like a proper young woman should before he takes notice of her. All she wants to do is dig in the dirt and steal away his toys. She has not made a good impression on a potential future husband."

Laurent had doted on his wife and little girl, and now he and Whispering Waters were both gone, murdered by Oliver Sabin out of revenge for what Laurent had done to his eye.

"At least they're together," Evie whispered. "But what about Sophia?" Their daughter was missing, along with Byron Yancey who had lived with them.

"If Yancey can get her to safety, Sabin won't find her. He won't go as far as Boston for a young child."

"That evil man is capable of anything," Evie hissed.

Alex squeezed her hand. "And if he shows himself in these parts again, I will find him."

"But what's to become of their little girl?"

"Yancey loved Sophia as his own. That's why Laurent entrusted her to him before he died."

Alex wrapped Evie in his arms. Together, they walked to their secluded cabin along the lake. Joseph ran in front of them, while two-year-old Lucas tried to keep up with his brother.

"Life here is harsh and unforgiving, but I couldn't imagine living anywhere else." Evie gazed from looking at the tall peaks of the mighty Tetons to her husband, smiling at the love reflected in his eyes. "And I am grateful every day that I have you and our sons."

Alex leaned toward her, and kissed her on the forehead. He smiled proudly, looking at his boys. "Joseph and Lucas will grow up in this land, and know how to survive here. I see changes coming, but they will have the freedom to choose what path they want to take in life. Who knows what their future holds, but I know they will grow to be honorable men and accomplish great things."

The adventure continues with Teton Splendor, the story of Laurent and Whispering Waters' daughter….

Dear Reader

Thank you for purchasing and reading Teton Sunrise. I hope you enjoyed the book. Please consider letting other readers know about the book by leaving a quick review on Amazon. The adventure continues with Teton Splendor, the story of Laurent and Whispering Waters' daughter.

To be the first to hear about new book releases, special announcements, and deals, please join my newsletter

*I*f you enjoy romance set in the wilderness, you might enjoy the Yellowstone Romance Series, and my newest series, Wilderness Brides. Several of the characters who make cameo appearances in the Teton Trilogy are the main characters in the Yellowstone Series, and characters from the Teton Series make appearances in the Yellowstone and Wilderness Brides Series. The Yellowstone Series begins with Yellowstone Heart Song, and the Wilderness Brides Series begins with Cora's Pride. You can find all my books at my Author Page

*M*any of my readers have asked for a timeline for both the Yellowstone series as well as the Teton series (any my new series, Wilderness Brides), since they are somewhat related (by setting and time period) and characters from one series make cameo appearances in the other. You can download a PDF here.

*T*eton Sunrise is set in the 1820's, the decade when the fur trapper and mountain man era west of the Mississippi was at its peak. By the 1840's, the beaver was nearly trapped to extinction, and silk replaced beaver fur for hats. In 1822, William Henry Ashley advertised in the Missouri Gazette for "enterprising young men to ascend the river Missouri" to trap for beaver. The group of men who joined the expedition became known as Ashley's Hundred, and included Jim Bridger, Jedediah Smith, Hugh Glass, and Thomas Fitzpatrick, among others who would become famous mountain men later on. This was the beginning of the fur companies who employed men to venture into the Rocky Mountains and bring back beaver pelts that were in high demand in the east and overseas. A "company man" was no more than a day laborer, outfitted by the company he worked for, and paid roughly $200 per year for his hard and dangerous work. Everything these trappers caught belonged to the company. A "free trapper" was exactly that. He answered to no one, and made his own decisions. He might join up with a group of other trappers for safety, but he traveled and trapped where he chose, and sold his furs, or plews, to whomever he wanted.

Jackson Hole was named for trapper David Jackson, who spent a lot of time trapping the area. A "hole" is a general term that was used by mountain men to describe a valley surrounded by mountains, and so the area where the town of Jackson, Wyoming sits today, was referred to as Jackson's Hole in the days of the trappers.

Competition between fur companies was fierce, and larger companies used ruthless tactics to break the backs of some of the smaller companies. The Rocky Mountain Fur Company and the American Fur Company were two of the largest outfits.

The annual trapper rendezvous was first held in 1826, when William Ashley led a pack train of supplies from St. Louis into the Rockies to outfit his men. This became an annual event, with trappers and Indians coming to trade goods, swap stories, buy supplies, sell their furs, and generally have a good time.

Fascinating tales of the mountain men abound. Whenever I come across a story that piques my interest, I try and find a way to incorporate some of it into my books. For instance, I used the story of John Colter and his escape from the Blackfoot Indians in one of my other novels, Yellowstone Redemption.

Another story I came across that was too good not to incorporate into Teton Sunrise, was an incident that happened to mountain man Joe Meeks. While traveling with fellow trappers and his Indian wife, a group of hostile Indians kidnapped his wife when she fell behind in their travels. Joe Meeks charged after the kidnappers, and lost control of his horse. The Indians were so impressed by Joe's show of "bravery" at riding headlong into their midst, that they gave the wife back to him. It didn't happen quite like that to Alex in Teton Sunrise, but I thought it was a great little tidbit.

The Teton mountain range is one of the youngest in North America. It was formed some 9 million years ago due largely to the uplift of several faults in the region. Earthquakes in the area are due largely to the nearby Yellowstone caldera.

The Grand Tetons were named *Les Trois Tetons* by early French trappers, and the range of mountains was called the Teewinots (many pinnacles) by the Shoshone Indians.

Find out more about me and my stories here:
http://peggylhenderson.blogspot.com

Join me on Facebook. I love interacting with my readers, and you can stay current on my book projects and happenings.

. . .

For even more behind-the scenes news, interaction and discussions with other readers about my books, and just general fun, consider joining my closed Facebook Group.

I'm always happy to hear from my readers. Tell me what you liked, or didn't like in the story. I can be reached via email here: peggy@peggylhenderson.com

I want to thank all the people behind the scenes who helped make this trilogy a reality.

My editor, Barbara Ouradnik – thank you for your countless hours of pouring over the manuscripts, offering your input and opinions on everything, and making sure the story shines.

Carol Spradling, my critique partner, and my great team of beta readers: Heather Belleguelle, Lisa Bynum, Sonja Carroll, Shirl Deems, Becky Fetzer, and Hilarie Smith. Thank you for your opinions, your nagging, spotting typos, and your overall impressions of the story.

Cover by: Collin Henderson

Also by Peggy L Henderson

Author Page

Teton Romance Trilogy
Teton Sunrise
Teton Splendor
Teton Sunset
Teton Season of Joy
Teton Season of Promise

Yellowstone Romance Series: (in recommended reading order)
Yellowstone Heart Song
Return To Yellowstone
A Yellowstone Christmas (novella)
Yellowstone Redemption
Yellowstone Reflections (coming 2018)
Yellowstone Season of Love (coming 2018)
Yellowstone Homecoming (novella)
Yellowstone Awakening
Yellowstone Dawn
Yellowstone Deception
A Yellowstone Promise (novella)
A Yellowstone Season of Giving (short story)
Yellowstone Origins
Yellowstone Legacy
Yellowstone Legends (coming 2018)

Second Chances Time Travel Romance Series
Come Home to Me
Ain't No Angel
Diamond in the Dust

. . .

Blemished Brides Series (western historical romance)

In His Eyes
In His Touch
In His Arms
In His Kiss

Wilderness Brides (western historical romance)

Cora's Pride
Anna's Heart
Caroline's Passion
Josie's Valor (coming soon)

FROM THE AUTHOR

Thank you for purchasing and reading Teton Sunrise. I hope you enjoyed the book. Please consider letting other readers know about the book by leaving a quick review.

The adventure continues with Teton Splendor, the story of Laurent and Whispering Waters' daughter.

If you enjoy romance set in the wilderness, you might enjoy the Yellowstone Romance Series, and my newest series, Wilderness Brides. Several of the characters who make cameo appearances in the Teton Trilogy are the main characters in the Yellowstone Series, and characters from the Teton Series make appearances in the Yellowstone and Wilderness Brides Series. The Yellowstone Series begins with Yellowstone Heart Song, and the Wilderness Brides Series begins with Cora's Pride.

Many of my readers have asked for a timeline for both the Yellowstone series as well as the Teton series (and my new series, Wilderness Brides), since they are somewhat related (by setting and time period) and characters from one series make cameo appearances in the other. You can request a pdf of this list by emailing me at:

peggy@peggylhenderson.com

Teton Sunrise is set in the 1820's, the decade when the fur trapper and mountain man era west of the Mississippi was at its peak. By the 1840's, the beaver was nearly trapped to extinction, and silk replaced beaver fur for hats. In 1822, William Henry Ashley advertised in the Missouri Gazette for "enterprising young men to ascend the river Missouri" to trap for beaver. The group of men who joined the expedition became known as Ashley's Hundred, and included Jim Bridger, Jedediah Smith, Hugh Glass, and Thomas Fitzpatrick, among others who would become famous mountain men later on. This was the beginning of the fur companies who employed men to venture into the Rocky Mountains and bring back beaver pelts that were in high demand in the east and overseas. A "company man" was no more than a day laborer, outfitted by the company he worked for, and paid roughly $200 per year for his hard and dangerous work. Everything these trappers caught belonged to the company. A "free trapper" was exactly that. He answered to no one, and made his own decisions. He might join up with a group of other trappers for safety, but he traveled and trapped where he chose, and sold his furs, or plews, to whomever he wanted.

Jackson Hole was named for trapper David Jackson, who spent a lot of time trapping the area. A "hole" is a general term that was used by mountain men to describe a valley surrounded by mountains, and so the area where the town of Jackson, Wyoming sits today, was referred to as Jackson's Hole in the days of the trappers.

Competition between fur companies was fierce, and larger companies used ruthless tactics to break the backs of some of the smaller companies. The Rocky Mountain Fur Company and the American Fur Company were two of the largest outfits.

The annual trapper rendezvous was first held in 1826, when William Ashley led a pack train of supplies from St. Louis into the Rockies to outfit his men. This became an annual event, with trappers and Indians coming to trade goods, swap stories, buy supplies, sell their furs, and generally have a good time.

Fascinating tales of the mountain men abound. Whenever I come across a story that piques my interest, I try and find a way to incorporate some of it into my books. For instance, I used the story of John Colter and his escape from the Blackfoot Indians in one of my other novels, Yellowstone Redemption.

Another story I came across that was too good not to incorporate into Teton Sunrise, was an incident that happened to mountain man Joe Meeks. While traveling with fellow trappers and his Indian wife, a group of hostile Indians kidnapped his wife when she fell behind in their travels. Joe Meeks charged after the kidnappers, and lost control of his horse. The Indians were so impressed by Joe's show of "bravery" at riding headlong into their midst, that they gave the wife back to him. It didn't happen quite like that to Alex in Teton Sunrise, but I thought it was a great little tidbit.

The Teton mountain range is one of the youngest in North America. It was formed some 9 million years ago due largely to the uplift of several faults in the region. Earthquakes in the area are due largely to the nearby Yellowstone caldera.

The Grand Tetons were named *Les Trois Tetons* by early French trappers, and the range of mountains was called the Teewinots (many pinnacles) by the Shoshone Indians.

Find out more about me and my stories here:
peggylhenderson.com

I'm always happy to hear from my readers. Tell me what you liked, or didn't like in the story. I can be reached via email here:

peggy@peggylhenderson.com

I want to thank all the people behind the scenes who helped make this trilogy a reality.

My editor, Barbara Ouradnik – thank you for your countless hours of pouring over the manuscripts, offering your input and opinions on everything, and making sure the story shines.

Carol Spradling, my critique partner, and my great team of beta readers: Heather Belleguelle, Lisa Bynum, Sonja Carroll, Shirl Deems, Becky Fetzer, and Hilarie Smith. Thank you for your opinions, your nagging, spotting typos, and your overall impressions of the story.

Cover by: Collin Henderson

ABOUT THE AUTHOR

Peggy L Henderson is an award-winning, best-selling western historical and time travel romance author of the Yellowstone Romance Series, Second Chances Time Travel Romance Series, Teton Romance Trilogy, and Wilderness Brides Series. She was also a contributing author in the unprecedented 50-book American Mail Order Brides Series, contributing Book #15, Emma: Bride of Kentucky, the multi-authorTimeless Hearts Time Travel Series, and the multi-author Burnt River Contemporary Western Series.

When she's not writing about Yellowstone, the Tetons, or the old west, she's out hiking the trails, spending time with her family and pets, or catching up on much-needed sleep. She is happily married to her high school sweetheart. They live in Yellowstone National Park, where many of her books are set.

Peggy is always happy to hear from her readers!

To get in touch with Peggy:
www.peggylhenderson.com
peggy@peggylhenderson.com

ALSO BY PEGGY L HENDERSON

The Teton Romance books started as a trilogy but has turned into a series of five books.

The Teton Romance Series is my first spin-off series from the **Yellowstone Romance Series**. After the Teton Series, I started writing the **Wilderness Brides Series**, and I'm currently writing another spin-off to the Teton books in the **Wild Mountain Hearts Series.** (the first book in the series, The Pathfinders, releases on 5/1/19). Characters frequently get mentioned and cross over, and storylines even get inter-woven occasionally.

Would you like to know more about Alex Walker when he was new in the mountains and was almost killed by a bear? **The Pathfinders (Prequel to the Wild Mountain Hearts)** starts off a new spin-off series, and tells the story of Alex Walker's comrades in the aftermath of Alex Walker's bear mauling incident. This book will release on May 1, 2019.

Yellowstone Romance Series: (in recommended reading order)

Yellowstone Heart Song

Return to Yellowstone

Yellowstone Christmas

Yellowstone Redemption

Yellowstone Reflections

Yellowstone Homecoming

Yellowstone Love Notes

Yellowstone Season of Giving

Yellowstone Awakening

Yellowstone Dawn

Yellowstone Deception

Yellowstone Promise

Yellowstone Origins

Yellowstone Legacy

Yellowstone Legends

Wilderness Brides Series

Cora's Pride

Anna's Heart

Caroline's Passion

Josie's Valor

Teton Romance Series

Teton Sunrise

Teton Splendor

Teton Sunset

Teton Season of Joy (Teton and Yellowstone Romance Series crossover)

Teton Season of Promise

Coming Spring/Summer 2019:

Wild Mountain Hearts

The Pathfinders (series prologue)

The Eagle

The Bear

The Fox

The Hawk

The Wolf

Made in the USA
Las Vegas, NV
16 December 2022